Badland Bride
The Quinter Brides, Book Two

by

Lauri Robinson

This is a work of fiction. Names, characters, places, and incidents either are the product of the author's imagination or are used fictitiously, and any resemblance to actual persons living or dead, business establishments, events, or locales, is entirely coincidental.

Badland Bride: The Quinter Brides, Book Two

Cover Art by *Nicola Martinez*

The Wild Rose Press
PO Box 708
Adams Basin, NY 14410-0706
Visit us at www.thewildrosepress.com

Publishing History
First Cactus Rose Edition, 2009
Print ISBN 1-60154-613-0

Published in the United States of America

Dedication

To my sister, Cheri.
Thanks for being my best friend.

Chapter One

Western Kansas
2008

Trembling from head to toe, Lila Scott prayed
for a miracle.

Her heart beat faster than the eight cylinders
beneath the hood of her cherry-red Ford Mustang.
The car was new, still had that showroom smell and
smooth, sleek leather, but Lila wasn't focused on the
smell or the softness of the driver's seat. With a
death grip on the padded steering wheel, she
concentrated on driving and took the corner at
seventy.

The curve ended, she straightened the wheel
and stole a glance into the review mirror. A thick
cloud of dust from the white gyp road blocked her
vision, giving no clue if Pete followed or not.

Had his big pickup made the swift exit off the
interstate? Drawing in a shaky breath, she slammed
her foot down, pushing the gas pedal all the way to
the floor. The engine hummed louder, roaring like a
lion instead of its normal kitten purr.

She kept both hands on the wheel. Worry of
loosing control of the car overrode the need to wipe
at the sweat dripping into her eyes. Frosty air
spewed out of the air conditioning vents, but it
wasn't the summer heat causing her to sweat

profusely. Fear of being murdered by a madman had her nerves in high gear.

Little more than a blur, the immense wheat fields of western Kansas flew by. Tiny, tasseled heads created a fuzzy sea of gold. Lila sent quick sideway glances in search of the old telephone poles she'd seen from the highway. The wireless, broken posts signified a homestead out here somewhere.

A few miles up the road, steep cliffs and the unusual, bleached-white pillars of sandstone creating the Kansas Badlands rose from the flat, mid-western plains. She kept her foot on the gas, raced ahead and hoped nature's bizarre groundwork would provide a safe hideaway. Before long all four tires bounced haphazardly and forced her to ease up on the gas. Nerves on edge, and darting glances between the rearview mirror and the windshield, she guided the little car over the gyp road plagued with hills and deep ruts.

The unmaintained trail curved ahead. Squinting into the mirror, she wondered if the small, dark object far behind was real or an illusion. The back of her throat burned, and the film of tears grew thicker in her eyes. "Please, please, don't let it be him," she begged, and turned the wheel to follow the road around the first of the moonscape cliffs.

****

Skeeter Quinter peered beyond the ruins of the outbuildings, waiting for whatever made the low rumbling noise to pull into the yard of the deserted farm house. His heart thudded with excitement. *What would it look like this time?* He'd seen so many odd and unusual contraptions since becoming a ghost. Even his mind, which was extraordinarily overactive, had a hard time conjuring up anything comparable to some of the images he'd witnessed the past few days. Or was it weeks? Months? Years maybe?

Leaning further out the top story window, Skeeter wished he was the kind of ghost that could fly. But he couldn't. All he could do was float through this old house. With ease, he drifted through doors, walls, even the ceiling and floors, but he couldn't penetrate the odd, invisible shield surrounding the outside exterior of the house.

He crossed his legs then folded his arms to hover over the window sill. His position had to be somewhat akin to Old Chief Smokey overlooking The People's great prairie. The sun, high in the sky, radiated heat onto the rolling fields of buffalo grass, and the massive sandstone pyramids, irregular anywhere except for here, near Castle Rock and the Kansas Badlands. Dozens of sun-bleached pillars stood hundreds of feet high, their spiral shapes grouped in unusual, mismatched clumps. He could almost imagine they were a tribe of warriors awaiting his next command.

Skeeter chuckled aloud then snapped his mouth shut, listening. *Dang!* He knew the sound had left his throat, he'd felt the chuckle vibrate his vocal cords, but only his mind had heard it, not his ears. He refolded his arms across his chest. "This ghost shit is for the birds."

The rumbling noise grew closer. A disgusted huff left his chest. He could hear the contraption, hear the ever-blowing wind whistling through the outcroppings of sandstone and rustling the leaves of the singular elm next to the sagging roof of the porch, so why couldn't he hear himself? Evidently, ghosts couldn't talk. Just hear and...breathe. That was the other odd thing—he could still feel air flowing in and out of his lungs. Ghosts didn't breathe, did they?

His elbows settled somewhere near where his knees should be, and his chin imitated resting on his palms. It was logical—him being a ghost. Ma always said you gotta be good to see the pearly gates, and, well, out of all the Quinter boys, Kid, Skeeter, Snake, Hog, and Bug, he'd probably been the worst. Had he known what his afterlife would be like, he would've taken care to be a better person. Twenty-three was too young to die, and being a ghost was awfully boring.

Truth be told, he hadn't been a bad person. He'd never killed anyone, never cheated, never stole, nor committed any other outrageous sins. Sure he'd picked on his younger brothers a time or too, but it had all been in good-natured fun.

Sorrow swirled in his gut. He missed his family. Even before becoming a ghost, he'd longed for Kid's guidance, Snake's knowledge, Hog's cooking, and Bug's enthusiasm. Heck, he even missed how Ma whacked them all upside the head when their rough-housing got out of hand. A raw sigh stung his chest. He'd never see any of them again. Somehow fate had sealed him inside this rotting, old house.

"If I was the kind of ghost who could fly, I'd be haunting Buffalo Killer right now," he grumbled. The Sioux brave had pretended to be a friend, and Skeeter had believed he was sincere. A frown tugged at his brows. He knew better, and shouldn't have trusted the brave. Years ago, Buffalo Killer's grandfather, Pawnee Killer, had convinced Custer he was a friend of the white man too, and that hadn't turned out too good for Custer either.

Buffalo Killer had said the Badlands held special powers and promised Skeeter would see them if he participated in a ghost dance. The ritual included drinking the rot gut whiskey the army supplied the few lingering bands of Plainsmen, and eating the magical peyote. Skeeter now knew why it was called a ghost dance. "Cause it kills ya," he mumbled.

The object making the noise rounded the corner.

He rose, and like he'd done as a child to the front glass of the mercantile in Nixon, pressed his hands and nose against the invisible shield. The excited thud of his heart pounded just as hard as it had all those years ago, anxious to get a peek, knowing odd sightings were likely the most thrilling things ghosts could encounter.

A bright red flash shot up the road faster than a falling star shooting across the sky at midnight. "Dang," he moaned with disappointment. If only he could get close enough to touch one of these horseless carriages. Gravel crunched and shot out like stray bullets as the object skidded to a halt. The wheels were wide and black with shinny metal hubs. They were quite remarkable, didn't have any spokes, but had bold, white letters that spelled *Good Year*. "Maybe for you," he said sarcastically.

Sunlight reflected off the chrome on the front end of the carriage, the brightness almost blinded him. He squinted against the glare and continued his assessment. Dark glass around the sitting area made it impossible to see more than a shadowy figure. Right in the middle of the front end, in between what looked like two huge eyes, was a carved, silver horse, and down the side of the red paint white writing said *Mustang GT*.

His nose pressed harder against the shield. He'd give anything to see how the contraption moved without horses. A loud vroom split the air as gravel blasted out from beneath the wheels and the carriage shot around the side of the house.

He twisted, glided through the air and walls like an arrow. Without warning he smacked the shield outside the far side of the house so hard it sent him back though the wall. "Damn! Good thing ghosts can't feel anything, 'cause that had to hurt," he muttered, slowly moving back to the wall. This side of the house didn't have any windows, so he poked just his face through the wood and tried to catch a glimpse of where the red carriage had gone. Weather-worn and tattered shingles of the porch roof blocked his view.

"Damn, damn and damn! That was the most unusual one yet!" He closed his eyes and floated downward, through dilapidated floorboards and the ceiling of the ground floor. Perhaps he could see the contraption from a downstairs window. The other two carriages he'd seen during his ghost life had stopped near one of the outbuildings, each time men had gotten out, and after wondering around a bit had climbed back in their carriages and rolled away. One of the vehicles had been green, the other white, with splotches of what looked like rust near the bottom. Each of those carriages had had a large wagon box behind the enclosed area.

A loud bang made Skeeter almost jump out of his skin, if that were possible for a ghost. He glided toward the sound, through the wall and into the kitchen of the old house. Good thing he was a ghost, the rotting lumber of the floors would never hold the weight of a live man.

The sight of the woman standing in the middle of the room made his heart swell, press against his ribs. She wasn't as tall as his six foot height, but she wasn't as short as his ma, or sister-in-law, either. He held his breath, hoping the boards below her wouldn't give out. What would he do if she did fall through? He couldn't catch her, couldn't even ease her plunge through the rotten wood. Arms out, as if they could prevent the inevitable, he floated closer.

Tight curls, much like his hair when it was wet, covered her head and fell to brush over her shoulders as she twisted her neck to peer around the room. The sunlight shining through the glassless windows made the red-hued curls dance like the flames of a camp fire.

Air lodged in his chest. It wasn't her height or the ball of fire dancing around her head that made it hard for him to breathe, it was the fact she didn't have any clothes on. Well, she wasn't completely naked. A piece of green material, held by two small strips of lace over her shoulders, covered her upper torso, and below the odd shirt, were a pair of white pants, with the legs cut off.

Waving his arms, he floated closer.

She remained still, looked right though him.

While she continued to gaze around the room, he examined every inch of the exposed skin on her long and shapely arms and legs. He paused to gawk at the bright red paint on her toenails. A rope ran between two toes, holding nothing more than the flat soles of old shoes beneath her feet.

Had she been attacked by Indians? Could that be why she didn't have any clothes? He floated around her, looking for injuries. His appraisal stopped at her face, and the air once again caught in his chest. Large tears fell from the wild eyes scanning the area with urgency. Fear distorted her face with a wrinkled grimace.

His presence must have petrified her. He felt lower than a worn-out, flea-bitten dog, and realized since becoming a ghost there hadn't been a time when he wanted to be alive again more than right now. He dragged out a ragged sigh. "I'm not going to hurt you."

Her head snapped around, and her wide-eyed gaze searched the space behind him.

His heart began to race. "Can you hear me?"

She started to nod, then blinking she shook her head and flipped around to stare at the door.

He floated in front of her again. "Miss? Miss? I'm not going to hurt you. I'm...I'm here to help you." Drifting closer, he said, "Nod if you can hear me."

"Oh, dear God, please don't tease me like this,"

she whispered, raking her fingers through the curls bobbing around her head.

Excitement shook his body. "You can hear me, can't you?"

She opened her mouth, then shook her head and closed her eyes. A disheartening frown fell upon her face as it lowered until her chin touched her chest. "Please, Lord, I can't take much more. Please don't make me believe I'm hearing voices now."

"Yes!" He floated around her. "You can hear me, which is odd, because I can't hear myself. But that's all right, as long as you can hear me." His feet kicked with glee as he danced a tiny jig in mid-air. He settled down enough to ask, "So do you hear me like I'm talking to you, or do you hear me like I'm whispering?"

Her face lifted. A thoughtful gaze bounced around the room. Fine wrinkles formed between her eyes. "A real faint whisper," she murmured so softly he almost didn't hear her.

"Oh, well, I'll shout then!"

Her head snapped up, eyes clouded with fear again.

Skeeter frowned, but the way she ran to the broken window quickly told him it wasn't his shout that had startled her, it was the sound of another carriage. It was a distance away yet, but moving closer.

"Oh, no!" she gasped. "He's found me already." She twirled around clearly looking for an escape route.

"Who?" He floated to the window.

"Who?" She moved away, frantically searched the room. "If you're my guardian angel you should know."

"Angel? I'm not an angel. I'm a ghost." He followed as she crossed the room, hovering near her shoulder.

"Great! That figures, instead of an angel, I get a ghost!" She shoved a door open, hurried into another room.

He glanced at the floorboards and quickly flew to block her route. "Stop!"

A hot wave rippled his body as she walked right through him.

He shook off the feeling before whipping around to land in front of her again. "I said stop! The floors are rotten. You'll fall right through."

A flutter of relief washed over him as she stopped in her tracks.

Her gaze examined the old boards, tears falling from the big, green eyes faster than a spring rain. "I have to find a place to hide. He's here to kill me. Please whether you're a ghost or an angel, help me, please help me," she pleaded.

Real terror filled her eyes. He cursed his state of ghost-hood and raked his brain. The rumbling outside grew louder; the carriage would soon come around the corner of the sandstone bluff. "It's all right, I won't let him kill you," Skeeter said, not at all sure how a ghost could fight a man. Sweat began to run down his back, made him shudder. "That's funny, I haven't felt sweat since I became a ghost. I haven't felt hot, or cold, or hungry or tired."

"What?" she asked.

"Nothing, nothing. I was thinking, or at least I thought I was thinking," he said, feeling as useless as a dead rat.

The few pieces of glass in the old house began to vibrate. "Please!" she sobbed, "He's here! Please help me!" Her hands twisted together, and her body trembled from head to toe, as she once again searched the broken and sagging floor boards.

The seriousness of the situation chilled his spine. "All right," he said. "See that set of stairs? Underneath them is a small door. But to get there you have to walk around the edge of the room, don't step anywhere near the middle."

She nodded, quickly shuffled to the wall and on the tip of her toes, scampered toward the stairs. Gravel crunched outside, and a vroom noise cracked the air like thunder from a bolt of lightning.

"That's it," he encouraged, "stay close to the wall. Good girl. Now, the door is locked, but it's the middle panel, whoever built the house didn't want anyone to know about it. The key is hidden beneath the base board."

She pointed to the long board running along the bottom of the wall. "This one? How do I get it?" Panic filled her voice.

Another quiver shot down Skeeter's spine. "Just pull on the board. You can do it. I wish I could do it for you, but ghosts can't grab things." He hoped she understood his inability to be of more assistance. He floated closer, cursing his uselessness.

Broken windows continued to rattle. She tugged on the board. "Don't pull it all the way off." He stopped her before she lifted it away from the wall. "We don't want anyone to see it's been removed. Now, reach down, yes, right there. Pull out the key."

The noise outside ended abruptly, making the silence that followed ominous. She lifted up a large brass key. It shook in her fingers. "I got it," she whispered.

"Good, now carefully, slip that frame board off the side of the panel, the one right in the middle." At least his ghost days had given him the opportunity to examine the old house from top to bottom.

She did as instructed. The board slid over to expose a key hole at the same time a loud slam echoed through the house. "Oh, God!" she squeaked.

"You'll be all right," he assured. Having floated to the window, he watched a tall, burly man stomp toward the outbuildings. "Where did you hide your carriage?"

"My what?" Her quaking fingers tried to make the key slide into the key hole.

He returned his gaze to the yard. "That red thing you rode in."

"Oh, I parked it behind one of the clusters of rocks on the far side of the house. Got it!" she exclaimed softly, tugging open the small door.

The strange man had disappeared behind one of the buildings. "Good girl." Skeeter glided back to her. "Now, it's dark in there, and there's nothing we can do about it, but don't worry, it'll be all right. It's a long tunnel that leads to the cliffs behind the house. Just keep crawling, don't stop until you come to another wooden door. You'll need the key again, when that door opens crawl to the very end, and you'll be in a large cave."

"Thank you," she whispered.

"Stop!" he yelled before she climbed all the way in.

"What?"

"The side panel, flip that board back into place."

She gave a nod of understanding, slipped the board back in place and climbed in the little opening.

He couldn't help but admire the round shape of her bottom, covered with the short, white britches as it disappeared into the small doorway. A tightening that ghosts certainly shouldn't be able to feel tugged at his groin area. Figures—leave it to him to find the most beautiful girl on earth, after he'd left it.

A second later the fire-red curls popped back out the hole. The big, green eyes glanced around the room. "Are you coming?" she whispered.

"I'll be along shortly," he assured. "Shut the door and lock it behind you."

"But how will you get in?"

A smile played with his lips. "Ghosts don't need doors."

"Oh." She shot a worried look around the room before her head disappeared, and her arm pulled the door closed.

Skeeter waited until the lock clicked then floated to the kitchen to peer out another window. The husky man kicked open doors on the outbuildings, splinters of rotten wood fell as he stormed in and out each dilapidated shed.

Damn, this being a ghost shit is awful. What could he do to make sure the man didn't find the girl's escape route? He'd promised she'd be safe, and he never broke a promise. His mouth twisted, and one hand lowered to his hip. If he were still a man, he'd just draw his gun and shoot the bastard—but his gun was back in the cave, and he was nothing more than a liver-bellied ghost.

Floating up and down, around the room and back to the window, didn't help. A plan wouldn't form in his ghostly mind. "If only I could throw something at that shutter above his head, I could make it fall and—"

The words stalled in his throat as the large chunk of wood slipped from the building above the man. It landed square on his head, knocking off a hat that only had half a brim.

"Damn! Did I do that?" Skeeter muttered.

Dust flew up around the man as he collapsed to the ground. A loud curse echoed across the land before he pushed the scraps of wood away and grabbed the odd hat.

Skeeter glanced at the area around the man, searching the clumps of weeds. "If only I could make that hay rake rise up and smack him," he shouted.

The man rose, and as he stepped forward his foot landed on the forks of the rake. Swiftly, the long handle jumped forward and hit him right between the eyes. Arms flaying, the man stumbled backwards, hitting the side of the building with a loud thud. A deafening curse split the air.

"Who would have ever thought ghosts had such powers?" Skeeter mumbled with a faint hint of joy. "Let's see…If only I could make that log roll over and pin him against the building."

****

Refusing to think of all the creepy, crawly things that probably lived in the long tunnel, Lila crawled through the darkness. Her shoulders rubbed against the sides, and a pain, from keeping her neck bent for so long, tugged on stiff muscles. The tunnel went on and on. Had a ghost really shown her the escape route, or was her overactive mind playing tricks on her? The voice had been so soft, like a whisper in the wind. It wasn't like she really heard anything; it was as if she felt the words.

She shuddered and kept moving forward. Ghost or no ghost, she'd found a way to escape Pete—at least for the time being. A touch of hope settled her quaking. The space was tiny; Pete's wide frame wouldn't fit even if he did find the tunnel. Still, the thought of him following, made her increase her speed, even the gravel biting at her knees didn't slow her momentum.

A sting ripped across her knuckles as they encountered something solid, bringing her to a halt. She ran a palm over the dark, flat area in front of her. Hard, cool wood blocked her path. Her fingers felt for a key hole, and once she found it, she unclenched the other palm to insert the skeleton key.

The heightened, quick thuds of her pulse pounded in her ears. Thick darkness made everything twice as difficult. Finally, after several tries, the key slipped in and turned. The lock clicking open made her swallow the sour taste in her mouth. "You can do this, Lila," she whispered. "You can't give up now, not after what you've been through the past few months. Besides, you don't have just you to think about, there's the baby to protect."

Revived by the personal pep talk, she took a deep breath and pushed the door open. A fresh, cleansing wave of cool air floated over her. She gulped, filling every corner of her lungs before letting the fresh air exhale. Tugging her shoulders tight, she squeezed through the small opening. The area on the other side was wider, giving her plenty of room to twist around and lock the door before she turned about to crawl along the dirt tunnel.

How? When had everything gone so wrong? All she'd wanted to do was sell her old Toyota to help pay for the new Mustang. Putting an ad on the internet sounded like a simple, easy way to do it. When Pete had responded to her ad, she never gave the idea of giving him her address a second thought. Hays was a safe town, weirdos didn't scan the internet for unsuspecting females—or so she'd thought.

Not even after he'd seen her old car, saying it wasn't what he was looking for, did she feel threatened or nervous around him. Yes, he was big and burly, but pleasant enough. When he'd asked her to join him for a hamburger, she'd refused at first, but he'd insisted, said it was his way of paying her for taking the time to show him the Toyota.

It had been the next morning, when she woke, sore and groggy, and not remembering much of anything beyond entering the smoky bar he proclaimed made the best hamburgers in Kansas, that she'd realized her mistake. She couldn't remember eating the cheeseburger she'd ordered, couldn't remember how she got home, and certainly didn't remember having sex with him. Six weeks later, when a home pregnancy test came up positive, she went to the police. Since at that time, she didn't know Pete's real last name, the detective wrote her off as a loose woman, and told her to go have an abortion and get on with her life.

Appalled, and sickened by her own stupidity, she set out to trap Pete Hawkins herself—see he was stopped from violating other women. The plan had backfired, and now not only was Pete trying to silence her—with death—every person she knew thought she'd flipped her lid, and like the police officer, told her to quit being a drama queen, get an abortion, and get focused back on her college studies. She'd graduate this summer with an IT degree, and Professor Rutledge insisted a baby would make getting a decent paying job impossible.

Tears slipped from her eyes as she crawled over the dirt, sharp rocks dug into her tender knees every now and again. She couldn't kill an innocent baby; none of this was his or her fault. As soon as the little blue line had appeared on the strip, she knew what she had to do. It wouldn't be easy, but it was the right choice. Somewhere there was a couple who desperately wanted a child, and she would give them this little life. Until then it was her job to keep it safe.

The faint smell of a camp fire floated down the dark tunnel. Fear sent her heart a flutter. She flexed at the tension tickling her arms, and then twisted to glance back down the tunnel behind her. "Ghost?" she whispered into the darkness. A moment later, sincerely wanting to hear a faint whisper, she asked louder, "Ghost? Are you still with me?"

The silence was so deep it stung her nerves. Neither her ears, nor her mind picked up anything. "Evidently not," she muttered and a new wave of sadness sliced her chest. Having a guardian angel, or a guardian ghost, had been comforting, and the best thing that had happened to her in a long time. She closed her eyes. "Dear Lord, please, if you give me back the ghost, I promise to be a better person. I'll find this baby the perfect family, always be kind to others, and never, ever ask for anything again."

She waited, let her prayer settle, and listened for the ghost to announce himself. The eerie quiet became thick, gave her no choice but to accept the ghost was no longer—her prayer unanswered. She swallowed a solid lump of isolation, and huffing in a shaky breath, began to crawl forward again.

A tiny beam of light made her pause to squint against the darkness, the smell of smoke grew stronger, filled her nose with the distinct scent of smoldering wood. She pinched her trembling lips together and glanced over her shoulder before turning back toward the light. "You really don't have a choice," she mumbled. A shiver rippled her spine as she moved forward. "This must be how Marie Antoinette felt as they led her to the guillotine."

Chapter Two

Western Kansas
1882

Crawling out of the tunnel and into a large cavern, Lila blinked at the beam of sunlight shining through a narrow opening at the far end and cautiously surveyed the area. A fire had diminished into a pile of glowing, smoking ashes. An assortment of odd debris littered the surrounding area. A saddle, several wooden crates, tin cooking utensils and...

Her heart stopped dead in her chest, and the icy shiver racing up her spine made her want to turn around and crawl back into the long tunnel. She fought the urge and settled her gaze near the fire. The man lying there rolled over, a slight moan escaped his lips. Relief oozed, allowed her heart to begin to beat—it wasn't Pete.

She wiped at the sweat beading her forehead and rose to walk around the fire pit. The long body moved again, stretching. Muscled arms lengthened to flex at his sides and long legs shifted as if he was awakening from a restful sleep. He was tall. Being five-eight, height was the first thing she noticed about someone. Old fashioned, wool pants covered his legs, but nothing except glistening skin and curly dark hair sheltered his chest. She pulled her wondering gaze from the line of dark hair inching its way to the waist band of the pants.

Worn cowboy boots sat near his head which was covered with disheveled, brown-blond curls. His face had that chiseled look, like someone had painstakingly carved each feature. Her heart skipped a beat. His big, masculine build and old-fashioned clothing reminded her of the old western T.V. series *Gunsmoke*. She shrugged her shoulders. "If you live in Kansas long enough, someone is bound to remind you of Marshall Dillon."

His eyes snapped open, and Lila slapped a hand over her mouth. He blinked several times as if trying to focus. She kept her hand over her lips, hiding the way her teeth chattered. Why had she spoken aloud?

The man shook his head, rubbed his eyes. He pulled his hands away, looked at them strangely, and then began patting his body. The wide hands slapped at his chest, scratched at the curls on his head, and squeezed opposite arms. "Well, I'll be damned," he uttered with a hint of dismay.

A cold shower of shivers rippled her body at the familiar sound. Except this time, instead of being a faint whisper, the voice was deep and husky.

The man rose to his feet and stomped around, like he was testing his legs for use. His hands continued to rub and pat his body. "Well, God damn!" he exclaimed excitedly.

Her pounding heart leaped to her throat. Lila tried to swallow, but the lump was too large and caused her to cough. Instantly, the man turned toward her. A wide, friendly smile made his gray-green eyes twinkle with delight. "Glad to see you made it," he said, tipping his head in a friendly nod.

Her eyes bugged, she shut the lids against the strain, and rubbed her forehead. When she opened them, he still stood in front of her. His ear to ear smile was bright enough to light a Christmas tree. "Excuse me?" Lila croaked.

"Glad you made it through tunnel," he said.

She glanced to the hole in the wall behind her. The narrow opening made her question if it was the same one she'd crawled through. "Yes, I made it," she admitted, not quite sure if she said it for him or for herself.

"I seem to have made it too," he said, clearly happy about it.

"Yes, you seem to have made it too." She couldn't help but smile. There was something about the man that filled the air. It was like he was happy to be alive, and it made her want to feel the same way.

"I don't think we introduced ourselves." He stretched one hand forward.

"No, no we didn't." She shook her head, feeling extremely light-headed.

"I'm Skeeter Quinter." He nudged his hand forward. "Well, actually my name is Steven Quinter, but everyone calls me Skeeter."

She extended an arm, and he instantly took her hand in a solid grasp, pumping it in greeting. Warmth from his palm flowed up her arm. "I- I'm Lila Scott."

"Lila. That's a pretty name."

His smiling eyes were mesmerizing. She squinted against the gleam, trying to think of a response. "Um...Thank you. Skeeter's a nice name too."

He pulled his hand away, and a lilting laugh bubbled out of his chest. "No, it's not. But my Pa gave it to me, so I don't mind it none. He said I was as pesky as a mosquito when I was growing up." He stretched his arms over his head. "Damn, it's good to be alive, ain't it?"

At that Lila had to chuckle, something she hadn't done in some time. "Yes, Mr. Quinter, being alive is a good thing."

"Ah, come on now, none of that mister stuff." He reached down to pluck a shirt from the floor of the cave. "My older brother, Kid, now there's a mister, and everyone knows it. But me, I'm just Skeeter."

Lila turned to keep from staring at the muscles bulging as he slid his arms in the sleeves of a plaid shirt. The debris lying around appeared to be rustic camping gear, a beat-up coffee pot, some very old cans, a canteen, a wooden bowl filled with some odd, brown chunks. She frowned and bent down to examine the container closer.

"Don't touch those!"

Startled by his screech, she held her hands up and froze, precariously balancing her crouched position.

He hopped, tugging on his boots, then reached over and grabbed the bowl. "Those things are dangerous. Buffalo Killer should be shot for giving them to me." His fingers wrapped around her arm. "Come on, let's get some fresh air, while I contemplate shooting him. I don't care if he is the chief's son."

"Shooting him?" She wobbled, rising beside him.

"Naw, I won't really shoot him, but I might let him believe it for a while."

Lila shot a couple curious glances at the bowl he carried as they walked through the cave. His fingers, still holding her arm, were gentle, not forceful, and his voice was light and carefree, making her wonder more about his statement.

The opening at the end grew larger the closer they got to it. Hot, dry air greeted them before they stepped out of the cave. He led her through the opening, and she quelled an intriguing sense of wonder—as if she was entering a different dimension. The summer sun heated the sandstone outside the cave to the point she could feel it through the bottom of her flip-flops—evidence she was still in

Kansas.

Skeeter let go of her arm, walked to the side of the cliff, and dumped the contents of the bowl over the edge. Lila let her gaze float beyond him, to the rough terrain and jagged edges of the badlands. She'd never stood atop the ruins before, and the view was awesome, breathtaking. Castle Rock, the tall cluster of sandstone pyramids, stood a short distance away. She paused, wondering. It looked taller than she remembered.

The area, though not widely visited, was fairly well-known since it proved thousands of years ago the United States was the bottom of an ocean. For centuries the chalk has given paleontologist some of the finest fossils ever found. She'd visited the place more than once on school field trips, and many claim you can still find Mosasaurs teeth lying about.

It had been the memory of one of those field trips that made her exit I-70. Pete's huge truck, close on the tail of her little Mustang, hadn't been able to slow in time for the corner and had continued to fly down the interstate. Evidentially, not far enough, for she had no sooner found the old abandoned farm house when his truck barreled down the rough and rutted driveway.

Lila walked to the edge of the cliff, she should be able to see the house from here, but unless Pete had binoculars, he wouldn't be able to pick her out amongst the ragged cliffs.

Her forehead tightened with a frown. The badlands gave way to nothing more than rolling prairies. Where were the fields of wheat dancing like a sea of gold, the old telephone poles, the house and other ruins? "I must be turned around," she murmured.

"What?" Skeeter looked at her expectantly.

"Oh, I said I must be turned around, the house should be right over there."

His gaze followed the direction she pointed. A deep scowl covered his face. Silently, slowly, he stepped closer to gaze over the land before them. He lifted one hand, scratched at the scalp below his windswept hair, and then spun around to take a long, thorough look at the landscape. "Uh...Lila..."

"Yes?"

Softly, as if nervous—or thinking hard, he punched one fist into the palm of his other hand, wrapped his fingers around his fist before drawing it out and then plunged it forward again. He continued punching his palm and a cloudy mask covered his face, making her believe a deep, uncertain thought flitted around in his head.

She never took her eyes off him. What was it? Did he know Pete? No, he'd helped her escape Pete. But that didn't mean he didn't know Pete. Did it? She squelched her mind from tumbling about haphazardly and scrutinized his actions, his gaze. He knew something—that was as clear as the sky above. But what was it? What was he contemplating so hard?

Squinting at the sun, he turned to her and repeated, "Lila..."

"Yes?" she said when his pause became extremely long.

He turned to point at two boulders of sandstone sticking out of the buffalo grass growing across the top of the cliff. "Let's go sit on those rocks for a minute." His face softened, gave an impression he was apologizing for something.

After the experience she'd had with Pete, she knew she should be cautious of strange men, but not a single red flag flashed. Matter of fact, there was something about Skeeter Quinter that made her feel tranquil and comfortable, as if she trusted him. She'd swear on her grandmother's grave it had been his voice that guided her through the old house and into the tunnel.

Testing her instincts, she let her gaze wander his tall frame, from head to toe, one more time, and waited for a tremor of apprehension, or a hard knot of intuition to twist in her stomach. Nothing, not a quiver nor ounce of uneasiness or fear formed. She bit her lips together, holding in a thought that said he definitely stimulated her. Moisture formed in her mouth. *Sheesh! It wasn't her fault!* A body that sculptured would have stirred Mother Teresa. She tossed the speck of self-justification aside, glancing upwards. Had her prayer been answered? Was he her guardian ghost?

His hand settled on her elbow. "Come on," he coaxed.

Her feet, as if they knew better than her mind, stepped forward.

They arrived beside the boulders, and he ran a hand over the top of the rock.

"Maybe we should sit on the ground, I bet you could fry an egg on that," Lila said.

He let out a clean, unrestrained laugh. "Yes, you probably could. Let's go around to the back side, there'll be some shade there."

Settled on the ground, she ran both hands under the tight curls at the back of her neck and lifted her hair, hoping a cool breeze would float over the sweat trickling down. Had Skeeter seen her enter the house from the top of the hill? Perhaps he'd been hollering at her through the deep tunnel, giving her instructions of where to find the key. She shook her head, letting the curls flip back into place. That was crazy, the tunnel was too long. Not even his deep voice could carry that far. But then again, there is no such thing as ghosts, or answered prayers—is there? She snuck a quick side glance.

He ran a hand over the five o'clock shadow across his jaw, once again looking deep in thought.

The gesture, along with his swanky, lanky frame, gave him that genuine cowboy appearance—a very good-looking cowboy. The wind tugged at his wayward curls, forcing them to flip and fall across his forehead in a carefree manner, and his clothes fit him like aged-old jeans Tom Cruise would pay a fortune for. A wave of heat racing up her neck made her pull her gaze away. There was nothing fake or store bought about his image. All in all it made her stomach gurgle with enchantment. The sensation made a frown tug at her brows. Ghost or no ghost, another man was the last thing she needed in her screwed up life.

"L-i-l-a..." He stretched her name out, made it sound longer than a ten syllable word.

The sound tickled her funny bone. She let out a small laugh and dragged his name out just as long. "S-k-ee-t-er..."

A cocky grin flashed across his face, one that made her heart flip, before he grew serious. "What year were you born?"

She tilted her head and met his gaze. "If you want to know how old I am, I'll tell you, that way you don't have to do the math. I'm twenty-two."

"That's good," he said with an obligatory nod. "It's a right fine age," his face grew somber again, "but what year were you born?"

His genuineness made her forehead crinkled. She relaxed the tight muscles and answered, "Nineteen-eighty-five."

He let out a slow whistle.

Taken aback, she huffed, "What? It's not like I'm an old maid or something, nor some teenage chick either."

He held up one hand in defense. "No, no, you're definitely not an old maid, nor a chicken." The cocky smile was back, brightening his face in a charismatic, magical way that warmed her heart.

"Chick, not chicken," she said, giggling at his delightful, dry sense of humor. Apprehension no longer distressed her body, a result of his friendliness. He most likely could make a nervous turkey feel at ease the day before Thanksgiving.

"Yes, chick. All righty then...Well, Lila..."

"Yes, Skeeter..." His conversation game was as charming as his humor. She probably shouldn't be enjoying it as much as she was, but it had been sometime since she'd been able to have fun verbally sparring with a man. And something about him made her want to flirt with earnest.

"What would you say if I told you I was born in eighteen-fifty-nine?"

She laughed, and purposely elevated her eyebrows. "I'd say you look damn good for your age." *He was a character.*

His cute, crooked smile displayed Crest commercial teeth. "Well, twenty-three ain't all that old," he said, shrugging his broad shoulders casually.

"No, it's not," she quickly did the math, trying to keep the banter going, "but that would mean you were born in nineteen-eighty-four."

"No." He shook his head. A curl fell over one eye and he pushed it aside. "I was born in eighteen-fifty-nine." His gaze had grown serious, somber even.

Something inside Lila flipped. She wasn't sure if it was her heart or her stomach, but something in the way Skeeter looked at her said he told the truth. The temperature of the summer air had to be close to one hundred degrees, but she all of sudden she could have sworn she stood in the middle of a January blizzard. "H-how can that be?"

Skeeter took a deep breath. Being a ghost had been hard, but telling an adorable, half-naked girl she's in eighteen-eighty-two, why that's almost impossible. It was all kind of farfetched, even to his open mind. "It's a long story—" the daze clouding her eyes made him rethink his explanation, "I'll try to make it as short as possible."

"No." She shook her head. "No, I think I'd like the long version."

She was even prettier now that he was alive again. Her eyes were a brighter green than spring grass, and the wind tossed the red-tipped curls about her head like petals on a flower. Several fluttered across her forehead, catching the sunshine. They sparkled brighter than icicles on a roof top in December. The shape of her face was flawless, gracefully curved and each feature naturally flowed into the next with perfection. Every time she spoke, shiny lips framed tiny, white teeth, and when she smiled, his heart kicked harder than an ornery old mule.

"Skeeter?" Concern filled her eyes, and she rubbed both hands over her upper arms, as if warding off a chill.

The sight brought his galloping mind to a halt, and the urge to comfort her fear forced him to recall their conversation. "Uh, oh, all right, the long version. Well, let's see. My older brother Kid, he married Jessie about two years ago now. She's a right fine gal, we all love her." His cheeks burned a touch at the declaration. He shook off the flush and continued, "Like a sister, we all love her like a sister. Anyway, her brother, Russell, well, you see, he wasn't treating Jessie very well, and to save Kid from killing him, I took Russ out to check some land. I knew Kid wasn't interested in more land, he owns half of Kansas now, but I wanted a little time alone with Russ to explain how he should be treating his little sister. It didn't take long for Russell to figure if he wanted to live to a ripe old age, he'd better shape up." Realizing he was blabbing like the town drunk, Otis Murphy, on a Saturday night, he glanced at Lila to make sure she followed his story.

She gave him a little nod, but a frown still pulled on her face. A faint, tiny band of freckles dotted her nose right below a wrinkle the grimace caused. Regret, knowing he was causing her grief, bubbled in his guts.

He sucked in a breath in order to rush through the rest of his tale. "Well, while Russell and I were out and about, we met a guy traveling to the Badlands and tagged along with him. Once we got here, we found all kinds of things," he dug in one pocket and drew out several small, black teeth, "including shark's teeth and dinosaur bones."

"Mosasaurs," she interrupted with the same tone Ma used when she was correcting their speech.

"What?" he asked as she plucked one tooth from his palm.

She pinched the tooth between her thumb and forefinger, examining it closely. "You said shark, but actually they're Mosasaurs. They were the predecessor to the modern day shark."

Her explanation caught him off guard. "Mosasaurs, you say?" He glanced at the other two teeth in his hand.

She nodded and replaced the tooth with the other ones.

None of the fossil's they found had been named Mosasaurs, or at least none he knew of. "I'll have to remember that," he mumbled, stuffing the teeth back in his pocket. Her self-assured gaze encouraged him to make a mental note to write a letter to Russell.

"Anyway," he continued, "this guy we'd met up with, he was all excited about our findings, and took off for New York to put together an expedition to come back. I figured whoever owned the land would make money from all these folks digging stuff off their property. Kid wasn't interested in owning the land, so I came back to find out if it was part of the land run or not. It just so happened it was, but no one had claimed it 'cause a band of Sioux had been keeping everyone off it."

"Sioux, like in Indians?" Her eyes had grown as round as silver dollars.

He'd hope to make even the long version short, but her startled look told him she needed as much information as possible. "Yes, Indians," he used what he hoped was a calming tone, knowing some folks still feared the Sioux. "I put a claim down, and started to befriend The People. Not that long ago this part of the plains had every clan of the Redman roaming it, but since the Army drove most of them into Oklahoma, there's only a few tribes here and there." He paused for a moment. "Just those strong enough to keep one step ahead of the Army." Knowing how badly Buffalo Killer's family had been treated by the army never failed to irritate his craw. He swallowed the foul taste it always created in his mouth, squelching it for now. "Every trip out, I bring things for them, beads and such. They're good folks, and I thought we were getting along quite well, until this trip that is."

"What happened?" Her eyes shot across the badlands as if she expected a raid at any moment.

"Don't worry. We're still on friendly terms." A begrudged smile twisted his lips at the thought of what he'd experienced. "At least until I see Buffalo Killer again, once I settle the score with him, his clan may not be too happy with me."

The sound of her gasp split the air like a stray bullet.

He cringed, hadn't meant to frighten her again, and patted her knee. Smooth, bare skin filled his palm, and then a sting, sharper than a hornet's, shot up his arm. Instantly, he pulled the hand away. A woman's skin had never stung him before. He glanced at his palm sure he'd find a red welt.

Finding no sign of injury, he formed a fist, tightening the muscles around the zing shooting up his arm.

Still wanting to ease her fear, he said, "Don't worry, I'm not really gonna hurt him. All of us Quinter boys like to think we're mean, but in all honesty, we pretty kind-hearted." Blood, hotter than the sun above, raced into his cheeks. He bit down on his tongue. *Damn!* The stupid thing got away from him sometimes. Not only was his hand on fire, but he was as tongue-tied as a school boy in a brothel. A new wave of embarrassment washed over his neck, and this time he closed his eyes. Why the hell was he thinking of brothels? She wasn't the kind of gal in one of the houses in Dodge.

Lila let out a little giggle. It floated on the breeze, tickling his ears.

There was one thing for sure though—this little woman had him ready to jump out of his skin. He peeked at her with one eye.

Her face had lit up like a firefly. All shine and sparkle. "What happened? What did Buffalo Killer do to you?" she asked.

His skin shivered from head to toe. Dragging in a fortifying breath, he willed control. Thinking quick, he pointed to where his horses grazed in the shade of several tall buttes, hoped she'd take the twinkling gaze of those green eyes off his stinging cheeks. "Since my horses are still here, no worse for wear, I figure I wasn't a ghost for no more than a day or so." He took a deep breath to dispel the lingering cobwebs in his head. "It sure seemed longer." His gaze settled on the horses. Worry about who'd take care of them had been foremost on his mind while being a ghost. They were fine animals, and he'd hated the thought of them left to their own.

"They're very pretty," she said, but a new frown had formed. Actually she looked quite shocked.

"I've been here about three months this time. My family lives over by Nixon," he explained.

"Nixon?"

"Yes, down on the White Woman," he said.

"Oh, I've never heard of Nixon, I thought Scott City was near the White Woman basin," she said.

"Nope, it's Nixon. Anyway, this time when I gave Buffalo Killer the gifts I had and said I was going to be scouting the land for the next few months, looking for a site to build on, he asked if he could help. I said sure." He searched the corners of his mind, trying to recall as much as possible. "What I'm assuming was last night or maybe the night before he came by for another visit." He pointed in the direction of the tall sandstone structure. "His tribe claims the area around Castle Rock has magical powers, and he knows I like hearing the stories. Well, he came by with some whiskey he got from the Army, and he also brought along peyote."

"Peyote buttons?" Her eyes grew wide. "That's what was in the bowl isn't it?"

"Yes, those are some nasty little things." He shook away the quiver racing up his spine. "Buffalo Killer called it a ghost dance. Said I'd see unbelievable things. He was right. I saw unbelievable things."

Something akin to excitement lit her face. "G-ghost dance? What happened? What did you see?"

"I don't really know how it all happened. One minute I was eating the awful tasting cactus, and the next minute, I was a ghost floating around an old house. I couldn't get outside the building, other than the tunnel I showed you. I couldn't get back into the cave either. It was the tunnel or the house. Those were my only choices." He scratched his head, looking back at the cave. Had it really happened? When his gaze fell back on Lila, he concluded it must have. She was proof.

Lila stared at him, face puckered, and blinking like she was trying to understand what he'd said. Pointing one finger at him, she asked, "You were a ghost? Or you are a ghost?"

He folded his hands onto his lap, and thought for a moment, took in all the sensations rippling his body and mind. "Was a ghost. I'm definitely human again now. There was a calendar on the wall in the kitchen. It said nineteen-thirty-nine, so I figured I had died and had been a ghost for over sixty years. The first time one of those horseless carriages pulled in, I almost died all over again. If that was possible," he added with a chuckle.

"A horse—oh, you mean a car?"

"Is that what they're called?"

She nodded.

"But yours said Mustang on it, and Good Year."

She smiled. "A Mustang is a kind of a car, and Goodyear is a brand of tires."

"But the other c-cars I saw had wagon beds."

A frown formed over her eyes for a moment before she said, "Oh, those would be pickup trucks."

"Like the one that guy chasing you had?"

"Yes, what happened to him? What happened to me? How'd I travel through time?" Her eyes grew wide. "How do you know it's not two-thousand-eight?"

This time Skeeter couldn't stop his hand from giving her knee a consoling pat. The soft, smooth skin made his calloused fingers tingle, but didn't sting him. "Whoa, one question at a time." He lifted the hand and pointed to the horses. "My horses, all my stuff in the cave." He shrugged. "I can only speculate on most of this, but I think this place is magical. I think when someone travels through that tunnel, they travel through time."

She slapped a hand against her breasts, the exact spot his eyes kept trying to focus on, and whipped her head around to look at the cave entrance. "Pete! Is he on his way here? To this time? What year is it anyway?"

He straightened out his twisted mind and answered her question, "Its eighteen-eighty-two. And I don't think you have to worry about Pete."

She gulped. "Yes, I do. He won't stop until he kills me. That tunnel isn't going to stop him." Her voice trembled with fear.

He wrapped an arm around her. The soft, silky skin of her upper arm filled his palm as her head settled on his shoulder. Her body trembled from head to toe. All of a sudden his heart picked up pace, rattled in his chest like the end button of a diamond back. "Don't fret. I won't let anyone hurt you. Besides, Pete won't find the tunnel."

"How can you be sure?"

"He'd never fit for one."

She sniffled and her head bobbed against his shoulder.

He tightened his hold around her. He'd never smelled anything sweeter than the scent floating from the curly locks of her hair. A warm, silly feeling tickled his insides. Then a protective, almost angry knot formed in his stomach. "Why would he want to kill you?"

"Because he's an evil man. I turned him into the police—the law—for um, um, hurting me, and now the law is after him."

"Why didn't they put him in jail? Sheriff Turley threw Kid in the old well likety-split when he was arrested."

"A well?"

He had to keep talking, keep his mind off the way his body was heating up, which had nothing to do with the sun over their heads. "Yes, Nixon didn't have a jail then, so they used the old dried up well. Kid was down there for three days. After he was cleared of the murder charges, he gave the town a donation to build a jail."

She leaned up and glistening green eyes looked at him curiously.

His body groaned, but he rustled up a smile. "That's another long story."

"It must be," she nodded, and then laid her head back on his shoulder.

A sigh of pleasure left his chest, he couldn't help it. She had to be the sweetest thing he'd ever met. He could get used to having her around. "So why didn't they put Pete in jail?"

"They didn't believe he hurt me, even after I showed them all the stuff I'd found out about him on the internet."

"On the what?"

"The internet," she sighed. "Never mind, I'd bet that's an even longer story than the well."

His hand roamed up and down her arm. Holding her felt so natural, like breathing, and talking with her was like talking to a trusted, old friend. The best-looking one he'd ever seen. "I was more surprised than a bear seeing snow when I woke up in that cave alive again."

"How'd you get back to the cave before me?"

He pondered her words for a second or two. "I don't think my body ever left the cave, I think just my ghost did. While I was at the house, I didn't have a body. It's hard to explain, but I just kind of floated around. I could still sort of feel my body, but I couldn't use it. I couldn't touch anything, but things inside still worked. I could see things and hear things." His nose tickled as her sweet scent wafted by again. "I don't think I could smell either. I don't remember if I could or not. Anyway, I was amazed when you could hear me, because I couldn't, I didn't think my voice worked."

"It was like a faint whistle in the wind, I don't

know if I heard you as much as I sensed what you were saying."

"Hmm, interesting." Skeeter rubbed his chin with his other hand. Stiff whiskers confirmed he'd only been asleep one night, and told him he needed to shave.

"What's interesting?"

"Well, Pete acted like it was more than a whisper in the wind," he chuckled.

She glanced his way. "He did?"

He nodded, lifted one eyebrow to tease her.

A grin made her eyes squint. "Tell me, oh, please tell me."

Her wide, excited smile made his whole body tingle. The blood flowing through his veins felt as hot as the sun blazing down on the rocks. Something swelled in his chest, as if her smile had made his heart double in size, and damn, if it didn't feel good. "After you locked the door under the stairs, I found out ghosts can make things happen with their minds. All they have to do is think about them hard enough."

"Oh?"

"Yes, I thought about a shutter on the old barn falling on him and it did. I thought about a rake handle hitting him in the face, and it did. I made a log roll over and pin him to the barn, and while he was trapped, I made all kinds of scary, ghostly sounds. By the time he got out from behind the log, he ran to his...what did you call it, pickup truck?"

She nodded.

"He ran to his pickup truck like the devil with a red-hot pitchfork was chasing him."

"Oh, I wish I could have seen it." Her light, happy laughter was contagious, and he soon found his laugh echoing with hers over the buttes. *Ole' Pete had been a sight to see.*

After the ever-present Kansas wind carried the

sounds far away she sighed, then pulled out of his embrace and stood up. "Skeeter Quinter, thank you very much for rescuing me today. I don't think I've ever met a nicer man." She held her hand out for him to shake.

He stood, wrapped his hand around hers. Her fingers fit inside his palm perfectly. "You're very welcome, Lila Scott. I don't think I could have rescued a more delightful or beautiful lady."

The way her cheeks turned cherry red made him chuckle. She pulled her hand away, ran it down her narrow hip. "Well, I better be on my way."

"On your way?"

"Yes, on my way."

"Where to?"

"Back to the future." She giggled again, flashed him a silly grin. "There's a movie called that, it was pretty good, actually had sequels. I even think they traveled back to the old west in one of them."

He frowned, not only because he had no idea what she was talking about, but also because he had to tell her something else. "Lila," he sighed.

"Skeeter," she said with a smile that made her eyebrows rise in a way that sent his heart rattling again.

Looking into her deep green eyes, he grimaced, not wanting to be the one to disappoint her. She was the prettiest thing he'd ever seen. A lump formed in his throat as he explained, "Lila, I'm sorry, but you can't go back to the future."

"Yes, I can." She dug into a pocket of the short, white pants. "I still have the key. I'll just crawl back down the tunnel. And thanks to you Pete is probably half way to Wichita by now, I'll be able to go to the police again. I'll file an order for protection or something."

"While I was a ghost..." he started.

She nodded, waited for him to go on.

35

"I, uh." He swallowed, cleared his throat. "Well, I sort of told the house to collapse. It was the last thing I did before floating into the tunnel. I heard it behind me, rumbling and tumbling, and then the tunnel caved in. The next thing I remember is waking up next to the fire."

She pressed both hands against her stomach. "But Skeeter, I have to go back to the future." Her eyes became glassy and wide. "Now!"

The terror on her face made a tingle rip up his back. He reached out, wrapped his hands around her upper arms. Willing to do whatever it took to ease her fear, he said, "Lila, settle down. I can try to dig out the tunnel, but it's going to take some time."

"I don't have time!" She shot a nervous glance between him and the cave.

"You don't have to worry. Pete can't get to the tunnel either."

"No, it's not that." Tears started to trickle down her cheeks.

The sight made his heart melt. He stepped forward, pulled her into an embrace. Warm breath tickled his chest as her face pressed against the opening of his shirt. His hands ran over the silky skin of her shoulders, then down her back, fitting her trembling body against his solid one. "Shh, don't cry. It's going to be all right."

"No, it's not." She lifted her face to peer at him. Tear drops glistened in the sun. "I'm pregnant," she whispered. "I can't have a baby in eighteen-eighty-two. Women die during childbirth in this century."

Chapter Three

If his solid arms hadn't been holding her, she would have collapsed to the ground. Her trembling knees knocked harder than a Jehovah's Witness with a station wagon full of Watchtower flyers to distribute. The beat of her heart pounded in her ears. Lila wrapped both arms around his tall, brawny body, holding on for dear life. High school history lessons, long lost in the caverns of her brain, leaped forward. More pioneer women lost their lives during childbirth than anything else. Not Indian raids, not diseases, not accidents, snake bites, gun shots...

She twisted her face, knowing her tears were soaking the front of his shirt. His hand, firm, yet gentle, ran over her hair, pressed her cheek back in place. "Shh, don't cry." He settled his chin on the top of her head. "It'll be all right. I promise."

It was as if he was a tall oak, and she a little sprig, sprouting near its roots, protected by an encompassing shelter. Her emotional breakdown began to ease. Feeling a tad foolish for falling completely apart in front of such a wonderful man, she took a deep breath, and eased her grasp on his waist. His hands slipped to her hips, the hold soft and reassuring.

Unable to meet his gaze yet, she wiped away tear residue with both hands. Glancing down she realized her hands were quite grubby from crawling through the tunnel. Fearful dark streaks covered her face she rubbed the backs of her hands across her cheeks.

"Come on." His hold tugged at one of her hips as he twisted about.

Head down, she fell into step beside him, and they walked toward the cave. One of his strong arms remained wrapped around her waist. The cooler air inside the cavern was a needed relief. Her shoulders drooped in acceptance. With a gentle but reassuring squeeze, he left her side, and she snuck a peek as he walked toward the fire pit.

Skeeter Quinter was the picture of an ultimate man. Not modern-day, fitness-club built, but naturally formed into a body so perfect Hercules would be jealous. Broad, bulky shoulders looked as if they could easily carry the load of the world. Lean hips swaggered as he walked with an old west flare, yet, he stood straight and tall.

And his charismatic face—she pressed a hand to the rapid thud behind her breast bone. His five o'clock shadow would make any woman swoon, and his bedroom eyes... There isn't an actor out there whose lashes could match his, and the way his hazel-green eyes twinkled she wondered if they were flecked with real gold.

Lila closed her eyes, trying to gain some resemblance of control. How could she be agog over her rescuer, when his rescue had sent her a hundred and twenty-six years in the past? Her lids snapped open, and her gaze floated about the cave. Was it all a ruse?

There wasn't a modern trinket in sight.

"Here." Skeeter set a wooden bucket down near her feet. "It's fresh water. There's a natural spring in the back of the cave." He tugged her elbow, forcing her to turn his way. A small square cloth dangled from his fingers.

"Thank you." She took the washcloth, dipped it in the water. "Maybe the tunnel didn't cave all the way in." Wringing the water from the cloth, she added, "Maybe it only caved in in the future, but not in the past."

He looked at her, his gaze sad.

She pressed the cloth to her face.

His hand brushed her shoulder. "You wash up, I'll go check."

The material, though wet, absorbed the tears slipping out of her eyes. She pressed the cloth harder against her face, trying to force any more from flowing. It was all too much. There was no way she could live in the past. She was a child of the twenty-first century. A millennial.

When convinced she was in charge of her rolling emotions, Lila scrubbed her hands and knees before wiping the sweat from the rest of her exposed skin. By the time she was done, Skeeter had built up the fire to provide more light near the tunnel entrance. She swished out the cloth, hung it on the edge of the wooden bucket, and walked toward the blaze.

He crouched on his hands and knees, his head and shoulders stuck in the opening. Careful not to stand in his light, she asked. "Is it open? Can you see anything?"

Slowly, he inched back, pulling his head out then his hands. A boulder half the size of the opening rolled out beneath his fingers. He grunted, shoved the rock further away from the hole. "I'm sorry, Lila. It's blocked."

"Are you sure?" She knelt down and grimaced at the pain in her knees. Her hurried scrubbing had opened the abrasions caused by her long crawl, and left the skin tender and sensitive.

He moved over, giving her free rein to examine the small opening. The only clear space was where the huge boulder had been. Other large rocks, thick sand, and baseball size stones created a solid wall from top to bottom. "How?" She twisted to look at him. "I didn't hear anything, didn't feel anything." Glancing back to the tunnel, she added, "It's unbelievable."

"The whole event is a little unbelievable." His hand brushed her shoulder. "You, me, the tunnel."

"Yes, it is." She ran a hand through her hair, flipping the irritating curls away from her face. Her gaze snapped up. "What about the house? Maybe the other end of the tunnel is there." She leaped to her feet. "Do you know where it would be?"

He shrugged. "Sure, but I don't think you should get your hopes up."

A cold chill showered her body. "Sometimes hope is all a person has."

His hand, big and warm, wrapped around hers, encompassing it like a winter glove. With his other hand, he wiped a wayward curl from her face. "You're right. Let's go take a look."

Half an hour later, Lila would have traded her new Mustang for a touch of that cold chill she felt back in the cave. Sweat oozed from every pore. Her bra, glued to her body, chaffed her skin beneath the hot, wet elastic. Following Skeeter down the steep cliff, she paused, slipped her fingers beneath her shirt and tugged on the wide band to ease the discomfort. He stilled, as if he sensed she'd stopped.

Quickly, before he had a chance to turn around, she stepped forward, grabbed a protruding boulder near his shoulder and managed to fix an expectant look on her face.

"You doing all right?" he asked with a quizzical stare.

She nodded and glanced over his shoulder. "How much farther is it?"

"A ways yet. You want to sit down for a minute?"

"No, I'm fine." She tried to sound believable.

His gaze went to her feet. The flip-flops were not ideal walking shoes. Her toes ached from trying keep them on while they scaled the steep landscape.

He didn't comment verbally. Didn't need to, his look said enough.

She took another step forward. "We'll find some shade at the bottom to rest for a minute."

He nodded, turned, and continued to descend.

With a deep breath, she followed, cautiously stepping exactly were he had in order to avoid slipping on the sandstone crumbling beneath their feet. It wasn't long before he jumped off the final stepping stone. Though it was only about a two foot jump, she paused. He grabbed her waist and lifted her down before she had a chance to determine if her shoes would stay on or not.

Once again his hand took hers, and he pulled her along the base of the high cliff to a shaded area. The ground was barren. Nothing could grow in the layers of the white, powdery stone. "Sit down and rest a bit," he suggested.

"Good idea. You must be hot." She pointed at his long sleeved shirt.

He knelt down, balanced on his toes. "Naw, I'm used to it. Is Kansas not as hot in the future?"

Knowing when she got up the back side of her white shorts would be covered with baby-fine sand, she thankfully sat down anyway. "Yes, we still have plenty of days well over one hundred degrees. I just usually don't scale mountains in the heat of the day." She stretched out her legs. "Not in flip-flops anyway."

"Flip-flops?"

She pulled off one sandal, held it up. "This is a flip-flop. The ultimate summer shoe."

"Looks like an old shoe a dog got a hold of," he touched the thong, "and piece of rope."

Despite how the scorching sun had made her head throb, she giggled. "They kind of do, don't they? Believe it or not, even men wear them in my time."

"Really?" He picked up a small rock, tossed it aside. "I think I'll stick with my boots." His gaze lingered on where the stone had landed before it touched on her clothing.

She read his mind and pointed at her attire. "These are shorts, and this is a tank top."

With an endearing, crooked grin, he followed suit. "Britches and a shirt."

The shade had relieved the exhausting heat and refueled her energy. A full laugh expelled from her lungs. "We still have britches and shirts in the future."

"That's good." He tried to look serious, but his chuckle said otherwise. He pulled the hat from his head, flopped it on hers. "Here, that'll keep the sun off your head. You won't feel as hot." His hand wrapped around her elbow, helping her rise. "It's not much farther."

The hat was big; the inside rim fell over her ears. She was about to say he should keep it as they stepped out of the shade. The wide brim kept the sun off her face, and a selfish bout made her want to keep it on. "Thank you," she mumbled.

He glanced at her.

"For the hat. Thank you."

"Out here a good hat is worth its weight in gold."

Her selfish bout grew.

He winked at her. "You're welcome."

The action flushed her system with heat more intense than the sun's. She tried to ignore it and focus on the sandy trail. They walked what her feet could have sworn were at least ten miles, but the sensible part of her mind said it was no more than a few hundred yards or so. The leather strap between her toes had gnawed the skin into blisters. She let out a long sigh when they came to a stop.

"This is where the house is, or will be. Over there is where the one outbuilding is, and the other over there. That's the butte you parked behind." He pointed as he talked.

None of it looked familiar. "Are you sure? That butte didn't seem so large."

"It isn't, or wasn't. I'm sure it eroded some over the years. And with the house near, it would look smaller."

"I suspect you're right." She moved forward, wincing as she walked along the side of a hill covered with buffalo grass. "So, where would the tunnel be?"

He'd stayed where they had stopped. "Right here."

"Oh." She moved back, searching the short, grassy stubble. The terrain of the badlands changes every foot, the merger slight and strong at the same time, going from barren, hard sandstone, to prairie grasses and back again. "What are we looking for?"

"A tunnel?" he asked with a teasing tone.

"I know that!"

His lop-sided grin grew before he turned to gaze at the hill. "An indention, a large boulder, a shrub, anything that could hide an opening."

Even sweating buckets, she wanted to flirt with him. The sun must really be getting to her. She tugged the hat lower, and followed his gaze. They searched far and near before she admitted, "It's not here."

He shook his head. "I'm sorry."

She walked to a lone tree nearby, sat down in the shade. "You knew it wouldn't be here, didn't you?" Pulling the hat from her head, she played with the brim for a moment, before pushing her hair from her face. The shade did little to prevent the hot wind from feeling as if she sat in front of a furnace vent.

His long legs folded beneath him gracefully as he sat next to her. "I suspected."

"Why did you come to look then?"

"Because you had to see for yourself," he answered as if it were a simple matter of fact.

Her gaze went to the horizon. She'd long ago learned it was impossible to describe the plains of Kansas to someone who'd never seen them. No where else in the universe is there a sea of land for as far as your eyes can focus. She knew the sight well, had taken it for granted for years. Soft, low-rolling hills and wide, flat spans created a magnificent merger of land with a sky so blue it appeared imaginary, yet at this moment it seemed different—indescribable. Not the outlay, the grass, or the badland carvings, nor even the sky above, but for some reason the soul of the land felt different.

She squeezed her eyes closed, rubbed at the lids with both hands before opening them again. Untouched. There was this overwhelming sense of purity around her. A thick, heavy glob formed in her throat. Pictures of her parents flashed before her eyes. Friends, acquaintances, fellow students. When the vision of Tabby, her cat, emerged, she bowed her head. "Oh, God, what am I going to do?"

Skeeter felt as if he'd just been stabbed in the heart. Her wail, though barely uttered, shot through him like a hot knife. Unsure what else to do, he accepted an internal instinct and took her shaking body into a cradling embrace. He didn't talk, didn't tell her not to cry, just held her as the sobs continued to come. Rocking her back and forth, he let her cry until her weeping eased into small sniffles.

After a heavy sigh left her chest, her breathing grew deep and even. Realizing she'd cried herself to sleep, he leaned back against the tree trunk. It seemed so right, cradling her as she slept. Poor little thing, she had to be exhausted. Of their own accord, his arms tightened, and he nestled his chin upon the top of her head.

What was he going to do with her? He wasn't averse to helping a stranger in need, but a young, pregnant girl from the future—what could he do to help her? His mind searched, but came up empty at every corner, other than the unexpected awareness he enjoyed her company. His gaze went to the sky above. Normally not a selfish person, he contemplated the situation. It was as if he'd been given an astonishing gift, one he didn't ever want to have to give back.

She struggled, just a mite, but enough for him to ease his hold as her slumbering form found a more comfortable position. Lush, soft, yet firm curves molded against his frame, fitting in like the comfort of a feather tick. His arms resettled, held her close. It was almost as unbelievable as the rest of the day—him, Skeeter Quinter sitting under a tree holding a gorgeous girl in his arms. Yet, it felt natural, almost like it should happen every day. And was a whole lot more fun than being a ghost.

He leaned the back of his head against the tree. Natural or not, he had to figure out a way to help her. The summer breeze blew around the tree, rustling the oval leaves and keeping her sleeping form comfortable as he thought...and thought.

He could try and dig out the tunnel, but that would take a month of Sundays and there was no guarantee the tunnel would still be magical. And even if he did start digging, she couldn't stay here. He'd been living in the cave on each trip to his land—didn't have a need for a house, but a woman, especially one as fine as Lila Scott couldn't live in a cave. A woman this fine needed a house. A big fine one like his older brother Kid owned.

It was as if a light went on in his head. Of

course! He'd take her home to Ma. She could stay there, and he'd have his brothers come back and help him dig. Kid wouldn't be able to come, he'd be too busy with his ranch, but the younger boys, Snake, Hog, and Bug would come. With four of them working, it wouldn't take long to dig out the tunnel, and he could test it, see if it still held the magic. Then go back and get her.

He knew the moment she woke. An eyelash didn't flutter, nor did she squirm, but her breathing changed. His arms relaxed, gave her room to sit up. A few moments later, she did so. As soon as her head lifted from his chest, an empty, vacant sensation took its place. He wanted to rub at the spot.

Skeeter watched, not saying anything as she sat up and looked around. After a couple minutes, her green eyes turned toward him, the gaze questioning. "It wasn't a dream was it?" she whispered.

She hadn't slept long, no more than half an hour. "No," he said, softly, not wanting to frighten her.

She crossed her legs, placed her elbows on her knees, and resting her chin in the palms of her hands, asked, "What am I going to do?"

Her face was stricken with sadness. At that moment, he would have paid all the money in the world to find her a ride home. But there was no ride to the future, no horse, no train, or carriage could carry her a hundred and twenty-six years away. Skeeter filled his lungs with a long, deep breath and held it for a moment. He forced a smile to emit, and touched the end of her button nose with the tip of one finger. "Well, I've been thinking about that."

Hope flashed in her eyes for a brief moment. It made his heart tumble.

"I can try and dig the tunnel out."

"You can?" Her face brightened a touch more. "I'll help."

"No, it's going to be a lot of work. Work that's not fit for a woman." He picked up a twig to give his fingers something to do. "And it's going to take some time. So, I'll take you to my mother's house. You can stay there with her, and I'll bring my three younger brothers back here to help me. When the tunnel is done…" The twig snapped between his fingers. He tossed it aside. "I'll come and get you."

"But I could stay here, with you, and help. I'm stronger than I look."

Her assurance tickled him, made a wide smile tug on his lips. "I'm sure you are plenty strong enough, but digging a hole isn't woman's work." He stood, held out one hand.

She took it and threaded her fingers between his after she rose beside him. "What is woman's work?"

Her fingertips floated over the back of his hand. The way her closeness awoke every sensation in his body was amazing, something he'd never experienced. It was all quite overwhelming, and enticing. He knew sexual urges. From about the time a boy turned ten, he recognized arousal, and learned how to contend with it on a regular basis. This was different. It was more of an awakening, a gentle and caring awareness that filled his entire body. It wasn't uncomfortable, actually it was quite pleasant.

"Skeeter?"

He shook the assessing thoughts from his mind. "Sorry, I-I was contemplating on women's work," he lied, feeling his cheeks burn a touch.

"What?"

He reached down, plucked his hat off the ground and placed it on her head. Tugging their entwined hands, encouraging her to follow him out of the shade, he said, "Well, in our time woman's work may be different than in your time, I didn't want to offend you."

She pressed her head against his shoulder in a playful manner. "You are quite the gentleman, aren't you Skeeter Quinter?"

Either it was the light, happy feeling her closeness caused, or the image of him being called a gentleman, he laughed aloud. "I don't think anyone's ever called me a gentleman before."

"Well, then I guess they don't know you like I do."

The wide hat prevented him from seeing her face, but he could have sworn her words came from a smiling mouth. She took a step and stiffened. He paused, glanced to see if she'd stepped on something. Her toes wiggled. "Sore feet?" he asked, looking at the leather thong running between her red-tipped toes.

She nodded.

"Sit down," he instructed and pulled off her silly shoes when she did. Large, white blisters covered the insides of her toes where the leather ran between them. He pulled a bandana from his back pocket and tore it in two. After wrapping the strips around the leather, he handed the shoes back to her. "It might be a bit uncomfortable, but will ease the pain of the blisters.

She slipped the shoes on, stood, and took a couple testing steps. "Much better, thanks." Her hand wrapped around his again.

Content, he laced his fingers between hers, and they walked in comfortable silence. When the cliff appeared before them, he trudged up without letting go of her hand. The climb became steeper; reluctantly he released his hold and stepped behind so he could catch her in case she fell. By the time they scaled the top, his eyes had gone dry from staring at her backside for so long, and his britches had become awfully tight.

Not paying attention, he had to dodge her still

form seconds later. She stood as stiff as a new board. Sidestepping beside her, he turned to follow her shocked stare.

Buffalo Killer waved from his stance near the cave. Skeeter took her hand, glanced her way. "Don't worry. I was just kidding about killing him."

Lila tried to keep her mouth from gapping, but it was an impossible task. The Native American standing several yards ahead of them was dressed in nothing more than tight hide pants. The span of bare chest wasn't shocking. It was the savage look on his face. A black-eyed gaze covered her from head to toe and was filled with something she couldn't read.

Skeeter tugged on her hand, but she couldn't move. He glanced at her, then back at the Native American. "It's all right. He's not as mean as he looks." Leaning closer he whispered, "He practices at looking as mean as his name sounds."

She glanced up, found comfort in the grey-green eyes, and asked, "Name?"

"That's Buffalo Killer, but I don't think he's ever killed a buffalo. They've been gone from these parts for many years. I told him they should change his name to Rabbit Killer."

A giggle stopped in her throat. "That's not funny," she half-heartedly protested. Skeeter had a way of making everything seem less serious. He had an attitude that said life was a game, and meant to be enjoyed. It was hard not to go along with his playfulness.

"Come on, I'll introduce you."

She tightened her hold on his hand, and wrapped her other hand around his forearm, hiding behind the solid span of his upper arm as they walked forward. Her flip-flops scuffed the ground as she dragged her feet. Skeeter kept his pace slow, as if giving her time to get use to the idea of coming face to face with a real American Indian. For that's what he was, not the politically correct Native Americans of the future, but a real, authentic Redman. They stopped a couple feet in front of him. She clutched Skeeter's arm tighter to her chest.

The dark-eyed gaze moved from her to Skeeter. "She from ghost dance." It was a statement, not a question.

Skeeter nodded. "Her name is Lila." He glanced at her. "Lila, this is Buffalo Killer."

Before she swallowed the log in her throat, Buffalo Killer said, "She breeding."

The log choked her. Stifling the coughs ripping at her esophagus made her eyes and nose sting.

"Yes," Skeeter admitted.

"What you do with her?"

"I'm keeping her."

Lila snapped her head up to look at Skeeter. His gaze didn't falter from Buffalo Killer, but his hand holding hers tightened.

"I take her."

"No, I said, I'm keeping her."

The wind whistled, a crow called, echoing in the distinct, heavy silence. After a few long moments, Buffalo Killer uncrossed his arms and kicked his knee high moccasins at the ground. Dust fluttered then resettled around his feet. "How you get her?"

Skeeter's arm had grown solid during the silence and now it relaxed, but Lila still clutch it with both hands. "I'm not telling," he said. Humor laced his words.

"I showed you ghost dance." Buffalo Killer's voice sounded like a child's whine. Lila had to take a second look. She blinked. He no longer looked menacing. An odd, almost comical pout covered his face.

"Yeah! We have to talk about that," Skeeter said.

"Why?"

"It almost killed me."

A smile broke out on the man's face. "You got her."

Skeeter looked down. The gold flecks in his eyes danced in the sunlight. "Yes, I did, didn't I?"

A warm flush filled her face. She dropped her chin, hoping the floppy brim of his hat would hide her red cheeks from his view. Why did his statement make happiness race across her chest?

"How?" Buffalo Killer asked. "I had ghost dance, too."

"I must just be lucky," Skeeter said.

"You share?"

"No, I will not share her. You best remember that, and tell the others as well."

Holding her breath, she snuck a peek from beneath the hat in time to see Buffalo Killer raise his eyebrows as he thoroughly assessed her body with his eyes. A tight, constricting knot formed in her stomach, making her clutch Skeeter's arm harder.

Chapter Four

Lila lifted an extremely sore butt out of the saddle by pressing the balls of her feet against the stirrups. The insides of her legs felt raw. Thank goodness Skeeter had insisted she put on his extra pair of pants, otherwise her thighs probably wouldn't have any skin left. She didn't want to complain, but they'd been traveling for almost two days. "How much farther is it to your mother's house?"

He pulled his horse to a halt. Hers automatically stopped. Skeeter looked apologetic as he said, "Do you want to get down for a few minutes?"

"Could we? Just a few minutes out of this saddle would be heaven." The words had no sooner left her mouth when a wave of guilt spread across her chest. He didn't even have a saddle on his horse. Since there was only one he'd insisted she use it. For two days he'd been sitting on nothing more than a folded blanket.

His hands wrapped around her waist. Their solid strength was as warm and comforting as his presence. Lila laid her hands on his shoulders, and pulled her feet from the stirrups as he lifted her to the ground. Men like Skeeter Quinter didn't exist in two-thousand-eight, which was an extremely sad fact. A sigh left her chest when her feet touched the ground. His hands gave her sides a gentle squeeze before slipping away.

The sun had lowered in the western sky, and the constant wind held a touch of cooler, evening air. Lila lifted damp curls off her neck, hoping the breeze would not only chase away the heat from the blazing sun, but also the amorous warmth being near him sent across every inch of her body.

Skeeter handed her the canteen. "It's not too much farther. We'll be there before night fall."

The water was hot, but it quenched her thirst, and after taking a second swallow she handed the container back to him. "I'm sorry for being such a ninny. I'm sure women of your time are much more resilient than I." She shrugged out of the shirt he'd given her to protect her skin from the sun, tucked it into the saddle bag.

When she was little her father had been obsessed with the popular T.V. show of the nineties, *Quantum Leap*, so accepting she was a time traveler was easy. Even living in the age old century wasn't difficult, but the possibility she may never see her parents, friends, and cat, again, caused a pain in her chest. That is whenever her eyes quit ogling her companion and gave her mind a chance to think of something besides him.

He took a long drink, after wiping a few drops off his chin, said, "There's nothing to be sorry about. You're doing a great job. I don't know many people who'd be willing to travel two days across the prairie in the July heat, and not complain about it." One of his fingers flipped a drooping ringlet away from her eyes. "You've been a good partner, haven't complained at all."

"Yes, I have. I've been whining the entire trip." Her college friends called her the drama queen. Said she turned molehills into mountains faster than a politician.

"Then someone else must be hearing it, because I haven't," Skeeter said as he turned to tie the canteen back onto the saddle horn.

"You are much too nice to me, Skeeter Quinter."

He gave her a saucy, sexy wink that made her knees go weak. Instantly, his hand reached over to settle her wobbling. "Here, let's sit down for a minute."

"No, no, my knees are just stiff from riding. I'll walk around for a minute before we leave again," she said, grimacing at her own lie.

Skeeter settled his hand on her elbow and led her in a small jaunt around the grassy trail as romantically as a finely dressed man might lead a woman across a ballroom dance floor. As they turned to walk back toward the horses he asked, "Have you thought any more about what I asked you last night?"

Lila lowered her head, not wanting to refuse his offer a second time. He'd been so sweet, and it had been terribly romantic. A longing sigh bubbled out of her mouth. It seemed eons ago, not just last night.

The stars had been twinkling overhead, and though the heat of a Kansas summer day was sweltering, there was rarely a night where a blanket wasn't needed. They had been snuggled together, one blanket below them, while the other covered them, his chest her pillow.

She'd told him about Pete, about her car, the date rape, the baby, all the nitty-gritty details she'd told few others. His arms had tightened around her like protective bands of steal. Simply, softly, he'd whispered, "Marry me, Lila."

It had taken her several minutes before reality had settled, and the loving spell surrounding her shattered. Disheartened, she'd been forced to decline.

He hadn't argued her reasoning just kissed her temple and held her until slumber overtook her. When the morning light came, awakening them, he hadn't broached the subject again. Throughout the day, she'd wondered if it had been a dream.

Now she knew it hadn't been. Her stomach hiccupped, and her eyes stung. "I can't marry you." Her reason was the most honest answer she'd ever given. "If we were to get married, it would make my going back all the more difficult." It was going to be hard enough, she'd never found someone she wanted to be with more than Skeeter.

"Lila, you saw that tunnel. It's completely collapsed, all the way to the cave. I can't guarantee I'll be able to dig it out, find the portal. But that's only one issue. You can't—people will—your preg—"

The one thing keeping her mind locked on the future—fear of giving birth without medical aid—overtook her thoughts, made her body quake. "But you said you'd try to dig it out. You said your brothers will help you, and you'll try."

Skeeter's hand slipped from her elbow to fold around her waist. He tugged her close to his side. "Yes, we'll try. I'll dig all the way to China if that's what it takes."

Relief flooded her system. "Thank you." She laid her head against his shoulder as they walked back to the horses. He was the rock in her topsy-turvy world. There was no doubt she would have already collapsed into a puddle without his strength and support, which was odd, because she'd been self-sufficient for years—a fact she was quite proud of. Yet, from the moment she'd met Skeeter, there was this...this bond between them that was indescribable, invisible, but very real—her salvation.

Stopping near the animals, he held her for a few seconds longer. She snuggled in, completely enjoying the embrace, but it wasn't long before realism set in. If she married him, she'd spend her entire life on guard duty. Leeches would forever be trying to steal him away. It really didn't matter what century it was, being married to a man such as he, one who was sure to turn the heads of every woman around would be exhausting. Utterly depressed, she stepped out of his embrace, and despite instantly missing his hold, moved farther away.

While she did a few knee bends, he bent down, lifted the blanket his horse had shaken off. He gave it a hard flip. Dried bits of grass, hair, and dust motes hung in the air for a few seconds before the wind blew them away. The sight caused a touch of remorse, just like her, here one minute, gone the next. Why had this happened to her? Why was she given this opportunity to meet someone so wonderful, to experience something so grand and unusual just to leave it behind?

He laid the cloth across the back of the saddle on her horse. Without a word he tied the reins of his horse together and flipped the loop over the animal's long neck.

She gave him a quizzical look. Surely he wasn't going to ride completely bare-back.

He stepped forward and lifted her onto the saddle. Both of her legs hung over one side. "I'll ride behind you for awhile. That way you can sit like this, and perhaps rest a bit." His hands patted her knees.

Her butt was tremendously sore, and the change of position felt good. "What about your horse?" More than willing to try the new arrangement, she pulled the flip-flops off her feet and hung them on the saddle horn by the bandana wrapped thongs.

"He'll follow."

"I wish you lived in two-thousand-eight," she admitted.

Skeeter laughed, climbing up behind her. "After all the things you've told me, I have to admit, I like the eighteen hundreds just fine."

He settled in and reached around to take the reins. Lila let her head rest against his chest. "I think I must have only told you about the bad things. There are some wonderful modern conveniences."

His free hand massaged her bare shoulder and arm, the rough skin of his fingertips lightly scratched the area. The action made her close her eyes, and a sigh of pleasure emptied her lungs.

"Why don't you tell me about some of them as we ride the last few miles?" he asked.

"Hmm, let's see, oh, I know. Many people have what we call hot tubs or whirlpools. They are big bath tubs that two, three, even as many as ten people can sit in all at the same time, and hot, bubbling water swirls around, easing all the aches and pains from your body." Her muscles began to relax as she described the soothing effects of a Jacuzzi.

"Are you saying you didn't like the pool of water we found yesterday?" he asked.

She could tell by the chuckle rumbling his chest beneath her ear he was teasing. "That was heaven. There was nothing more I wanted at that precise moment in time." Lila leaned back so she could give him a flirting gaze. "I still don't know why you didn't want to go skinny-dipping together. I told you in the future—"

"Yeah, I know," he interrupted, "groups as large as ten and twenty do it together in the future." He pressed her head back into his chest. "Like I said, I like the eighteen hundreds just fine."

The slow, steady sway of the horse, and the solid, protective body holding her, lulled her like a porch swing. Covering a yawn, she mumbled, "I think I might take a nap."

Her sleepy mind believed his lips touched her head before she nodded off, then again it could have been a dream already forming.

Skeeter, on the other hand, wide awake,

tightened his hold around the girl in his arms, and for some reason his mind floated back several years, to when he was about ten or so and had found a little bird down by the creek. One of its tiny wings had been broken, and the poor thing had been hobbling about the tall grass, just waiting to be snuffed up by a snake. He'd caught the meadowlark and took it home where Ma helped him splinter the wing. For a couple weeks he'd kept it in a box in his room, fed it smashed up worms and corn mash. Even with a broken wing the little bird had welcomed each new day with a silly song every morning, and would sit upon his shoulder as he went about doing his chores throughout the days.

A knot formed in his throat, like his heart remembered that one specific day and now rose up to choke him just like it had all those years ago. The wing had healed, and he knew he had to let the meadowlark go, everyone had told him the bird belonged in the wild, not in the crate in his room. And he knew they were right, but all the same it hurt, a real deep down hurt, when he let that little bird go. There were still days when he'd see a meadowlark and wonder about the little one he'd had.

He rested his chin on Lila's sun-kissed curls. Would she be like that little bird? Only in his life for a few days, but remain with him forever. She'd told him so many incredible things about the future, he couldn't stop from asking her questions, all sorts of questions, since he found it all so amazing. Then again, so was she, amazing, that is. And so loveable, just like his little bird. Not that she had a broken wing, but she was broken. He could feel it—there was something besides being from a different time, from being pregnant, and from the terror she'd experienced. No, it was deeper, like there was a part of her that had been broken and had never healed.

The thought stuck in his head, and his chest, as the horses trudged down the trail leading to his Ma's place.

****

The cool night air licking Skeeter quickly dried the water from his long legs before he pulled on a clean pair of pants. The echoing thuds of horse hooves, made him slip on his boots and grab the new shirt from the fence post before walking around the back side of the wash house. Lila had settled into the brass bathing tub his mother always used in the house before he came out to use the big one Snake had made for him and the boys outside.

One of his brothers, from this distance he couldn't tell if it was Snake, Hog, or Bug raced down the driveway like they were being chased by Indians. Skeeter glanced toward the barn, frowning. What would take them away this time of night? He and Lila had arrived an hour ago, and just as he'd suspected, Ma had begun clucking around the girl as if she were a long lost chick.

The barn door flew open, the hinges creaking as the heavy wood swung wide. The broad door hit against the outside wall of the barn with a solid thud. Ma Quinter, all five feet of her covered in a brightly flowered dress that almost glowed in the moonlight, stomped out. He smiled at the sight of her marching form. She was a tough, little lady, who could outshoot all five of her sons. His grin widened. It was good to be home. Good to see everyone.

As she came to a halt beside him, the glint in her eye made him take a step back. He took another step, reading body language that said she wanted to cuff the back of his head. Slightly miffed, he scowled, "Come on, Ma. I'm too old for you to be cuffin'."

"Yeah, well, maybe you're right. Ain't seemed to have done a lick of good any way." Her eyes snapped like fireflies.

"What's that suppose to mean?"

"That lil' gal in there!" She pointed to the house. "I think you got a bit more explainin' ta do."

Skeeter shuffled his feet. What was it about his mother that always made him feel he was about nine and still wet behind the ears? He'd told her as much as he could. Hell, he was still trying to figure it all out. After all, a ghost dance that produced a girl from the future, who in their right mind would believe it?

"Well?" she asked.

"Ma—"

"Don't Ma me!" She stepped forward, lifted her nose so her eyes could glare into his. "That gal's gonna have a baby."

A bucket of cold water couldn't have been more shock inducing. "H-how—d-did—"

"How do I know? I've had four babies. I know what a woman's body looks like when it's expecting. Poor little gal's probably embarrassed as ole-git-outs about the way yer treatin' her. Yer Pa's turning over in his grave, thinking this is how you care for a woman."

Skeeter took a quick side step, making sure he was out of her arm's reach. "Ma," he started. "It's not like that. Yes, she is goin' to have a baby, but it's not mine."

"Well, then, whose is it?"

"Some man who took her against her will," Skeeter admitted, trying to hide the rage boiling in his gut. Once Lila had told him what happened, he'd wished that shutter had been larger, split the man's head wide open. Never had he encountered the type of hatred he felt for Pete Hawkins.

"The devil you say!"

"Yes, I think he's as close to the devil as you can get."

"Well, you're gonna marry her anyway," Ma said

with solid resolution.

He glanced toward the house, wished things were different. "I've asked her Ma, but she doesn't want to get married."

"We'll what's wantin' got to do with anything?"

"Wh—" Before Skeeter could complete his response, a loud ringing filled his ears and pain exploded across the back of his head. The world became colorful, swirling out of control, and then everything went black.

****

Lila sat in a straight-back, wooden chair, dressed in a gorgeous gown of lilac, embellished with lace, eyelet and ruffles. In some ways it reminded her of the dress she wore to her senior prom. But she couldn't enjoy this ensemble. Twenty-five feet of thick, hemp rope tied her to the chair.

Stephanie Quinter had been kind about the whole thing, even to the point of giving her a soft, embroidered pillow to sit on, but nonetheless, bound and gagged, Lila sat at Ma Quinter's kitchen table.

Skeeter, in somewhat the same predicament as she—only worse, gave a low, pain-filled groan. Her heart jolted. She wanted to reach out to run a comforting hand over his shoulder, but the bindings made it impossible. She swallowed a lump of shame, and justified, at least the back of his head had quit bleeding. The white bandage his mother had wrapped around the top of his head, and tied with a bow above his eyebrows, covered the gash the iron frying pan had caused. Until tonight, Lila had always thought stories about women hitting men with a skillet were old wives tales. A new bout of regret slapped her. He probably needed stitches.

Her heart began to thud harder as he moaned again, indicating he was coming to. His head rolled her way, his eyelids lifted. "I'm so sorry," Lila mumbled through the cloth covering her mouth.

Knowing full well he couldn't understand she tried to apologize with her eyes. It was all her fault, and she'd gladly take the blame. She's the one who should have been thumped, not him.

He blinked and squinted, his gaze moving from the ropes around her shoulders to the gag over her mouth. His eyes bugged, then shot daggers toward his mother as his chair started to bounce around. One of the boys had tied the chair to a table leg, and his fierce actions made the table slide. It hit her chest, causing her to give a small yelp of surprise.

Skeeter's gaze landed on her, and he calmed instantly. Eyes full of sorrow, the cloth stretched over his mouth fluttered as he mumbled.

She nodded, accepting his apology. His eyes flashed around the room, and landing on his mother, he began to mumble again. The rag over his mouth billowed in and out with frenzy.

"Settle down, Skeeter! You're gonna make your head start bleedin' again," Stephanie Quinter carried a cup of coffee to the table and sat down. "The boys have gone to get Reverend Kirkpatrick as well as Kid and Jessie. I thought they might like to be at the wedding." She registered her reasoning with a stiff nod.

Lila started coughing, gagging on the extra saliva the wet rag produced in her mouth. Swallowing, she peered at Skeeter, who'd started yelling, the gag in his mouth greatly muffled the noise. However, his movements sent the table askew again.

Through cough-induced, stinging tears, Lila watched Stephanie grab her coffee cup seconds before it tumbled. "Skeeter!" the woman shouted, "You're making the table hit Lila."

Skeeter stopped thrashing and once again looked at her with apologetic eyes. The way his shoulders drooped made the tears in Lila's eyes burn

with empathy. He'd told her his family was a little
rough, but this was beyond belief.

Stephanie Quinter had been a beacon of
kindness when they'd arrived, satisfying their
hunger with a meal of stew and biscuits while the
three brothers filled the high-back, brass bathtub in
one of the bedrooms with steaming water. The
woman had insisted Lila put on the pale purple
dress, and even supplied her with an array of lacy,
somewhat confusing, undergarments. She had on
more layers than she wore in the dead of winter, and
would never have figured out all of the strings and
buttons without the woman's help.

After assisting her dressing, Stephanie had left
the room, only to return a short time later
transformed into a Holy Roller. Quoting the Bible
and totting a shotgun half the size of a cannon, she
burst into the room and marched Lila to the kitchen
table. She tied her to the chair, while one of the
brothers tied an unconscious Skeeter to another
chair. Scared out of her wits, and more confused
than driving in Wichita made her, Lila had barely
uttered a protest. Her vocal cords had become
paralyzed by the way Stephanie Quinter ranted and
raved no grandchild of hers would be born out of
wedlock.

Lila had even gone so far as to click her heels
together three times, praying she'd wake up and the
wicked witch would be gone. Guilt made her
stomach roll, bile burned the back of her throat. She
shot a glance toward Skeeter. His head slowly shook
back and forth, as if he couldn't believe it all either.

He hadn't betrayed her by telling his mother of
her condition. She'd known the moment the older
woman had seen her darkened breasts her secret
was out. Taking a bath at the Quinter house had
provided less privacy than showers in seventh grade
gym class. And the short, round, pioneer woman was

more attentive than any physical education teacher had ever been. Caught off guard when Stephanie carried in another bucket of hot water, Lila hadn't been quick enough to cover herself. Now Skeeter's family thought he'd wronged her, and they were set on making it right.

"The baby isn't his," Lila muffled through the cloth, once again trying to explain his innocence.

Skeeter mumbled something at the same time while gesturing toward her with his head.

"I can't understand a word either of you is sayin', so you might as well hush up. The boys will be back soon." Stephanie took a long drink from her cup.

Behind the woman, leaning against a long cupboard, stood what Lila imagined could only be called an elephant gun. The huge double-barrels were large enough to make any beast die of a heart attack long before it was shot. A shiver ran up her spine. Skeeter gave her a worried glance. She tried to give him a reassuring smile, but the quivers raking her body wouldn't quell. How on earth was she going to get out of this one?

The answer seemed to have come a moment later, when the door flipped open, and a man and woman, followed by the youngest Quinter brother, Bug, rushed in the house. "Stephanie, what the hell is going on here?" a tall, broad shouldered man asked.

Lila's heart leaped to her throat.

The petite woman with golden brown hair hanging almost to her waist beside the man patted his arm. Her voice was warm, but held warning. "Kid."

The man glanced down at the woman. His dark eyes instantly softened. "I'm sorry, love. Are you feeling all right? The ride wasn't too much for you was it?" One of his hands went around the woman's shoulder while the other began to caress her stomach.

Lila felt her eyes widen. The woman was pregnant. The pounding of her heart became almost painful. Skeeter had told her about his brother Kid, and his wife Jessie, but he hadn't said how pretty Jessie was, or that she was pregnant. Lila surveyed the woman with interest. Jessie Quinter appeared to be very young, younger than she. A depressing sigh left Lila's chest. The odds of the girl surviving a pregnancy in this day and age were gravely against her.

"I'm fine," Jessie said, and tilted her head upwards, accepting a gentle kiss, before she turned to Stephanie Quinter. "Ma, why are this girl and Skeeter tied up?" Her voice was once again light, but it held underlying authority that rang surprisingly loud and clear.

Stephanie had leaped to her feet when the trio entered. She wrapped an arm around the woman. "Here, sweetie, have a seat. I'd have thought you'd have brought a wagon in your condition." She frowned at the man as she continued, "Kid, you should have known better than to have her ride over."

"He tried, Ma, but I insisted we ride. I thought we needed to get here as soon as possible." Jessie lowered herself into the chair at the end of the table. Her husband's hands settled on her shoulders and she reached up, resting a hand on one of his. "Now, what's going on here?"

"These here two are gonna have a baby," Stephanie said, pointing to her and Skeeter. "And no grandchild of mine is gonna be born a bastard."

The skin on Lila's cheeks prickled with heat, and she wished with all her might she could just disappear. Skeeter started shouting. The rag over his mouth billowed and rough mumbles filled the room. The ropes binding him strained against his trouncing and his chair legs bounced a time or two.

"Is that true, Skeeter?" Kid asked angrily.

Skeeter started to mumble at the same time she jumped to his defense. Fighting the gag, as well as the thick rope wound around her, Lila tried to say none of it was Skeeter's doing, but between the rag and Skeeter's loud sounds, no one could understand her.

Kid held up one hand. "A simple yes or no is all I need."

"It's not his baby," Lila said against the cloth, shaking her head.

The older brother frowned, clearly not understanding what she'd said, and then glanced to Skeeter.

He mumbled beside her, long and loud the whole time gesturing with his head. Tails of the billowing white bow tied against his forehead fluttered and fell over his eyes. He flipped it aside, and Lila grimaced, afraid his wound would start bleeding again at his thrashing.

"Just nod your head," Kid said, staring at Skeeter. "Yes, she's going to have a baby? Or no, she's not?"

Simultaneously, she and Skeeter nodded their heads.

Kid bowed his head, slowly shaking it from side to side. His long, eerie sigh filled the room with a stinging silence.

Skeeter started talking again, but Lila hung her head. This was somewhat the same scene she'd imagined would happen when her father learned about the pregnancy; and a major part why she had yet to tell her parents. She was a chicken. Hated conflicts; always had—which was probably the reason the whole scheme to catch Pete hadn't worked either.

"Told ya!" Stephanie slapped the table. "Hog should be back with the reverend any time now."

"Ma, pregnant or not, you can't keep tying people up at your table and marrying them," Jessie said.

"Why not? It worked out just fine for the two of you. I ain't heard either of ya complain a'tall," the older woman responded.

Skeeter and Kid both started talking at the same time. Lila tried to block the sounds from entering her ears. Tears threatened to spill behind closed lids, her throat burned, and her head felt like a bee hive—full of angry, humming bees.

"Hush now! You're upsetting the girl," Jessie said.

The room instantly became quiet. All except for the bee's buzzing.

Jessie's voice sounded again, "Kid, cut the ropes off her."

"No!" Stephanie insisted.

Chapter Five

Skeeter let Kid help him into the chair on the front porch. His head stung as if it was on fire, and his gut churned. He untied the bow flapping across his forehead and unwrapped the bandage circling his scalp. After tossing the blood stained rag on the small table, he ran a hand over the back of his neck, pinching at the tension. He flinched as a new, sharp pain shot up the back of his skull.

"You doing all right?" Kid asked. "You look awfully white."

"I'm still seeing stars, among other things," Skeeter admitted. The wallop from his mother's frying pan was the least of his worries.

"I wish there was time for you to recuperate, but as Ma said, the reverend's on his way. You gotta tell me what's going on so I know what to do when he gets here."

He looked up at his brother. Kid leaned against the porch railing, his arms folded over his chest. The oldest Quinter brother had a way of making the rest of them feel like saplings next to a tall oak—always had.

Skeeter lifted his gaze, to meet the dark eyes he knew would be condemning him. Startled, he looked deeper into Kid's eyes. They were full of compassion, not critical at all. He frowned. Then a twitch tried to pull his lip into a grin.

Jessie had worked her magic on Kid. The little slip of a girl, he—Skeeter, had hauled home and forced Kid to marry, had turned his brother into a real human being. If his life wasn't in such disarray he may have chuckled at the transformation.

Kid raised an eyebrow.

The smile tugging hard on his lips slipped from his face as he recalled the predicament at hand. In twenty-three years he'd never thought of a woman the way he thought of Lila. Had never been willing to do whatever it would take to protect her. He took a deep breath, and thankful his brother was here to help said, "Damn, Kid, you could of knocked me over with a feather when she told me she was gonna have a baby."

"I know the feeling," Kid said with a deep laugh. "That's exactly how I felt when Jessie told me. Still feel that way some days."

A twinge, somewhat like regret touched his heart. Skeeter breathed past the pang. "The baby isn't mine, Kid." He shook his head. "Lila and I haven't...well you know."

Kid bit his lower lip as he nodded.

He'd rather die than have Kid think badly of Lila. "A man raped her, and...ah hell, Kid, it's hard to explain."

Stepping away from the rail, Kid pulled up a chair. "Well, Skeeter, I'm here to listen."

He couldn't tell Kid Lila was from the future, couldn't tell him Buffalo Killer's ghost dance had turned him into a ghost. He'd never believe it, no one would. Yet, he had to help Lila. She was so sweet and innocent and didn't deserve to be treated badly. He turned to his brother. "I think I'm in love with her."

Skeeter felt his eyes bulge as the words emitted. Where had they come from? Hell, he didn't even know what love was, and certainly had no idea what being in love meant. Or did he? Had he made the discovery two days ago when he awoke? From the moment he'd met her, his life had changed. His thoughts, feelings...everything was different. A good kind of different.

Kid rubbed his chin. "And?"

As long as he was being completely honest, he might as well tell all. "And I want to marry her. Buffalo Killer might steal her if I don't. I asked her." His shoulders drooped. "But she doesn't want to marry me."

"Has she said why?"

He nodded.

After an extended amount of time Kid said, "Skeeter, a few years ago I probably would have carried that girl out of here, as far from you and this family as possible, pregnant or not. But that was before Jessie, and before I really got to know you. You're a good man, an honest, upright citizen, one I like knowing is on my side every day." He reached over and laid a hand on Skeeter's shoulder. "I can't help you if you aren't going to tell me what's going on. I need the whole story."

It felt as if he'd been riding in the wind all day and fine grains of sand had embedded themselves in his eyeballs. He blinked at the stinging, tried to swallow the stump in his throat. He lowered his head, shaking it from side to side. "Kid, you won't believe it. No one will."

"Try me, brother." Kid's grip on his shoulder tightened. "You can trust me. I trusted you with my life, and you didn't let me down."

Skeeter twisted, looked deep into the honest, sincere eyes of his brother. A warm sense of camaraderie filled his body. If anyone could help it would be Kid. Kid Quinter never let anyone down. His shoulders squared at the next thought. He was ready, and willing, to follow in his brother's footsteps.

****

Lila sat on the edge of the bed. She'd wrung her hands together until her knuckles hurt. She lifted her gaze as the latch sounded and watched the door to the room open.

Jessie entered carrying a cup and saucer. "Here." Holding them out, she added, "Its tea. How are you feeling?"

"Awful," Lila admitted.

Jessie smiled and sat down beside her. "And I bet it has nothing to do with the pregnancy."

She gave a slight shrug and took a sip of the tea.

"How far along are you?" Jessie asked.

"Not quite three months. You?"

"Almost six months." Jessie patted her stomach. "It's wonderful isn't it?"

Lila blinked, somewhat confused. "Uh?"

"Have you felt the baby move yet?"

"No." Lila set the cup and saucer on the small table beside the bed. "I don't think so, anyway."

"Oh, you'll know when you do." Jessie's face took on a warm, pink glow. "But even before then, just knowing a life is growing inside you is wonderful, isn't it?"

Lila laid her hand on her stomach. She hadn't even told her mother about the pregnancy yet. There hadn't been anyone to whom she could share her thoughts about being pregnant. "Yes, it is," she admitted.

"Can you tell me about? Tell me what happened?" Jessie ran a hand over Lila's shoulder.

Lila wanted to cry. The woman's kindness was almost more disconcerting than Stephanie Quinter's righteousness. She shrugged her shoulders. "You wouldn't believe me."

"How do you know until you try?"

"Would you believe me if I said I was from the

71

future? That until two days ago, I lived in the year two-thousand-eight?" Lila almost quivered at the tone of her own voice. She hadn't meant to snap at the other woman. The bitter statement had just shot out of her mouth.

A smile formed on Jessie's face, but it wasn't in disbelief, or humor. It was a smile of compassion. "Yes, I'd believe you."

Lila felt her chin drop. She slapped her mouth shut, swallowed, wondering how to respond.

"I know Skeeter. For him to bring home a girl from the future wouldn't surprise me in the least." Jessie raised a hand, reached over to push the hair out of Lila's eyes. Her fingers were gentle as she settled the curls behind one ear. "And I'm very intrigued. Please tell me all about it."

Lila's brows tugged together, she rubbed a hand over her forehead. Talking to Skeeter was one thing, but to tell someone else she was from the future was, well, weird. Besides, where would she even start? How much would she need to say to make the story sound believable? The whole thing was unbelievable. Lila sighed, a long, deep, confusing sigh that did little to ease her frustration.

"Where did you live in the future? What was the name of the town?" Jessie asked.

"Hays," Lila answered unsurely.

"Fort Hays?"

In for a penny, in for a pound, Lila thought. She glanced at Jessie. "Yes, but in the future it's just known as Hays. I think it was changed from Fort Hays to Hays sometime in the eighteen-eighties." She let out an odd laugh. "Any day now, I guess."

"Really? Do they still have boot hill there?" Jessie asked with wide, interested eyes.

Lila nodded. "But people in the future think boot hill is in Dodge."

"They have one there too, but it's not as large as

the one in Hays. My brother Russell and I spent a winter in Hays, a few years ago." Jessie gave a little shiver and rubbed her arms. "It was a rough town."

"Worse than Dodge?" Lila asked. History had made Dodge City the wildest cow town in Kansas.

"Oh, yes." Jessie nodded.

"Hmm, interesting," Lila murmured. Living in the past was quite fascinating. Too bad she hadn't majored in history. "They change the name of Nixon too, it's Scott City in my time. Actually most of the towns and counties around here have different names in two-thousand-eight."

"Oh?" Jessie asked.

She nodded. "I attend the State University in Hays. I'm working on an I T degree."

"Really? Kid tried to send me to the University in Boston, but I chose not to go," Jessie said, and then asked, "What's I T?"

Lila frowned. Though she and Jessie were close in age, they were generations apart. She was a millennium baby, a member of the Y generation, the generation that was giving the baby boomers more trouble than the Xer's ever thought of. Millennials crave technology, and therefore crave college. She couldn't imagine someone choosing not to go. She also didn't know how to begin to explain computers. "It stands for Information Technology." She shrugged her shoulders, "It's really hard to explain."

"It sounds like it." Jessie reached over, patted her knee. "So, how did you meet Skeeter."

She wanted a friend she could spill the beans to, and Jessie's kindness made the perfect companion for her—a scared, pregnant girl from the future. She twisted, looked Jessie in the eye. "This guy named Pete had given me a drug and raped me. Six weeks later I found out I was pregnant and tried to have him arrested. It didn't work out, and he's been stalking me ever since. Yesterday morning, he was chasing me down the highway, and I took a side road, it led me too an old homestead. I hid my car behind the sandstone bluffs and ran into the abandoned house."

Jessie blinked a couple of times. "Then what happened?"

"A voice or a feeling told me to crawl through a small door and into a tunnel. When I got to the end of the tunnel, Skeeter was there sleeping next to a fire. He said he'd participated in a ghost dance with an Indian named Buffalo Killer and he'd become a ghost in the house. He scared Pete away and made the house fall down, and when that happened the tunnel caved in, so I had no way to get back to the future."

Jessie's finger's felt cool against Lila's heated skin as they brushed over her forehead.

Lila reached up and clasped the hand, squeezing it. "I know it sounds unbelievable. It is unbelievable, but that's what happened. I swear to you. That's what happened."

"I believe you," Jessie whispered.

She looked at Jessie seriously. "Why? Why would you believe me?"

Jessie looked extremely sad for a moment. "Because I know how it feels to have people not believe."

"Do you also believe me when I say I can't marry Skeeter? That I have to get back to the future?" The statement tore at her heart.

With a frown Jessie asked, "To go back to the man who raped you?"

"No, no, I'll get an order for protection or something. I have to go back so I can have the baby and give it away." A new pain made her throat burn.

"What?" Jessie's solemn eyes popped wide open. "Give your baby away?"

Lila nodded. Her decision hadn't come lightly,

but another thing about the millennium generation, thanks to divorce, single parents and latchkey life, was their independence and empowerment. The baby boomers called them selfish and lazy. She didn't believe she was selfish, just had a different attitude than other generations. "Yes, I'm not ready to be a mom." She repeated the excuse she'd hoped to soon believe. Letting go of Jessie's hand, she rose to walk around the small room.

The large brass tub had been removed. A bed, a dresser, a chair, and the table beside the bed filled Stephanie Quinter's bedroom. It was tidy and quaint. Jessie had led her in here after Kid cut the ropes binding her and Skeeter. Stephanie hadn't been happy about the happenings at all.

Lila twisted to face the bed again. "Nor am I willing to have a baby in the eighteen-eighties."

"Why not?"

She threw her hands in the air. "It's dangerous for one."

"Having babies is dangerous? How? It's a natural process," Jessie said.

"It's changed a lot between now and two-thousand-eight." Lila knelt down in front of Jessie and took both of her hands. She liked Skeeter's sister-in-law, a lot. And she didn't want the girl to go through labor without modern medicine any more than she wanted to herself. "Jessie, women die during childbirth in this day and age."

"There's always that possibility, I guess."

"In the future, they have specialists, and ultrasounds, and neonatal units." Her mind took a detour. "You should come back to the future with me," Lila said.

"But you said you can't get back to the future. That the tunnel caved in."

Lila let go of Jessie's hands and began to pace the room again. "It did, but Skeeter promised he'd dig it out. That's why we came here. He needs his brothers to come help with the digging. It'll take him too long by himself."

Jessie patted the brightly patterned quilt covering the bed.

Lila sat down. "You don't believe me do you?"

"I never said that. But, Lila, what about before you go back to the future? You aren't going to be able to hide your condition for much longer. And—well, people are not very pleasant to unwed pregnant women. A matter of fact, it's dangerous for you to go anywhere in your condition as a single woman." Jessie wrapped an arm around her shoulders. "Believe me. I've seen it with my own eyes."

Lila twirled the lace perfectly stitched onto the edge of one sleeve. "I hadn't thought of that. It is really bad for an unwed woman to be pregnant in this time isn't it?"

Jessie nodded. "I'm not trying to scare you, but when I lived in Dodge, I helped a woman sneak girls out of town who were pregnant." She gave a long, sad sigh before saying, "Some, who refused to leave didn't live to have their babies, and others were treated very, very badly." Her eyes met Lila's. "Those that died didn't die in childbirth. They were murdered, and even then the town folks refused to bury the girls inside the church cemetery. They had to be buried outside of town."

Ice cold, Lila whispered, "Oh, my God."

****

Skeeter didn't know feet could tremble, but his were. He curled his toes and tried to focus on what Reverend Kirkpatrick said. It was no use. He couldn't make out the man's mumbling. All he could think about was the fact Lila had agreed to marry him. She was marrying him. Right here, right now in his mother's kitchen. Whatever Jessie had said to her had changed her mind. He'd thank his sister-in-law until the day he died.

After he'd admitted to Kid he was in love, the thought had settled, and ultimately made him quiver with happiness. He hoped Lila was happy about it too. Tilting his head, he snuck a glance.

Her green eyes glistened and a soft smile covered her face as she looked back at him. His heart leaped, he curled his toes tighter. Did that mean she was happy? Was it possible she could love him? Surely not, most folks didn't take a quick liking to him, let alone fall in love with him.

But that was before. Before he'd been a ghost. Before he'd met Lila. From now on, he was a new man. He was going to spend the rest of his life making her the happiest woman on earth, waiting for the day Lila would look at him the way Jessie looked at Kid—like he'd hung the moon just for her.

A weight landed on his shoulder. Skeeter glanced to his side. Standing next to him, Kid leaned closer and whispered, "Go ahead little brother, kiss your bride."

Skeeter whipped his head around, met Lila's smiling, expectant gaze. His heart raced so fast it was sure to beat its way right out of his chest, fall to the floor, and race out the front door. Taking a quick breath and hoping it would help keep the organ in his chest, he leaned down to press his lips to hers.

He'd kissed women before, he'd even given Lila a quick peck over the past couple of days, but nothing had prepared him for this. As soon as his lips touched hers, excitement raced through his body like a wild fire in August. It left no area untouched or uncharred.

Sweeter than honey, her soft, sweet lips moved beneath his. His arms folded around her. Gently, he tugged her lithe body against his burning frame and twisted his head so he could get a deeper taste.

Her arms, wrapped around his neck, clung to

him as her fingers ran through his hair, encouraging him to delve deeper. When her lips parted, and his tongue entered the sweet cavern of her mouth, he wondered if he died again, but this time he'd gone to heaven. He could almost hear angels singing.

Someone clearing their throat, loud and obnoxiously, broke the sweet song. Skeeter scowled and opened one eye to see who was interrupting his bliss. The unhappy glare of Reverend Kirkpatrick made both of his eyes pop open. Abruptly, and regretfully, he ended the kiss.

Lila sighed as they separated. Her cheeks were redder than the roses his brother, Snake, grew out back. She didn't open her eyes, just laid her head against his chest. Skeeter ran a protective hand over her back as he glared back at the man of the cloth. Reverend or not, the man had no right to embarrass his wife.

A wide smile formed as the thought set in. Lila was his wife. He glanced down, and her face lifted. A smile tugged on her wet lips.

"Yahoo!" He shouted and not caring what anyone else thought, he lifted his new wife into the air and swung her around, making a full circle. The room filled with laughter. After he settled her back onto the floor, he turned to Reverend Kirkpatrick and thrust a hand forward. "Thank you, Reverend," he said with earnest.

"You're welcome," the preacher said then turned to the others in the room, "May I present Mr. and Mrs. Steven Quinter."

The audience began to clap, and Jessie stepped forward. She planted a little kiss on Skeeter's cheek and said, "Congratulations."

She turned to embrace Lila, and Kid stepped forward with an outstretched hand. "Congratulations."

"Thank you, thank you both very much," Skeeter

said through the smile pulling hard on his lips. His heart had to be as big as a water bucket, and full to the brim with happiness.

Lila looked up at him, smiled and said, "Yes, thank you both very much."

The bucket overflowed.

"Well, I think some cake and coffee is in order," Stephanie Quinter said. "Hog baked a brown sugar and molasses one this morning."

Lila's head was still spinning as Skeeter led her to the table. His kiss had almost knocked her socks off, and the tumbles in her stomach had nothing to do with the baby.

He'd been so sweet and kind to her the past couple of days. She'd thought it was just because that was the kind of man he was. Even when he'd asked her to marry him, she'd believed it was out of kindness. But his kiss hadn't been thoughtful. It had a much deeper core.

Her fingers touched her lips, caressing the puffiness his passion had instilled. She covered her mouth, not wanting anyone to hear her intake of breath. *Skeeter had fallen in love with her!* A deep sinking feeling hit her stomach like a rock, and her shoulders drooped. Her life had just gone from bad to worse.

Chapter Six

How had she let it happen? How did it happen? They'd only known each other for two days. She'd recognized the love she felt for him growing in her chest. But she loved everything—chocolate ice cream; long, hot showers; *American Idol*, and numerous other things. She could deal with her love. But his love...She sighed. It meant the one thing she didn't want to happen would. She'd hurt him. If he was in love with her when the time came for her to return to the future, her leaving would break his heart. She'd had her heart broken—the night of her junior prom, when Mike Schmidt had stood her up, took Heather Reins to the prom instead. That had been an awful experience. She'd cried for months.

She reached over, clutched Skeeter's hand. He turned and the smile on his face made her heart flip and beat faster than a rock and roll song. Her blood began to bubble, sending a happy, light feeling to her head. The sad memories disappeared. She grinned back and leaned against his broad shoulder. His was so very handsome, and being married to him would be wonderful.

Professor Rutledge came to mind, the teacher whose psychology class she'd just completed, the one where she'd studied the generations. He'd said since birth millennials had been told, by both the media and over indulgent parents, they could have it all.

Maybe he was right. Skeeter was the man of her dreams, and the universe had seen a way to bring them together, surely it would also find a way for them to stay together.

Her heart fluttered. *He could come back to the future with her.* A wide smile made her cheekbones raise. The other thing about her generation; they are extremely optimistic. And believed there was no sense waiting until tomorrow for what they can have today.

She pressed her lips to the hard bulge of his bicep beneath her cheek. He leaned down, kissed the top of her head. As she sat up, their eyes met, and at that moment the year two-thousand-eight ceased to exist. It didn't matter what century it was, she was married to the most wonderful man on earth, and it was her wedding day.

Happiness bubbled from her chest as she glanced about the room. Everyone had been served cake and coffee. She broke off a large piece of her slice, and held it up to Skeeter's lips. "It's tradition, the bride and groom have to feed each other their first bites."

His cheeks turned slightly pink. "Really?"

She nodded and glanced to his plate.

He broke off a chunk, held it before her mouth. The rest of the occupants in the room became little more than wallflowers. Her skin, pricked with pleasure, tingled as they fed each other. They took the time to lick sweet, sticky, leftover frosting from each others fingertips. Lila didn't know which was more overwhelming, tasting his skin, or the way his tongue sensually curled around her fingers, but she felt herself melting.

Since it was already extremely late, the wedding party didn't last long. After saying farewell and good night, Skeeter led her to a bedroom on the wall opposite from the one she'd been in earlier. He pushed the door open. Every inch of her pulsed with excitement and anticipation. The room was rustic, and the flickering light from the oil lamp, sitting on a highboy chest beside the bed, made everything look extremely romantic.

Skeeter closed the door behind them. She twirled around to wrap her arms around his waist. The steady beat of his heart thudded against her ear.

It was surreal, the world around them extremely quiet. No horns honked or voices from a T.V. filled the air. She lifted her face, looked at him. "Please tell me I'm not dreaming. Please tell me this isn't some kind of virtual reality video game."

He chuckled. "I assure you it's not a dream, or whatever kind of game you just mentioned."

"Kiss me," she whispered.

"Gladly."

If possible the merger was stronger, more intense than his wedding kiss. She consumed the sweet, savory taste that was all him; overtaken by the acute and demanding need surging from the pit of her being. Her fingers worked the buttons of his shirt, her hands searching for the hot, rippled contours of his chest. She kneaded the hills and valleys before reaching around to grasp his hips and tug him forward as she walked backwards, toward the bed.

He broke the kiss, lifting his lips and gasping for air. She giggled and turned around, presenting the long row of buttons down her back. "You have to help me out of this contraption."

Very slowly, his fingers unlatched the long row of minuscule buttons, the material loosening a bit with each movement. She wiggled, anticipation killing her.

"Hold still. You're squirming like a cat in a bag." He kissed the back of her neck.

She twisted her head, wanting to catch his lips. "I feel more like a firecracker, and someone has already lit the fuse."

His lips brushed over hers as his hands slipped the dress off her shoulders.

She turned around, facing him with a sly smile. Slowly, teasingly, she tugged her arms out of the material and let the gown flutter to the floor. Her fingers walked up the front of his shirt. Then back down so she could tug the material out of his pants. It was surprising—how forward she was behaving, but it was all so incredible, this overwhelming need she had for him.

Since the moment her eyes had settled on his bare chest yesterday, her sexual desires had been kicked into high gear. For the past two days she'd barely stopped thinking about this moment. Wondering, fantasizing how it would feel to have his weight settled atop her.

His hands slipped around her neck, massaging and caressing until they came to rest on her cheeks. She gazed into his face. Something there made her hands grow still on his hips. "What? What is it?" she asked, holding her breath.

He wanted her, the evidence was as clear as the nose on his face, yet something was making him appear reluctant. His face held almost a painful expression. "Oh, your head! Does it still hurt?"

"No, I'm fine. But, you...Your, um, condition, the baby. I don't know if we..."

Relieved, she smiled. "It's perfectly safe. Besides pregnant woman are supposed to get plenty of exercise."

His eyes sparkled, but his gaze still held a touch of doubt. "You're sure?"

"Positive." She ran her hands around to his back, pulling the rest of the shirt tail out of his britches. Pushing the shirt aside, she roamed both hands over his hard, hot chest. "You aren't considering denying me my wedding night, are you?"

He laughed, and for a moment she wondered if the rest of the house heard the joyful sound. The next instant, and in one swift movement, he picked her up, twisted and gently lowered her to the bed. He leaned over her, caressed her cheeks gently. "I don't plan on denying you anything my sweet wife."

She grabbed his neck, pulling his head downward. "I'm so glad to hear that."

****

Sunshine, bright and hot, the following morning made everything look as full of light and as happy as Skeeter felt. After eating a hearty meal with his mother and younger brothers, he led Lila from the house, stealing a kiss as they walked across the front yard.

When the merger ended, he wrapped his hands around her trim waist, and lifted her into the buckboard. It was unimaginable a baby could grow in area so tiny. His big hands easily spanned Lila's middle. Her stomach was firm and flat. He'd never felt anything as silky smooth as her skin. Memories of the night before made his loins tighten.

It was so amazing they were married. He'd told Kid everything. How he'd participated in Buffalo Killer's ghost dance. How he'd saved Lila; how the tunnel had caved in, Pete chasing her—all of it. His brother had helped him come up with a plan, and this morning they were going to Kid and Jessie's to gather supplies for the trip back to their land. His chest swelled with pride at the thought of sharing his land with Lila. He glanced up.

She smiled and scooted over, making room for him on the seat and settling the long skirt of her purple dress over her knees. He climbed onto the driver's seat and as he took the reins, she settled a hand on his thigh. The bulge in his britches grew.

Their wedding night had been beautiful. He almost chuckled aloud at the thought. He'd never used the word beautiful before in his life, but he couldn't think of another way to describe it. And not even the devil himself could wipe the smile off his face this morning.

"So, where are we going?"

"Like I said at breakfast, over to Kid's then we'll drive into Nixon and get you some decent shoes," he glanced at the feet she'd settled on the front base board. "I thought we'd stop by Willamina's on the way. See if there's anything she needs from town."

"Who?"

"Willamina and Eva. They're friends of the family."

She nodded, glanced about the area. "How far is it to Kid's house?"

"Not far. Kid has a big, fancy house. You'll like it." He clucked his tongue, setting the horses in motion. With a firm hold on the reins, he kept the pace slow, trying to keep the dust floating up from beneath the team's feet to a minimum. July was always hot and dry, and this year was no different. He pulled off his hat, plopped it on her head. "We'll have to get you a hat, too," he said, wondering about the temperature in her time. Was the landscape still the same? The wide open spaces did something for a man—gave him a sense of pride that was hard to explain. He'd hate to think it was all gone.

"Have I told you I'm a millennial?" She broke the silence a few minutes later.

"A what?"

"Some people call it generation y."

He glanced her way, waiting to hear more.

"You see, each generation is very different, they have different thoughts, wants, needs. I don't really know what generation you are, they never taught us about those born before nineteen hundred. You

85

might be rolled into the lost generation. That was the one before the great generation. Then came the baby boomers, then generation x, then the millennials, that's me, and now there's the generation z or vistas."

"Who taught you all this?"

"A professor at the college I attend. He also owns the apartment building where I rent." She shrugged. "The reason I'm telling you all this is because I may not like Kid's big house. I don't want you to be offended but know where I'm coming from." She twisted, pointed a finger at her chest. "You see, Professor Rutledge says my generation are multi-taskers and don't plan on staying anywhere for a long time, so therefore, we don't really care for the big houses the generations before us did. We like small, compact places that are easy to take care of so we can get on with life."

Skeeter didn't comment. She'd talked about this professor yesterday too, and he once again noticed how her eyes became glassy when she did so, and he didn't like it. It was as if everything the man had said was the gospel—Skeeter already concluded this professor must be some sort of Bible pusher, all hell and brimstone, and someone he'd like to knock into next week—but right now he wasn't focused on that. His mind had become stuck on one line. The one where she said she didn't plan on staying anywhere for a long time. Like a wallop it reminded him their time together would be short lived. She needed to go back to her time, and he would have to let her—just like his bird.

Funny, he'd always been carefree. Ma called him happy-go-lucky. That was because most things hadn't meant a lot, there was always tomorrow. But in Lila he'd found something he wanted to last forever, and he didn't like the thought of her leaving. It squeezed his guts into tight knots. She was so delightful, so loveable. With a shake of his head, he tried to clear his mind, and sent an encouraging glance her way, silently asking her to go on. He didn't want to dampen their time together with worrisome thoughts.

"My generation is also quite blunt, and we question authority. I mean, think about it, who is the *government*? And why should we *trust* them? All they are is a bunch of old geezers from the great generation who don't know when to retire." She wrapped her hands around his arm, hugging it. "Anyway, I'll try to bite my tongue, but please don't be offended if I don't like Kid's big house."

There was this way about her that made him happy. So happy. He laughed, pulled his arm from her grasp and wrapped it around her shoulders. "I won't be offended." Placing a kiss on the top of her head, he said, "Tell me more."

She scooted closer and wrapped her arm around his back. "I don't know what it is about you that turns me into a Chatty Cathy doll." She frowned, looked at him seriously. "I thought men didn't like women who talk all the time."

Despite the fact he had no idea what a Chatty Cathy doll was, he laughed. "I don't know about other men, but I like hearing you talk. I like listening to what you have to say." He'd always enjoyed learning about new places and things, had read most every book he could get his hands on, but her tales were better than any story. Listening to her voice was music to his ears.

"Hmm...maybe it's because you don't have a radio, CD, or MP3 player." Lila laid her head on his shoulder. "Did I tell you my generation is really techno-savvy?" His hard, solid body felt so good, and last night had left her floating on cloud nine. Nothing could dampen her happiness.

"Tell me more," he encouraged.

She giggled and took great delight in telling him about every invention she could possibly think of, from televisions to space shuttles and everything in between. Without stopping she talked until the wagon rolled around two large pens full of calves and their mommas. Then whatever she'd been saying completely escaped her.

Followed by a huge black lab, Jessie walked across the yard. The loose, white blouse floating around her rounding stomach was like a slap of reality.

Lila glanced around. Yes, she had married the man of her dreams, was being escorted in a horse drawn carriage by the ruggedly, handsome cowboy. But this wasn't some fairytale. It was real. She was in the nineteenth century where they had very few hospitals, no medical insurance, and just like Jessie, she was pregnant. But she had hope—the other girl didn't.

Her joyous, festive mood faded as Skeeter eased the wagon to a halt. He twisted to gaze at her. The wide smile on his face slowly slipped away. "What's wrong?" he asked.

A lump the size of Mount Everest formed in her throat. She couldn't tell him his sister-in-law would most likely die in childbirth. "Nothing," she lied. "It-it's just the size of their house. You're right it's big, and—and very nice." She glanced to the house for the first time.

He wrapped her in a solid, hard hug. "It'll be all right. I promise you, everything is going to be all right."

She nodded and hid her face in his chest for a brief moment, wishing she could believe him. Wished everything in this topsy-turvy world she'd been thrown into would be all right. She willed a deep breath to ease her frustration. Knowing Kid and Jessie waited for them forced her to lift her head and smile a greeting.

"Hello," Jessie said brightly.

"Hi," she responded. Her heart ached for the couple.

Skeeter helped her down, and the other woman instantly took her hand. "Come on into the house, it's already getting warm out."

"Oh, I guess I hadn't noticed," Lila said as they walked toward the house. Over her shoulder she watched Skeeter and Kid lead the horses to the barn. The harnesses jingled and hooves clomped. The sounds seemed to echo in her ears, emphasizing a world, a time, where she didn't belong.

"This is Sammy," Jessie introduced her to the large dog walking beside her knee. "He's never far from my side. I hope you don't mind."

"No, a friend of mine had a lab while we were growing up. They're great dogs." Lila sighed. "I have a cat, Tabby. He's the independent kind, easy to take care of." This dread on her shoulders was smothering. "I'm sorry. I guess I'm out of sorts this morning."

Jessie looped an arm through hers. "We'll go inside and have some tea. Maybe that will help. When I was first pregnant, I was so sick tea was the only thing that would stay down."

Lila didn't have the heart to say she wasn't morning sick. She picked up her feet, forced them not to shuffle, and walked up the porch steps. Jessie opened the wide front door and waited for her to enter first. She stepped over the threshold and paused, glancing around the great room. It reminded her of a lodge she'd stayed in while skiing in Colorado several winters ago.

A massive, stone fireplace covered one wall, but it was the picture hanging above the mantle that drew her gaze. A large, framed, canvas painting of Jessie and Kid hung prominently in the center of the stones. Several white-faced cattle dotted the field behind them. They gazed at one another, and the artist had displayed their love so richly it made Lila gasp.

"A young friend of ours painted it. Her name is Eva. She and Willamina live up the road a bit. I think she did a wonderful job."

"She certainly did," Lila admitted. The painting captured the image of love every ad agency in the future tried to use to sell products. They'd all failed. Something so real couldn't be reproduced with actors. She turned to Jessie. The woman would never leave her husband to come to the future and have her baby. That was as clear as the Kansas summer sky.

"Well, let's go have that tea," Jessie said, leading the way to the kitchen.

She followed. Her mind was a whirlwind. What could she do? There had to be someway she could assist Jessie, make sure the girl was prepared when her time came. Her heart skipped. Perhaps she did belong here—for a time anyways—long enough to teach Jessie about pregnancies. Yes, everything happens for a reason, and she'd bet her reason was to educate Jessie.

A determined mindset settled. "Do you have a doctor following your pregnancy?" Lila asked as soon as they sat down at a long kitchen table.

"I've seen Doctor Fields in Nixon. When the time comes, he'll ride out for the delivery. But of course I have Ma as well as Kid." Jessie set a kettle to boil on the wood stove.

Lila bit her lip and tried to think of all the things she'd read about pregnancy. "Are you taking prenatal vitamins?"

"Pre-what?"

She shook her head and sighed. She was going to have to start at square one.

****

Skeeter glanced toward the house, watching the door close behind Lila and Jessie.

"How are you doing today?" Kid asked as he walked into the barn.

"Fine." He turned to follow. "I have to ask a favor."

"Ask away."

He shuffled his feet. Admitting his faults all of sudden became extremely hard. They'd never bothered him before, but since he met Lila, he didn't want to be a failure at anything. The way she'd clammed up once she'd seen Kid's house had made him aware of what little he had to offer. He bit his tongue, tried to keep the shame out of his voice. "I don't even have a house, Kid. I've been living in a cave on the land. It's been fine and dandy for just me." He shook his head. "I can't take Lila back there to live in a cave."

"Well, then I guess we need to load up the boys and some supplies and build you and your bride a house." Kid slapped his back and turned to unhitch the team.

He stepped over, loosened the other horse's harness. Kid sounded so matter of fact. Like he'd just said gotta unhitch the team, or shoe the gelding. Building a house was a huge undertaking. He glanced at his brother. Was it as simple as Kid made it sound? "I have plenty of money, I've—"

"How is the Bone War going?" Kid interrupted.

His brows furrowed. Maybe he hadn't heard right. This being responsible for someone else was a bit overwhelming. And the love in his chest made keeping his feet on the ground a constant battle.

Kid looked at him expectantly. His mind paused for a moment before he remembered his brother's question. The Bone War had been a bit mind-boggling when he first found out about it, too. He switched trails, answered Kid's question. "Those two fools might kill each other. Cope has hired armies of diggers, and Marsh is only one step behind him."

He'd been astonished when Russell took their first load of dinosaur bones east. Their discovery instantly became the center of attraction for two rich men who were each set on becoming the country's leading authority in the new field of dinosaur paleontology. Each one wanted to be the first to name and claim credit to the findings of new species of dinosaurs. The two men also seemed to have never ending pocketbooks. Through the process, he and Russell were well on their way to becoming very rich men themselves. Scholars out east named the battle between Cope and Marsh, The Bone War, and Skeeter had to agree. The two were certainly at war with each other over old bones, and there were times he felt caught in the cross fire.

"Jessie got a wire from Russell a few days ago. Said it'll be a few more months before he returns."

Skeeter hung a harness over a stall post. "Yeah, he'll stay out there until Cope's men finish the dig to collect payment for their finds."

Kid led one horse, he the other, to the paddock. Frisky at being unhitched, the team raced across the dirt, tails lifted like sails in the wind and clouds of dust swirled beneath their galloping hooves.

"I have to admit, when you two first returned with your dinosaur bones and sharks teeth, I was a bit skeptical." Kid shook his head.

"A bit?" Skeeter laughed. He knew full well his brother thought he was loco two years ago when he returned with a pocket full of sharks teeth.

Kid nodded. A wide smile covered his face. "Well, maybe more than a bit. But now, I have to admit, I'm right proud of you, Skeeter."

Taken aback, he could do nothing more than ask, "You are?"

"Of course I am. We make our own luck in life." Kid leaned against the barn door. "You knew what you wanted and went after it. I'm proud of you for doing so, and I'm proud of you for succeeding."

Something puffed in his chest. It felt good. He watched one of the horses lie down to roll on the dry ground, unsure about the feeling. "But I just told you I don't have a house."

"At one time I didn't either. We all start somewhere. You have money."

He nodded. "Plenty."

"Then let's build you a house. It's slow around here right now. I'll leave a couple hands behind to take care of this place and Ma's. Between all of us it won't take long." Kid turned, walked back inside the barn.

Skeeter stayed put, watching the horses.

"What's really bothering you?" Kid asked from inside the barn.

He turned, glanced around. "You had all this when you married Jessie. I don't have anything to offer Lila."

"That didn't seem to stop her from marrying you."

"Ma's shotgun may have had something to do with that."

Kid laughed. "It played a part in my marriage as well."

He grinned. "That's true."

"I was so scared." Kid walked back to the doorway, gazed across the pasture.

"What? When were you scared?" He'd have bet his last dollar his older brother had never been afraid of anything in his life.

"Lots of times. When we first got married. When Jessie disappeared. When I was arrested. When she told me she was pregnant." Kid shrugged. "I'm sure there'll be plenty of more times too."

"Really? *You* were scared?" He couldn't believe it. Kid never showed fear.

"Yup, we all get scared at times." Kid smiled, slapped his shoulder. "But the happy times are worth all the fear in the world. Come on, let's go up to the house and draw a building plan for your place."

Skeeter fell into step beside Kid, and they walked through the barn. For the first time in his life, he didn't feel towered by his older brother. It was a bit odd, but he felt equal to Kid, like they were both successful men. A grin pulled at his cheeks. As they walked out of the barn and into the warm sun, he let the smile cover his face. "Lila says she wants a compact house. One that's easy to take care of."

"Compact?"

"That's what she said. A small place that's easy to take care of."

Kid shrugged. "Good thinking, I keep telling Jessie we need to hire someone to help her, but she refuses. I'll have to once the baby comes whether she likes it or not. And though I'm glad she'll have the help, I'll miss our time alone together." Kid flicked his eyebrows. "A small house, especially when you're newly married, is an extremely smart choice."

Skeeter caught his underlying message, and his chest grew again. This camaraderie he felt with Kid increased his happiness and pride. Lila had completely altered his world. The thought of living with her every day, and loving her every night made him giggle with glee.

He slapped Kid's shoulder. "You got a point there, big brother."

****

Four days later, a small caravan of covered wagons left the Quinter farm. Lila sat beside her husband on the bouncy seat. She felt like an actress from *Little House on the Prairie*. The whole family was coming with them back to the Badlands, where they would help build a house and dig the tunnel that would take her and Skeeter back to the future.

She'd told him a house wasn't necessary, but he'd insisted. Said since the rest of the family didn't know about the future, it would be best to build a house, let them all think they were getting settled. In the darkness of their room, where her mind had a hard time distinguishing between fantasy and reality, his enthusiasm had caught her hook, line, and sinker, and ultimately, she'd agreed to the adventure.

The sun was still rising, a golden globe sending long shafts of light over the horizon. The loving mist of spending the night in her husband's arms still surrounded her. A satisfying sigh escaped her lips, and she leaned her head on his shoulder.

He wrapped an arm around her. "Sorry it's so early, but it's best to get a timely start. The summer heat forces the horses to be sluggish after noon."

"I know. It's fine." She glanced over her shoulder, through the arched openings of canvas. A dozen wagons, full of building materials, furniture, supplies, and family followed. Kid drove the second team, Jessie sat next to him with their dog, Sammy, comfortably perched on her other side. "I hope it all isn't too much for Jessie."

"Don't worry, Jessie will be fine. Kid will make sure."

She grinned. "Are all men in the eighteen eighties like you Quinter boys? Think you're so big and strong there's nothing you can't handle?"

"I suspect so. If a man doesn't take care of what he has who will?"

"In the future..." She paused, trying to find the right words. "It seems people don't take the responsibility to take care of what they have. I mean they do, when it comes to possessions, but when it comes to actions they depend on lawyers, the government, even doctors to make everything all right." She shrugged. "It's hard to explain, but it seems like the things we depend the most on in the future, don't matter a whole lot in this time."

"I guess it doesn't rightly matter what century a person lives in, there's good and bad in all of them. I'd say all that really matters are the people you're with."

The thick, heavy gloom that settled on her every time she thought of Jessie and her baby dying was back. Along with it came the tears to burn the backs of eyes. She sniffled trying to keep them at bay. Almost wished she could tell Skeeter all she knew, things might be easier if he knew.

Skeeter squeezed her harder. "Ah, sweetheart, I didn't mean to make you cry."

"You didn't. It must just be the pregnancy. I read it makes women overly emotional."

"Do you want to know what I think?"

She nodded, her cheek rubbing against his shoulder.

"I think you worry too much. Think about it. What does it get you?" He nodded his head. "I mean look around, a person can worry about anything, but all the worry in the world, doesn't change anything. But faith, now that's something a person should have. Faith in the horse beneath you to get you where you're going, faith in the sun to light your way, faith in the people around you, to aid you along the way."

Lifting her face so she could see his, she asked, "Are you telling me not to worry?"

He reached over, ran a gentle hand through her hair. "I'm telling you to have faith in me. I won't let you down, I promise."

She leaned forward, pressed her lips to his. "I believe you. I don't know what it is about you, but I believe you." The uneven ride of the wagon made it impossible to make the kiss as deep as she'd like. She settled for a quick brushing of lips. "I think I love you, Skeeter Quinter," she whispered.

His lips caught hers again before he said, "I know I love you, Lila Quinter."

She giggled, his proclamation filling her with unexplainable joy.

"Promise me something?" he said as she nestled her head back on his shoulder.

"Sure, if I can, anyway."

"Promise me, you'll try to forget about the future for a bit. I don't mean the future you lived in, but the one when it'll be time for you to go back. It's going to take us a few weeks to build the house and dig out the tunnel. During that time I want you to just live. Have faith, and enjoy our time together. Don't worry about doctors and hospitals."

She sat up, glancing around. He thought she was sad about leaving. She wasn't. Though she hadn't yet asked him to return to the future with her, somehow she knew he would.

It was the fact Jessie wouldn't live through childbirth. No matter how hard she tried to educate Jessie on her condition, the girl would just shrug it off; continuously insisting Kid would take care of her. It was driving Lila batty. Both Jessie's lack of concern, and how the whole family thought Kid walked on water. He was a nice guy and all, she liked him, but it was his authority that irked her.

She hadn't meant for her behavior to make Skeeter think she wasn't happy here. The thought tugged at her heart. Fact was she was almost too happy here, which would make leaving all the more difficult. The only thing keeping her feet on the ground was the baby. She had to do what was right for the baby. And that included getting back to the future as soon as possible.

Miles of wide open space surrounded them. In places the grass grew two feet tall, swayed in the wind like water ripples. Sunflowers with their bright yellow petals and brown centers poked their heads above the grass like children playing hide and seek. Two eagles, side by side, an unusual sight, flew overhead. The birds flapped their wings, and then caught the wind current to glide elegantly through the sky.

She didn't like feeling down in the dumps, it wasn't her way. But worry about Jessie's pending death was right there in front of her every day. The whole family watched over the young girl—just as they had started to do toward her. The thought made her forehead wrinkle.

He was right, it would be some time before they could leave, and they should be enjoying this time with his family. They would have to leave soon enough, and probably never see any of them again. Maybe while the men built the house, she would have enough time to educate Jessie on all she knew about childbirth. She had read quite a bit on the internet when she first learned of her pregnancy. Surely there wouldn't be much for her or Jessie to do, and she could have the girl's undivided attention.

Her heart swelled, and a smile tugged at her lips. "I promise. I promise to not think of the future for the next few weeks." She leaned over, hugging him with both arms. "You have to be the smartest man I've ever met."

Skeeter laughed and held her close. The way she could mold her body against his was incredible. His fingers cupped her side, caressing the soft curve of her hip beneath her dress. He'd say or do just about anything to see her smile. The last couple of days, she reminded him of a decorative oil lamp after someone blew out the flame. Though she was still pretty to look at, she didn't shine. The last four days—ever since their marriage—she'd acted like the weight of the world sat on her shoulders.

At first he wondered if it was him—their marriage. But at night, when they explored each other's delights, she came to life. And it was then, in bed, when his heart would swell three times its usual size because those sparkling green eyes showered him with love. Not only could he see it, he felt it. It was like a whole other world. Long after she fell asleep, he'd wallow in thoughts, searching for what was making her so sad.

He couldn't fathom a reason, other than the future. She was worried over having the baby, afraid she'd die in the process without the doctors she talked about. He could understand her concern; he, too, worried about her health and wished there was more he could do, more he could say to make her understand worrying about it wouldn't help. Some things were just best left in God's hands. As long as she stayed healthy, things would be just fine. And part of being healthy was being happy.

He wanted to see her smile during the day, not just during those wonderful nights. He longed for the happy-go-lucky woman he fell in love with, the one who'd traveled from the cave to his mother's talking about hot tubs, skinny-dipping, and so many odd contraptions his head spun just recalling them. He leaned down, kissed the top of her head. He loved her happy, sad, and in between, and would until the day he died. Maybe even beyond then. He enjoyed every moment of being with her. He'd get her back to the future, but it would take some time, and a lot of work. The time would go quicker if she could enjoy it too.

Maybe building the house would help. Give her something to focus on. The rest of the family was ecstatic. His younger brothers had teased him mercilessly. He took it. Loved every minute of telling them they were just jealous. The pride he felt escorting her around the small town of Nixon, showing her off to friends and acquaintances, was more powerful than dynamite. The thought made him chuckle aloud.

She glanced toward him.

"Have I told you about our land?" he asked.

"No, not much. I've been the Chatty Cathy remember?"

He tucked her head on his shoulder again. "I homesteaded a couple hundred acres, and last year I purchased a few hundred more. A mile or so from the cave there's a great piece, lots of water, trees to slow the wind, good soil for a garden. I think it'll make a great place to build our house. There's a little train side-track a dozen or so miles away, Me-lo-te Switch. There's not much there, but they do have a small mercantile."

Her head snapped up. Wide, twinkling eyes stared at him.

"What?" he asked, knowing her adorable little brain was working full force.

"In the future Me-lo-te is known as Quinter."

He frowned, this once wondering if she told the truth. "Really?"

A wide smile covered her face. "How do you think that happens?"

He shrugged. "We'll have to wait and see."

"I've never known someone who had a town named after them."

Chapter Seven

Lila had camped as a child, but it had been in a Winnebago. An only child, born to baby boomers long after they'd had their careers and gave them up to travel the seven wonders of the United States. She'd been homeschooled until the eighth grade, and her world had completely changed when they moved to Hays for her to attend middle school. Now, living with a gaggle of family, traveling by covered wagon, she realized camping in the twenty-first century was a walk in the park. Not that she was complaining. She actually enjoyed living on the trail so to speak, and had always loved nature.

A smile tugged at her lips as she recalled the impromptu dance they'd had last night. Hog could give Charlie Daniels a run for his money when it came to the fiddle, and after the evening meal he'd pulled the instrument out. She'd always loved dancing. When the second song started she'd led Skeeter to the dirt to twirl with her. As the speed of the music picked up, so had she. The rhythm had taken over, and she'd danced around the fire pit, hips swaying, feet stomping and arms thrusting in the air. After the song ended and she looked up, the entire Quinter family, mouths agape, had stared at her as if she'd been pole dancing. She'd never laughed so hard in her life. True to form, Skeeter had joined in the laughter, and soon the whole family had joined them to boogie around the fire.

A warm giggle escaped her lips as her mind returned to the task at hand. She bent to swish the last tin plate in the flowing creek water. Familiar hands wrapped around her waist. Her husband's lips brushed the back of her neck, sending warm, sensual shivers down her shoulders. "Need some help?" he asked.

"Hmm, it depends on what type of help you're offering." She glanced at the small crop of trees running along the water. Her mind forever went in one direction when he was near.

His lips moved up to nibble on her ear. "Any type of help you need."

Leaning back against him, she said, "Well, when I first walked down here, I couldn't help but think how wonderful it would be if we could..." She twisted her neck to whisper in his ear, "Go skinny-dipping."

He twirled her around, pulled her into a tight hug. "God, I love you." His lips covered hers.

When the kiss ended, she raised her eyebrows, gave him a coy smile. "So you're willing?"

His fingers were already unbuttoning her gown. "Very."

In no time they were frolicking in the water, thoroughly enjoying a refreshing, playful game of underwater tag. She dove deep, quickly swam several yards closer to the shore before popping her head out of the water. The spot where she'd left him was smooth, not a ripple swirled the water. Her heart stopped for a moment. Worried, she planted her feet in the soft sand and twisted about to look for him. She gasped as firm hands grasped her waist. His head shot out of the water in front of her. The look in his eyes said it was time for the game to become serious.

She wrapped her arms around his neck, pressed her body against his hot, wet, flesh from knee to chest. His lips picked a trail across her shoulders, fueling her need for him until she withered. Wrapping her legs around his hips, she whispered, "Now, please, now."

He didn't disappoint her. His hands, lips, and body pleasured her until she held on for dear life. Ultimate quakes of ecstasy left her so weak, if by chance she slipped from his arms, she'd drown for sure.

The last bits of daylight were fading by the time he carried her out of the water, back to their misshapen pile of clothes. "Have I told you how happy you make me?" she asked.

His eyes widened, almost as if he was shocked by what she said.

She caressed his cheek. "Evidently, I haven't. Forgive me for being remiss."

His arms squeezed her so tight, for a split second she thought she might smother. Hot and delightful, his mouth settled on hers, breathed his very breath of life into her. The only thing that would make her happier was if the baby growing in her womb was his. The thought sent a chill up her spine, made her quiver.

He let her loose, quickly bent down for her clothes. "Here, I don't want you to catch a chill."

Disappointed, she sighed. Her rambling mind had broken the enchanted spell. She took the lacy, old fashioned undergarments. "That would be impossible. It had to be close to a hundred degrees today."

He stepped into his pants. "We'll be at the land about noon tomorrow."

"Really?" she asked, tying the wide string at the waist of her pantaloons. The floppy underwear was surprisingly comfortable, and the camisole wasn't nearly as sweat trapping as her bra.

"Yes, but as long as we're coming along the trail,

I want to make a quick detour to check on the bone excavation near the edge of our property line." He tugged his boots on.

"Bone excavation?"

"Yes, I told you about the bones."

She tugged the simple, light blue dress over her head. "Yes, but I didn't know an excavation was going on. What are they finding?"

"I won't know until we stop."

She giggled at his teasing, grabbed his shirt off the ground, and threw it at him. He caught it, laughing.

"We were wondering what was taking so long," Kid's voice sounded as he and Jessie walked around the trees.

"Decided a bath was in order," Skeeter said, shaking the water from his hair.

Kid and Jessie looked at each other. A knowing smile grew on their faces.

Lila ran her fingers through her hair, and then picked up a stack of dishes. "Jessie would you mind carrying the rest of these?" she asked, nodding at the few she'd left on the ground.

Jessie and Kid gave her a startled look.

Skeeter stepped forward. "I'll help."

She started to protest. He touched a finger to her lips. Irritated, Lila let out a little huff and began walking away. He quickly caught up, dishes in hand. Without a glance his way, she plodded toward the wagons.

"What's wrong?" he asked.

"Jessie shouldn't be swimming in her condition."

"Why not, you just did."

She rolled her eyes. "That's different."

"How?"

She thought quickly, trying to come up with an answer. "Because I'm not as far along as she is."

He grabbed her arm, his hold wasn't hard, but

still it forced her to stop and look at him. "Why are you so obsessed with Jessie's pregnancy?"

"I'm not obsessed—"

"Yes you are. She can't turn around without you telling her what she should be doing and what she can't. What she can eat, where she can sit, what she can carry—"

"I do not," she interrupted.

"Yes, you do."

"Well—she's pregnant and shouldn't be doing some things." She glanced at the trees, light giggles floated through the bushes. "Like swimming. Kid should know better."

"Kid's not going to let anything happen to Jessie."

In the past week, Skeeter had never raised her ire, but right now steam formed in her ears. "Kid's not God, Skeeter. When are you going to figure that out?" She tugged out of his grasp, walked away. Glancing over her shoulder, she added, "He can't save Jessie from everything."

He threw his empty hand in the air. "Now you're mad at me because Kid and Jessie went swimming?"

"It's true, men are ignorant no matter what century they live in," she muttered.

"What?" He'd caught up to her.

She balanced the dishes in one hand, used the other to grab the couple he held. "Just leave me alone."

"Lila—"

"Just leave me alone, Steven!" She'd never used his given name, but right now she was so mad at him he didn't seem like Skeeter to her. Stiff grass crumbled beneath her feet as she stomped toward the wagon. How on earth was she going to make sure Jessie's delivery wasn't fatal if no one else was willing to heed her warnings? People in the eighteen hundreds had to be the most stubborn people ever.

They all thought there was nothing they couldn't tackle.

After settling the dishes in the storage crates, Lila climbed in the back of their wagon, flopped down on the feather tick Skeeter had spread out for the night. Jessie was going to die, and nobody but her realized it. And even if by some miracle she didn't, the baby certainly would, which could be just as devastating. She stared at the canvas flopping overhead. The wind made it bubble like a parachute. The death of the baby would tear Jessie apart. The poor girl didn't deserve that. Losing a child was terribly hard on parents. She knew that first hand. When she'd been seven, her mother had a baby that died right after birth. He'd been named Charles after her father, and if it hadn't been for the medical care her mother had received, her mother would have died as well. Lila could still remember all the blood. Her mother had started hemorrhaging after she came home from the hospital, and gallons of bright-red blood had soaked right through the mattress on the bed before the ambulance had arrived with flashing red lights and whisked her away.

The back of her throat burned, her face scrunched, and with a loud sob, the tears began to flow with a grand force. She tried to blanket her mind, not think of the baby growing in her womb or the event that was sure to happen, but it was impossible. Just as not thinking about her parents was. She'd thought about them several times this past week. Reflected on how much her father will enjoy hearing about all she saw, all she did. Until this very moment, she hadn't thought of what they must be going through.

It was understandable; she wasn't prone to worry when separated from them. They traveled a lot. In May, they'd left to spend the summer in Alaska, and weren't due to return to Kansas until

October.

Her mind swirled. What if someone had found her car and called them?

"Lila?" Skeeter stuck his head in the back opening.

She rolled onto her side, hid her face behind both hands.

"Ah, honey." The wagon groaned as he climbed in. His hands tugged her close. Strong arms instantly gathered her into an embrace. "Shh, I'm sorry. I didn't mean to upset you."

Despite her previous anger, she was unable to resist the sheltered, loving comfort he offered. His chest felt so solid under her cheek, his arms so strong and consoling. Her emotions were in complete upheaval. With a renewed energy they peaked, her sniffles became uncontrollable. "My face is probably on milk cartons by now," she sobbed.

"What?"

"My...face. It's on a milk carton."

Gently, he rocked her back and forth. "Shh," he whispered.

The tears kept flowing, and she buried her face in his shirt. "Or maybe they stop doing that when the lost person is over eighteen. There was this kid from Minnesota, his name was Jacob, and they even had his picture on semi trailers." The memory made her sobs increase. A hot knot tightened in her chest.

Every missing person she'd ever heard of on CNN flashed in her mind. Pictures of their parents crying on national T.V. tore at her heart. Was that what her parents were doing? Her dad was almost seventy. The stress could cause a massive coronary. "Oh, God, it's going to kill him."

Skeeter grasped her cheeks, forced her to lift her head. "Kill who? What are you talking about?"

She didn't try to open her eyes. Knew she couldn't see anything through the burning tears.

"My father. It's going to give him a heart attack."

"Your father? Lila, you're not making any sense. What's going to give him a heart attack?"

She grabbed his wrists. "They're probably searching for shallow graves, looking for my remains."

His lips, warm and gentle brushed over her forehead. "Nobody is looking for your remains."

"You don't know that." She pulled her head back.

"Honey, you're sitting right here in front of me."

She snapped her eyes open, wiped at the tears with the heels of her hands. "In eighteen-eighty-two, but what about two-thousand-eight? My parents probably think I died, or at the very least I'm missing. Not knowing what happened to me has to be awful for them."

His face softened, his eyes filled with concern. "Oh, honey, I never thought of that." He wrapped his arms around her shoulders. "Come here."

She went willingly, snuggled into his chest. "I have to get home."

"I know. I'll get you back to the future. As soon as possible." His chin settled on her head. "I promise."

His assurance eased the pain gripping her body. There was nothing like the comfort his hold provided. Nothing she could compare to the way his presence wrapped her in a perfect, loved-filled shroud. Snuggled against his solid, welcomed strength, gradually her distress faded as if he absorbed her grief. He continued to cradle her, rocked her until a deep, tranquil peacefulness filled her.

****

The next morning as they rolled into the excavation area, Skeeter tried to shake a heavy tension from his shoulders. His guts were rolling like a rapid river again. Nothing had prepared him for loving someone. At least not this crazy up and down ride he was on. He went from riding high, to feeling lower than a snake's belly. Loving Lila was easy, wonderful, but trying to figure her out more confusing than reading the Bible upside down. He hadn't meant to upset her last night, had really just gone to help her with the dishes. Of course he hadn't been able to deny her suggestion of skinny-dipping anymore than he could deny his body of breathing. He still didn't know what had triggered her anger, and suspected he needed to try understanding it all a bit harder.

He'd been so engrossed in having her in his life he'd never considered those she left behind in the future. He reached over, wrapped her hand with his. The smile she tried to muster up didn't touch her eyes and filled him with a sense of uselessness more encompassing than the sky above.

No wonder she was so sad. She lived with extreme passion, yet had such a soft heart. Her concern for others was so apparent. His entire family already adored her, almost as much as he did. But missing her parents was tearing her apart. Therefore, it tore him apart. He had to find a way to get her to the future as soon as possible.

He glanced over his shoulder, to the wagons following his. Holding in the sigh burning his chest, he pressed a kiss to her temple and returned his gaze forward. Family was an odd thing. He'd left them many times, without ever giving it much thought. Things were different now. It was as if he was a different person, looked at things with new eyes. Felt things with a new heart.

As soon as they arrived, he'd send Bug up to start digging on the tunnel. His youngest brother wouldn't mind, he loved playing in the dirt. And he'd talk to Kid. Explain why Lila had been so concerned about Jessie's pregnancy. Anything that has to do with parents has her worried beyond control. Kid was sure to understand. Maybe he even had some pointers on this whole husband thing.

He pulled their wagon to a stop beside a high-sided U.S. Cavalry buckboard parked at the edge of the encampment. Half a dozen white, canvas tents covered an area of about two acres. Several yards beyond the tents, diggers paused, rested their hands on shovel handles to watch the caravan roll to a halt.

"Soldiers are digging for dinosaur bones?" Lila asked, her eyes canvassing the area.

He nodded, and needing something to concentrate on besides her unhappiness, explained, "Two men from out east started what some people are calling The Bone Wars, several years ago. Edward Cope and Othniel Marsh have been competing to see who can collect the most fossils. Each of them wants to become the country's best paleontologist. Last year Cope found a complete prehistoric bird about three miles from here. He was so excited he rushed back to New York to officially name it, and as soon as possible sent another gang of diggers out." He nodded toward several army men mingling about. "Afraid Marsh's diggers will try to steal some of the bones Cope hires noncommissioned units of the Cavalry to guard the sites."

"I remember reading about the Bone Wars, briefly, there's not a lot about it in Kansas history books." Her face pulled into a slight frown. "I wonder why? Have they found a lot on your property?"

Skeeter wrapped the reins around the wooden brake handle. He had no idea why Cope and Marsh weren't in history books, and pondered for the briefest moment if he'd ever be in a history book. He couldn't ask her, didn't want her to dwell on not being back in her time. Dang, if it wasn't hard. There were so many things he wanted to know about, so many things she mentioned that he speculated about, but her happiness was more important. He wasn't about to bring on melancholy just because he wondered about something.

Shaking off his wandering mind, he answered, "Yes, they've found a lot on our property." He took off his hat, wiped at the sweat. "Russell, Jessie's brother says Cope has barns full of bones in Philadelphia, but still he wants to buy every one we discover."

"You search for them too?" she asked, her gaze going back to the dig site.

"Not any more. I did in the beginning, but after Russell took the first specimens to New York, Cope paid us a goodly some so he could be the only one to dig here. He sends out experienced diggers. Besides, Russell and I had already found plenty, quite a stock pile actually. Russell is still out there selling them to museums and colleges."

He climbed down as two men exited a tent and approached the wagon. She scooted over, held her arms out for aid. Once settled on the ground, she asked, "Are they worth much?"

"The bones?"

She nodded.

"More than Russell or I ever imagined." Skeeter shrugged. It had been exciting at first, all the money rolling in. But it hadn't taken him long to realize a rich man is not the one with the most money, but the one who needs the least. At this moment in time he knew there was nothing he needed. He had it all. Lila and a good chunk of land that would provide every thing they'd require. Taking her arm, they walked to meet Yokel and his sidekick Johansson. The men's clothes were covered with the fine, white dust of the Badlands, and their eyes looked like two burnt red holes in a white blanket.

"Hello, Mr. Quinter," Nelson Yokel greeted.

"Ma'am," he added tipping his hat to Lila.

"Yokel," Skeeter extended his hand, "How's it going?"

Johansson stopped a few feet behind Nelson, and Skeeter didn't encourage him to step closer. The man was a shifty sort, and he'd just a soon Lila didn't have anything to do with him.

"Pretty good, but we're glad to see you. We've had some Indian trouble," Yokel said.

Lila stiffened beside him. He wrapped his arm around her waist, patted her side. "What sort of trouble?"

"Nothing really, just things missing and broken—" Yokel started.

"There's a band of Sioux watching us from the cliffs everyday. It has to be them," Johansson interrupted. The man was scrawny and always fidgeting, like he couldn't stand still.

Skeeter glanced around. A quick flash of light glistened from the ridge. The signal allowed him to relax. "It's just Buffalo Killer. I asked him to keep an eye on things for a few days." He scratched his jaw, wondering if he should voice his concern that the braves wouldn't break or steal things. If that was happening, it was someone besides the Sioux.

Yokel gave a short nod.

Johansson crossed his arms. "Who's Buffalo Killer?"

"A friend of mine," Skeeter said, his tone firmly ending the conversation.

Johansson lips puckered like he'd just sucked on a lemon, and then he flipped around, walked back toward the tent.

Skeeter remained silent. Yokel's glance roamed from the departing man to Lila. He looked between the two of them. When the man's gaze settled on him, Skeeter offered, "This is Mrs. Quinter, my wife." Pride filled his chest at the introduction. The boastfulness she instilled in him was still a bit confounding.

Yokel's eyes popped open like a frogs. "Oh, I didn't know you were married." He removed his hat, bowed his head with respect. "It's a pleasure, ma'am."

"Hello," she returned with a graceful tilt of her chin.

Skeeter nodded to the wagons behind them. "My family is with me. We're going to raise a house a few miles from here."

"Oh, well, let us know if there's something we can do to help," Yokel offered.

"How much longer will this dig last?" He glanced around the large camp, knowing when the time came the entire site could be packed up and lugged away in less than a day.

Yokel replaced his hat. "A month or so. We'll need to head out long before fall. Want to be well settled in New York before winter hits."

Skeeter offered his hand to the man. When Yokel took it, he said, "All right. We may take you up on your offer when we set the rafters."

"We'll look forward to the change in pace." He tipped his hat to Lila again. "Nice meeting you ma'am."

"Good-bye," she offered and they turned to walk back to the wagon. Away from the men, where no one else could hear, she asked, "Do you still have Indian attacks in this time?"

Her face was full of worry. His hand roamed up her back to cup her upper arm so he could tug her closer to his side. "No, there hasn't been an attack in several years. Easterners are still fearful from all the tales they've heard about the west. But you don't have anything to worry about; Buffalo Killer's band is friendly. And I brought several more gifts to keep them on our good side." He'd have traded all the dinosaur bones on earth to keep another worry from entering her mind. As it was she had way too many going on in that pretty little head of hers.

They stopped near the wagon. "It's just their ghost dances that are dangerous?" she asked.

He glanced at her face. A smile twitched his lips as he read the teasing glint in her eyes. His heart tumbled at seeing a touch of her happy spirit, the one he loved so much. Mindless of the twenty diggers and soldiers nearby, as well as his family sitting in the hot sun, he pulled her into a deep, long-lasting kiss. When they separated, smiling, he said, "Yes, it's just their wonderful ghost dances that are quite dangerous."

She giggled as he lifted her onto the wagon, and the way she snuggled next to him the rest of the way to the house site he'd picked out, made his heart soar like the eagles overhead. But his happiness was bittersweet. He couldn't be happy while she was so distraught. Wasn't that how it was suppose to be? When one partner isn't happy, neither is the other. His mind sought a way to balance it all. There had to be a way for him to ease her sorrow and accept the bliss she instilled in him at the same time.

As the horses plodded up the last hill, before they would circle around the thick grove of trees a notion came to him. Skeeter squeezed her shoulder. "Perhaps they don't know you're missing yet."

Lila glanced at him, brows furrowed with confusion.

"Your parents, perhaps they don't know you're missing yet."

"Oh," she murmured. A thoughtful gaze went back to the landscape. "I've been gone almost a week. We talk on the phone every few days. By now they'll at least be wondering why I haven't called."

"Well, I've been thinking and maybe time isn't the same there."

She shook her head, let out a little sigh. "Time is the same. There are still twenty-four hours in a day, seven days in a week."

"I know. But I was a ghost for a long time, yet when I got back, I had only been gone overnight. Maybe that's how it is for you."

Her eyes grew wide, and she nibbled on her bottom lip. After a bit, she said, "How long did it feel like you were in the house?"

He shrugged. "I don't know. But I saw a lot of things, and it felt like a very long time."

"Hmm," she mumbled.

The way one finger tapped her chin made a smile tugged at his lips. It had seemed like he was in the future for years, and yet, he'd only been gone a few hours. He crossed two fingers. If it was that way for her, too, he'd have time to get everything settled here before he took her home.

****

Lila folded her hands behind her back. Satisfaction of a job well done made her grin like a Cheshire cat. For the past three weeks, she'd been so busy she hadn't had time to think, let alone worry. Some of the diggers had come to help, not the ones trained to dig out the precious bones, but the ones with strong backs. A handful of soldiers had come as well. Between them, the ranch hands, and the brothers, a solid, quaint house had grown to stand tall and proud on the grassy prairie. Large sandstone blocks cut from the bluffs near the cave made the foundation, and timber had been cut from the large grove of trees near the twisting stream flowing behind the house site.

The women had been as busy as the men. Ma Quinter sewed curtains, braided rugs, and made cushions for parlor chairs Skeeter had unloaded from one of the wagons. Lila's grin widened at the memory. Two days ago, she'd laughed out loud at seeing the large crates full of chair parts. It appeared the nation had been founded on 'some assembly required.'

Not a person had been idle. Jessie had set about putting the kitchen in order, even before the house had been finished. She'd unpacked crates of dishes, pans, and utensils Lila stilled didn't recognize, and at times wondered about. Before they'd left Nixon, Skeeter had practically cleaned out the only store in town. What they hadn't had in stock, he'd ordered and paid to have it delivered to their new home when it arrived. A wagon load arrived every other day.

Lila lifted her face, let her gaze scrutinize the large structure—the house she'd designed. Kid had drawn a plan, but Skeeter insisted she approve each inch of the drawings and the construction. At first she'd been reluctant to say anything, but after her first few suggestions were taken favorably, she became bolder. The process not only amazed her, it enthralled. There wasn't a part of it she hadn't been engrossed in. Day by day the house had been pieced together like a 3-D puzzle.

The men had mixed handmade concrete this morning and now were constructing large blocks of sandstone into a stunning fireplace on the back wall of the living room. She stepped aside, making room for one of the ranch hands to push the wheelbarrow full of mud up the wide plank and onto the porch. She glanced about. One of the large cement trucks, with a turning drum and stinking diesel fuel like she'd often seen in the future, was no where in sight. The men had mixed natural materials from the earth to mold the blocks together. A deep satisfying sigh exhaled. She hadn't enjoyed participating in something so much in a very long time—not since she'd moved into her apartment, and met Professor Rutledge, who within that first year had convinced her to switch her degree from early childhood to Information Technology. A quiver touched her spine. Nothing about the career shift had been fun, but he'd explained there was no money in teaching, and if she wanted to be able to afford to live on her own, he'd said, she better go into computers.

"Lila, you have to see these!" Jessie, perched in the shade of a tall cottonwood tree, waved a hand.

A frown formed as she noticed the large crates surrounding her sister-in-law. No matter how much she encouraged Jessie to relax, the woman was forever finding something to do. Lila sent a final glance toward the men. Her gaze touched on the bronze back of her husband. Even from a distance, she could see the muscles moving as he hefted the blocks in place. He worked twice as hard as the other men, and yet every night he had the energy to love her inside out before she fell asleep in his solid embrace.

His head lifted, slowly turned until his gaze met hers. He winked at her, and a ripple of happiness made her giggle as she fluttered her fingers at him before turning to walk to the tree. She'd never known one person could make another so happy all the time. Her gaze landed on Jessie, and a heavy weight settled in her chest. Nor one who could frustrate the dickens out of her.

The other girl patted the quilt spread out on the ground. "Here, sit down. You must see this china. It's beautiful."

Lila sat. "You should be taking a nap."

"It's not even noon yet." Jessie held out a tea cup. "Look at this, it has gilded edges."

"Yes, that's nice. But I've told you before—you have to take it easy. And I don't think you should be breathing in all the dust from the straw these dishes are packed in."

The other woman let out a long sigh, set the cup

on top of a pile of stiff, yellow straw. "Lila, I love you like a sister. But you have to stop."

"Stop what?"

"Stop badgering me," she said more harshly than normal. With a hint of shame in her eyes, Jessie glanced around. "It's making Kid nervous."

Lila rolled her eyes. Kid was a nice man, a wonderful brother. But the way everyone bowed to his every word, drove her crazy. "Kid should know better than to let you work all the time. Your condition—"

"My baby is going to be fine. I'm going to be fine," Jessie snapped.

Shocked, Lila glanced at her sister-in-law.

Jessie covered her face with both hands, shook her head. The large dog at her side perked his ears and then laid his head on the pink material of her dress. Jessie patted his black head with one hand. "Lila, I didn't want to tell you this, but you give me no choice. Kid's mother died giving birth. All of your—*concern*—about me is making him question my safety, the baby's safety. You have to stop."

She knew it! Knew having a baby was incredibly dangerous. Finally someone else agreed with her. "So he understands what I've been saying?"

Jessie shook her head, almost as if she was frustrated, and then she reached over. Her fingers warm as they wrapped around Lila's hand. "I know you're worried about me and the baby. And about your own pregnancy. But please, you have to stop."

Lila didn't comment. Couldn't. She didn't want to cause Jessie more frustration by saying she wasn't worried about *her* baby. *She'd* be safe in the twenty-first century—with a gaggle of doctors to make sure—by the time her due date rolled around. Skeeter's declaration of how he'd been in the future for some time, but had returned to the past only a few hours after he'd left had convinced her that's what happened to her. When she and Skeeter traveled through the tunnel, they'd find her Mustang and go home to Hays in plenty of time for her to have a healthy pregnancy and delivery. Most likely it will be the same day she'd arrived in the past. No, she had nothing to worry about, but Jessie certainly did.

"Lila?" Jessie said. "You do understand what I'm saying, don't you?"

Lila let out a deep sigh, giving an agreeable nod. She'd have to be more cautious with her warnings. Jessie must be terribly worried. How dare Kid tell her about his mother? He should know better than to cause his wife extra concern.

"You have become the sister I never had. I don't want us to be cross with one another, but I can't have Kid worrying so either." Jessie squeezed her hand a touch tighter. "You do understand, don't you?"

"You don't want Kid worrying?"

"No, I don't want him worrying." Jessie's gaze wandered to her husband. "He's so wonderful. He's my whole world. And he's been working so hard." She glanced back. "I don't want him worrying about me when he has so many other things on his mind. I'm sure you feel the same way about Skeeter."

Needing a moment to think, Lila glanced toward the house. She hadn't thought about Skeeter worrying about her. Did he? Was that why he worked so hard?

"Lila?" Jessie asked.

She fluttered a hand. "Yes, yes, I understand what you're saying."

"Good. I know we're both going to be fine. As well as our babies. Nothing is going to happen. Trust me."

Lila bit her tongue. Why did everyone in the past put such trust in each other? Skeeter had no reason to worry. But Kid and Jessie did. If only the other girl would agree to go back to the future with her. Then they would both be fine. Maybe she could still find a way to convince Jessie. Now that the house was almost complete maybe she'd have time to design a plan. She reached over and laid her other hand on top of Jessie's to console her fears. "Yes, we are both going to be fine. And so are the babies."

"Thank you." Jessie picked a cup up. "Now look at this china. It's gorgeous."

Lila played along, not really interested in the china. Her mind searched for the information she'd read on the internet about pregnancy. She didn't want to do it, but perhaps fear factor would be the best route to get Jessie to go with her.

After she'd oohed and ahhed over every plate, bowl, and serving dish, she was happy to see Snake approaching. She needed some time to fully plan her new approach to Jessie's well-being.

"How is the hoeing coming?" she asked. The brother had tilled up a large patch of earth for a garden.

"I'm ready to start planting. Thought you'd like to see it," he said, stopping in front of them. Snake leaned down, patted the dog's head. Sammy laid his head back down on Jessie's knee. "It's getting late in the year for planting, but the growing season here is long, so you should still have a fair harvest."

Lila was on her feet, wrapped an arm around his elbow. "Thank you for all your work, and yes, I'd love to see it."

He looked at Jessie. "Care to join us?"

She shook her head, smiled at Lila. "No, thank you. I think I'll stay here in the shade."

Lila returned the grin. At least Jessie was making an attempt to heed her warnings. "We won't be long."

"Take your time," Jessie responded.

She fell into step beside Snake. Skeeter's younger brother was a master gardener. The family claimed there wasn't a plant, tree, nor flower he couldn't make grow in the sometimes desert heat of the grassland. The patch of earth he'd prepared was several yards behind the house, in direct sunlight all day. A low fence surrounded the entire area.

He noticed her gaze. "I built the fence to keep the critters out. Without it you won't have anything to pick." He pointed to two large barrels. "I also brought along some willow branches. Chopped up and left to soak, they make excellent fertilizer. After a couple weeks you can plant the mush and new willow trees will grow."

"Really? I've never heard of that."

"It's not widely known, but ask Jessie. She has a forest of weeping willows growing behind her house." He opened the narrow gate and led her up and down the rows, explaining where each seed should be planted.

Lila was interested. She had several indoor plants as well as an herb pot in her apartment. The thought of a real garden had her hoping it would take a couple months to dig out the tunnel so she could actually tend the tiny plants. As long as she got Jessie to the future before her ninth month, everything should be fine.

Snake bent down, picked up several round seeds. "In every hole you have to put three seeds."

"Why three?"

"One for the grub worm, one for the birds, and one to grow," he explained with a very no-nonsense tone.

"Oh, I never knew that."

"Remember it, and you'll always have plenty to eat." He handed her a trowel and a small container of seeds.

She nodded and set about planting her new

garden, while contemplating her plan of getting Jessie to the future. She might have to invite Kid along to make it work. She began to giggle. The thought of the two Quinter brothers living in two-thousand-eight was comical.

****

The next morning, as a cool breeze blew beneath the flap at the back of the wagon, Lila twisted her head on the pillow, opened her eyes. The sun hadn't risen yet, but was sending a few pale pink streaks in warning of its upcoming shine. Something out of the ordinary caught her attention. She peered closer and a smile tugged on her lips.

On her pillow, a few inches from the end of her nose sat a little, bright-green tree frog. His bugged-out eyes moved about as if he was a taking a good, long look at his new home. The floppy skin beneath his wide mouth billowed now and again.

Skeeter, curled against her back, slipped his hand out from beneath the quilt, and snatched up the little critter. He leaned over and let the frog go outside of the canvas stretched over their wagon.

Lila rolled over, snuggled in chest to chest. "He wasn't hurting anyone."

His lips, warm, his breath hot, brushed over her forehead, down her cheek. "I know, but I find I don't like the thought of anyone or anything sharing your bed. Except me."

She kissed his neck, nipped at the skin. "Not even a little tree frog?"

"Not even a tree frog," he muttered before his lips found hers.

Her hands began to knead the muscles beneath his balmy skin. She trailed her nails over his shoulders, down his muscled arms while fully participating in the kiss. It was amazing how his nearness sent her body into molten lava. Whether he was lying next to her, or half away across the yard, she craved his touch, his kiss. The mere sight of him made her breath catch and her stomach flip with anticipation.

She snuggled deeper into the feather tick and tugged on his hips, encouraging him to roll atop. Their naked bodies, ready for one another, joined together with such intensity she lost track of her thoughts, of time.

Later, sated, and basking in glory he found awe-inspiring, Skeeter caressed his wife as she snuggled in his arms, and placed a kiss on the top of her curls.

"Mmm," she moaned, low and sexy. "Good thing you shooed that little frog away, he may have got a lesson in life he wasn't old enough to see." Her lips pressed a light kiss to his chest. "He was just a baby."

He smiled and ran his hand over her stomach. A small, firm mound had grown between her hips bones. The thought of cradling the infant in his arms made his heart thud. "Speaking of babies, how are you doing? Feeling all right?"

"Yes, I'm fine." A deep, long sigh made her body rise and fall slightly. "It's Jessie who needs to slow down."

A chuckle rumbled over his vocal cords. "You've told her so plenty of times."

The fingertips roaming his chest stilled. "Not you too." She sounded disgruntled, irritated.

"Not me too, what?"

"Think I've been badgering Jessie." She tilted her head, caught his gaze.

He chose not to comment and kissed the tip of her nose. "You need to take it easy too."

"No, I'll be fine." She tucked her head back on his shoulder. "Jessie will be delivering her baby without modern medicine. That frightens me."

"Don't worry, K—"

Her hand covered his mouth. "I don't want to

hear that Kid will take care of her. He's a fine man, but he's not a doctor. Not the doctor she's going to need."

He kissed the palm, and when she pulled it away said, "Dr. Fields will be there when the time comes." Twisting so they laid face to face, he frowned, "You are quite the woman, worried about Jessie when you're facing the same thing."

Her face pulled into a scowl. "I'm not facing the same thing. I'll be having this baby in the future, long after we travel through the tunnel."

A chill snuck into his body. He refused to allow her to feel the shiver that wanted to shake his body, held it in with a deep breath. Bug and Hog or Snake, whenever they were free, had been digging on the tunnel, but he'd yet to tell her of the progress. Somehow keeping it from her seemed wrong, but he didn't want to get her hopes up if the portal to the future couldn't be opened again.

Kid had told him women were hard to figure out, and he'd discovered that had been putting it mildly. He felt as if he was walking on ice half the time, and finally concluded keeping his mouth shut may be his best approach.

He ran his hand down her side, resting his palm on her hip, and took the subject down a different trail. "Have you thought of any names? Kid and Jessie have several picked out."

"Yes, I know they do. But I don't. I don't think it would be right." Again, she let out a long sigh.

The icy chill was back. "Don't think it would be right? Why not?"

"Because when I give the baby away, the new parents might not want the name I pick out. I think it should be their choice to name it."

He tried to swallow, almost choking on his own saliva. "G-give the baby away? To who?"

"I hope I get some say in that, but I've only had

one meeting with the adoption agency so I don't know for sure. I'll find out after we get home."

Despite the quilt, the heat of her body, and the sunshine now filtering through the heavy canvas, the blood in his veins froze like a bucket of water in January. "Adoption agency?"

Chapter Eight

He flipped the flap open, climbed out the back of the wagon. His guts churned, his temples throbbed, and his heart felt like someone had just stabbed it with a dull knife.

"Skeeter, wait, what are you so upset about?" Lila, still in the wagon, pulled a dress over her head.

The gown, light green and covered with tiny, pink rosebuds, fell into place, and she began to button the front. Disheveled hair from their night wrapped in each others arms bounced about her shoulders as she peered between him and the buttons. His heart convulsed, tore. How could someone so beautiful, so loving, consider giving up the tiny life growing inside her body? A little human being she hadn't even got to know yet.

Feeling unexplainably weak, he sat on the chair near the back of the wagon, pulled his boots out from behind a back wheel. It was completely beyond understanding. Maybe she wasn't the person he thought her to be. What kind of woman wants to give away her baby? The most precious gift ever given. The one thing that meant more than all else combined.

She scooted out of the wagon, sat on the other chair to put on the new lace up shoes he'd bought for her in Nixon. "Skeeter?" Her look was perplexed. "What's up? I told you before I was giving the baby up for adoption."

His toes hit the ends of his boots with force. "No, Lila, I don't believe you ever mentioned that." He slapped his suspenders over his shoulders as he stood.

She tilted her head, as if contemplating something. "Hmm, maybe it was just Jessie I told. It's hard to remember what I can tell someone and what I can't." Fluffing her skirts she rose from her chair. "Sorry," she grimaced, "I thought you knew." Shrugging her shoulders, she added, "But it really doesn't matter."

The muscles in his neck tightened. "Doesn't matter?"

"I made the decision a long time ago." She stepped forward, placed a hand on his arm. "I've already signed the papers."

Her touch felt like fire. He twisted out of her reach, grabbed his hat from inside the wagon bed. "We're married now, shouldn't that change things?"

"But—it's not your baby."

His face twitched as his skin tightened, pulled into a scowl of confusion. Fire-like heat stung his eyes. "I feel like it is," he admitted.

"Someday, when we're ready, we'll have our own baby."

There were so many feelings raking his mind and body, he didn't know which one to define, which one to act on. "When we're ready?"

She nodded. "Yes, in a few years when we're settled, and have enough money in the bank to afford a baby."

"I have enough money to afford a hundred babies," he snapped.

Her face formed a silly grin, as if consoling him. "I'm sure you do for this century. But things are a lot more expensive in the future than they are now."

His molars clamped together. He had to get

away. Far, far away before the anger surging through his body exploded like a stick of dynamite. Pushing wayward curls away from his forehead he slapped his hat on his head and pivoted.

"Skeeter? Where are you going?"

He twisted, catching her view in the early morning light. It was amazing, how someone so beautiful, so charming, and hot blooded, could be so cold hearted. Skeeter forced his gaze to leave her, to look somewhere over the glistening curls of her head. "I have to go check the dig site."

"But we're moving into the house today. Don't you want to help?"

"No, no I don't." His gaze met her puzzled one.

"Don't you want to have a say in where all the furniture you bought goes?"

A bellow of disgust grunted up his throat. "It doesn't really matter, does it?" Without a second look back, he crossed the yard.

She appeared beside him before he had the gelding saddled. "Skeeter, I think we need to talk."

The steam in his head almost hissed as it flowed out his ears. He tugged on the leather cinch strap. The horse flinched, sidestepped. Relaxing his hold a touch, he ran a finger beneath the strap, loosened it and then threaded it through and around the metal loops, forming a solid tether.

"Skeeter?" she asked softly, her voice hesitant.

Unable to speak, not knowing which angry thought rolling around in his head might burst out his mouth, he stuck a foot in a stirrup, lifted himself into the saddle. His tongue clicked against the roof of his mouth, encouraging the gelding to move.

"Steven Quinter, don't you ride away from me when I'm talking to you!" she shouted as the horse started to trot. Skeeter didn't even look back as he slapped the brown rump with the ends of the reins.

A thick film of tears blurred her vision, making

him disappear long before Lila was ready to pull her eyes off his departing form. She could have sworn she'd told him about the adoption the first day they met.

What didn't he understand? Even in this century people had to realize you just didn't have a baby on a whim. You had to save, plan, be prepared. Her apartment only had one bedroom. She had her car to pay off, student loans, credit cards. It would be years before she could afford to have a baby—if ever.

Ah, hell, who was she trying to fool?

Her shoulders fell and sadness crept over her skin, settled in the pit of her stomach. More than once over the past few weeks she'd thought about keeping this baby. The little life growing inside had started to move. The flutters were gentle and made her tingle with delight. Jessie was right, it was amazing. The movements had also made her question her decision. She even dreamed about keeping the baby. Skeeter would make an awesome father.

She rubbed at the throbbing in her temple. But the people of her generation didn't keep babies just because they were pregnant. They thought about what was best for everyone involved. And in her case, with mounting debts, and the way the baby was conceived, the best alternative was giving the baby up for adoption. Let a couple who couldn't have children give this baby the love and life he or she deserved.

Twisting around, her steps faltered when she caught sight of the yard full of people staring her way. Tears pressed against her eyes. Bowing her head, she dodged around Kid as he strolled toward her.

"Lila?" he softly questioned.

She held up one hand, clearly stating she had nothing to say, and made a mad dash for the solitude of the wagon. Her chest and eyes burned when she finally climbed in and flopped onto the feather tick. Tucking her knees into her chest, she curled into a fetal position, and let the tears flow.

****

Skeeter crawled out of the long tunnel. He stood, and lifted his hat from where he'd left it on the dirt floor before climbing in the dark hole he'd been digging out for the past two days.

"We've almost dug clear through the hill," Bug said, pointing at the opening. "You sure there's bones in there?"

Brushing loose dirt off his knees, Skeeter glanced to his youngest brother. The other boys didn't know the real reason for digging the tunnel, and he felt that was best. "I must have been wrong," he said, patting Bug on the shoulder. "Come on, let's go out in the sunlight for a bit."

"What about the hole?"

"Forget about it. I must have been wrong. There aren't any dinosaur bones there." He tugged Bug's arm, forcing him to walk to the cave opening.

"Skeeter, are you feeling all right." Bug shifted his feet a touch. "I mean, you're acting, kind of, well, kind of sad."

A shiver ripped across his shoulders as they stepped into the bright sunlight. How did he tell his little brother he felt like a fly caught on a windowsill? He wasn't caught, there were ways out, but for some reason all he could do was fly against the glass pane, thinking that was the fastest way to the other side. "I guess I just have a lot on my mind," he admitted.

"I suspect you do." Bug grinned.

His younger brother's easy chuckle made Skeeter wish he could feel that carefree again. This heavy-heartedness was wearing him out.

Bug scowled, looked at him quizzically. "Lila's a

great gal."

"Yes," he sighed. "Yes, she is." Just one he couldn't—for the life of him—figure out.

"Our family is really growing, babies on the way and all." Bug picked up a rock, threw it over the side of the cliff.

Skeeter looked back at the cave. Their family would soon be declining as fast as it had grown. The ride across the prairie the other morning had given his mind a chance to mull and clear some of the haziness. That was when he remembered Lila kept saying 'we' when she talked of the future. At first he thought she meant the baby, but the more he thought, the more he realized she meant 'we' as in him and her.

He hadn't thought of going to the future with her, actually, he hadn't thought of any one going to the future. The excitement of building the house and barn had kept him rooted in this time. Yes, he'd worked on the tunnel, had engaged the boys to help him, but the end result hadn't really formed. Then. Now, it irritated him like a sliver just under the skin. One that hurt, but couldn't be seen or dug out. Instead it festered, gathered infection until it was a full blown wound.

He'd have to dig the rest of the tunnel out himself. Didn't want to take the chance that his younger brother would find the portal. And when he found it, he'd go to the future with Lila. Maybe there, with the modern medicine she talked so much about, he could convince her to keep the baby.

He already considered the child his, and the thought of being separated from either the infant, or Lila, painfully tore at his chest. He'd miss his family, but it couldn't be helped, just as the way she missed her parents right now couldn't be helped either. He was beyond questioning it all, beyond wondering why things couldn't be different—that's how life is.

He'd best just accept his fate, and make the best of it.

He slapped Bug's shoulder. "Let's go down to the dig site, see what they've found there."

"Sure," Bug said. "You know I've wanted to check the soil there. I'm sure you have oil under this ground. Lots and lots of oil."

Skeeter shook his head, but didn't comment. Lately Bug had become obsessed with a man named Rockefeller from Ohio and his Standard Oil Company. His little brother was forever scavenging for rock tar that everyone knew wasn't good for anything except greasing wagon hubs. Bug on the other hand, swore they were oil seeps, and claimed he'd become an oil man like Rockefeller someday.

Skeeter lifted his saddle and blanket from the beneath the shade tree, flipped them onto his horse. "Well, you can search for your oil while I check to make sure none of Marsh's men are planning an attack on Cope's digging army." Tightening the cinch, he added, "I never imagined digging bones could be so dangerous."

Bug saddled his horse, and side by side, they rode to the dig site, Skeeter keeping an eye on the waving sea of knee high grass for anything suspicious the entire way. A nagging itch in the back of his mind told him something was going to happen. Something bad. The feeling had been with him for sometime now, and had grown to the point it could no longer be ignored.

Marsh and Cope's Bone War had been going on for almost a decade. The two men stopped at nothing when they thought the other was about to best them. Yokel said they'd found a new species last month, and had sent word about it to Cope.

The trail proved clear and in no time they rode into the encampment. Men loaded several odd sized and shaped crates into the back of a wagon. The bones were packaged carefully before taken to the train to ship east. Each one was wrapped in burlap and nestled in straw before the crates were built around the cargo and nailed closed. Cavalry men guarded the crates twenty-four hours, until they arrived safely in Cope's care.

Slipping off his horse, Skeeter waved a greeting to Yokel.

"The men said your house and barn are almost done, just some finishing touches to be completed," Yokel said as he extended his hand.

"Yeah," Skeeter answered, shaking the man's hand, but refusing to converse about his house. The subject felt raw, made his stomach churn. "How it's going here? Any trouble?"

"No, things have been going real well. We'll have everything ready to ship sooner than expected."

Skeeter, at a loss for words, nodded. Now that he was at the site, he realized there was nothing for him to do here. It had just been filler, a time waster while he contemplated his life. Would there ever be a time he felt in control again? When he could just live?

He turned to Bug. "I forgot something back at the cave. And I ah—have to see if I can locate Buffalo Killer. You can hang around here or head to the house, which ever you prefer."

"You want me to come with you?" Bug frowned, looking utterly confused.

Skeeter couldn't fault him, he was confused, too. Yokel kicked a boot at the ground. The digger, too, probably wondered what he was doing at the site. Why he wasn't at his new house, with his new wife. Thankfully, neither man questioned him, for he had no idea what lie he would be able to come up with. "No, I'll be back tonight or tomorrow."

"Well, all right, I'll wait here for you. Hang around, check some soil samples." Bug glanced to the land surrounding the dig site.

Skeeter gave a slight wave to Yokel and remounted. All of a sudden an urgency to complete the tunnel tugged at him. He urged the horse into a canter. While he rode, his mind joggled and jostled, from Lila to the baby, from his family to hers. What would he do if the tunnel didn't work?

Halfway to the cave, a bareback rider crested the hill on the horizon. Skeeter tugged his rifle out of the scabbard hanging off his saddle, waved it above his head. The rider signaled back and turned his mount to descend the hill. Skeeter watched the rider maneuver around the buck brush and sandstone boulders with one eye, and used the other to gaze about, checking for any other riders.

Buffalo Killer stopped a few yards ahead of him. "I look for you."

"Why?"

"Strange man at cave."

"Did you talk to him?"

"No. I look for you."

"Maybe it was one of my brothers," Skeeter suggested.

"No, he like her."

"Like her?" Goosebumps rose on his arms. "Like Lila?"

"From future." Buffalo Killer nodded, turned his gaze in the direction of the cave.

An eerie sensation crept up his spine. Skeeter slapped the leather reins across his horse and hunched over the saddle horn. The tunnel wasn't done; no one could have climbed through it. Buffalo Killer's horse tore up the ground beside him as they raced ahead.

The Kansas weather can change in a heartbeat, and did so. Dark, thick storm clouds rolled in and hovered overhead, turning the sky a dark gray-green. Large drops of rain started to fall as they arrived at the Badlands. Dirt and dust flew about as they skidded to a halt just inside the cave opening. Buffalo Killer dismounted beside him, and silently they moved deeper into the cave.

Long flashes of lightning reflected off the walls. The quick strips of light lit the darkened area for split seconds. Long enough for Skeeter to recognize someone had been there. The gear he kept stowed was spewed about. He kicked the dented coffee pot out of the way, moved toward the tunnel entrance. Crouched down, he flipped his hat off before he crawled into the opening.

Thunder rumbled the ground, making loose dirt crumble as he moved forward. His mind searched, trying to figure out who Buffalo Killer could have seen. Was it someone else from the future, or was it one of his family or Kid's cowhands who'd come looking for him? A cool breeze brushed over his face, he increased his speed. A minute later, he came to an opening. How had this happened? When he and Bug left there'd still been a good three or four feet to dig through.

He stuck his head out. Rain beat against his cheeks, and lightning lit the sky. The opening was about two feet off the ground, up the side of the cliff. There was no farm house, no out buildings, no red horseless carriage with *Mustang GT* written on the side.

He wiped the rain trickling in his eyes, and felt the slime of mud streak his cheeks. Cupping his hands, he let the rain water fill them and then splashed his face.

Lightning continued to light the grassland and highlighted the whiteness of Castle Rock standing tall and proud in the middle of the prairie. He twisted and squirmed until he'd turned about, and began to crawl back toward the cave.

When he popped his head out, Buffalo Killer had

a fire blazing in the pit. Skeeter crawled out and grabbed his hat as he moved closer to the flames.

"What you see?"

"Nothing. The tunnel goes all the way to the side of the hill." He knelt down, poked at the flames with a narrow stick. "It had to have been one of my brothers or a ranch hand you saw."

"No," Buffalo Killer stated.

He threw the stick in the fire. "That tunnel goes no where my friend. Definitely not to the future."

Buffalo Killer shrugged.

"Which direction did the man you saw go?"

"To the bone ground."

"See, it had to be one of my family members. Probably looking for Bug and me."

"On foot?"

An eerie sensation walked over his neck, he snapped his head up. "What?"

"The man walked. No horse."

A large flash of lightning accompanied by an ear-piercing crack of thunder spooked the horses and prevented Skeeter from answering. He moved to where Buffalo Killer had staked their mounts near the cave entrance. The animals stomped at the ground, tugged on their reins. He stood between them, talking low and slow as their wild eyes gazed about. When they settled, hung their heads, he moved back to the fire. "What are you doing?"

Buffalo Killer looked up from the box he'd pulled closer to the light of the flames. "I hunger." His smile grew wide. Light bounced off his white teeth as he held up a can of peaches. "You hunger?"

"Yeah, give me a can," Skeeter said, pulling his knife from his boot.

They opened the cans and proceeded to eat the fruit off the tips of their knives. It was several hours, and long after Buffalo Killer ate half a dozen cans of peaches before the storm calmed enough for them to leave the cave.

A slight drizzle hung in the air and chunks of hail melted on the ground. Skeeter was thankful the storm had happened today, not some time during the past three weeks while they had been living in the wagons. Lila should be safe and dry in the new house they'd built. His heart gave a quick thud at the thought. How had he come to love her so much? She'd turned his life upside down. But it was a nice flop. He'd never really had big plans for the future, had been content to let life roll out as it may.

Since she'd arrived with her bright red curls and tickling laughter, he'd found himself dreaming and making goals, wanting things he'd never thought much about before. A house, furniture, hell, he even wanted the fancy dishes he bought.

He was no closer to understanding why she felt compelled to give away the baby. His heart rate increased. How was he going to let her give their baby to strangers? Having a son or daughter was the one thing he found he wanted the most. He thought of the baby as theirs. Already loved the child—couldn't wait to hold it in his arms. It didn't matter that he wasn't the father. Ma wasn't Kid's real mother, but she loved him no different from the rest of the boys.

"No trail," Buffalo Killer said, breaking the silence.

Skeeter blinked, brought his mind back to the task at hand. "No the storm washed any tracks there would have been away. We'll find who you saw when we get to the dig site."

Buffalo Killer pulled his horse to a halt. "I not go there."

"Why not?"

"It not right." His long, black hair waved in the wind as he shook his head. "Dig up bones."

"They're not human. They're dinosaurs," Skeeter

explained. A coyote several miles away yipped, the sound fading with the wind. His horse pranced and stomped the ground, ready to move on.

"Still not right. Anger Spirits."

The yip came again, closer, louder. He pulled tighter on the reins, trying to calm the horse. "The Spirits don't care about prehistoric bones."

"How you know?"

"How do you know?"

Buffalo Killer shrugged. "I know."

"You never said that before."

"I not go there."

He rubbed his temples, trying to have a conversation with Buffalo Killer was like talking to a tree. "But you've watched the area, Yokel and the diggers saw you and others on the hills."

Buffalo Killer nodded. "You asked."

"If I ask you to come with me tonight, will you?"

"Not close."

"All right. I understand. I won't ask you to do something you don't want to do. You can go home, just keep an eye out. I'm sure whoever you saw was a family member, but keep an eye out anyway."

Buffalo Killer nodded and without another word, he turned his mount and rode west.

The clouds had moved out behind the storm, giving the moon free rein to lighten the grassland with a muted glow. Few trees hampered his view as he traveled along. The coyote's song made the hair on his neck stand. They'd never bothered him before, but tonight they sounded odd and made him wonder if it was coyotes.

A heavy sigh of relief exhaled when the faint flickers of the excavation campfires came into sight. There were no signs of a man on foot anywhere between the cave and the dig site. Skeeter didn't know if he felt happy about that or not.

He unsaddled the gelding and tethered him with

the other horses, then walked into the quiet camp. The click of a trigger being cocked sliced the air. His feet stopped, and he spun his gaze toward the row of wagons.

A sentry stepped out from behind one.

Skeeter held up his hand. "It's me, Quinter. I'm here to spend the night."

The man lowered the gun. "Sorry, Mr. Quinter."

He walked closer to the wagon. "Have you had any trouble tonight?" Nodding toward the compound he continued, "Any strangers in camp?"

"No, Sir. You're brother is still here, though."

"The one who was with me earlier?"

The man nodded. "He's in the big tent."

Several canvas tents were scattered throughout the area, and Cavalry wagons dotted the outskirts. One overly large tent stood in the center of the camp. "How did you weather the storm?"

The man shuffled, rested his long gun across his arms. "No real problems, a few tents leaked, one went down in the wind."

"All right. I'm going to find a place to bed down."

"There's space in the big tent."

"Thanks," he said and meandered into the camp. Neither time, when he left the house two days ago, or when he left the cave tonight did he think of grabbing a blanket. Not that it mattered, without Lila by his side, he probably wouldn't sleep anyway.

As he pulled the tent flap open, the coyote sounded again. He twisted, searching the dark with no avail. Something about the sound wasn't right. The flap fell back into place as he moved away from the tent, back toward the sentry.

Chapter Nine

Lila drew a deep breath and let it out slowly as she twisted from the window. The sun danced across the earth, signaling another bright, clear day. In Lila's eyes it was dark, and dank, for it was the third day without Skeeter. Slowly, she glanced around her bedroom. It was quite lovely—very rustic and earthy. Stepping closer to the poster bed, she smoothed the thick coverlet spread across the feather tick.

Though Ma Quinter could be ornery and cantankerous, the woman was Michelangelo of the sewing machine. She'd made the boys load up her huge, heavy, treadle machine before they left her farm. Since arrival, while the men worked on the house, she'd sat in the shade of a cottonwood and created everything from diapers for the baby to the new coverlet and curtains to match. The material was soft, silky, something Lila hadn't thought of pioneers having. It was a dark, rich brown color with golden thread stitched in large swirling shapes across the top.

She sat on the bed, unable to control how her mind wondered if Skeeter would like it. How she wished he'd return. She'd never missed anyone with such ferocity. One hand ran over the front of cream colored dress she wore, one of the dozen Ma Quinter had made for her. Her palm flattened over the small hump of her belly. The flutters below were slight, too faint to be felt outside her body.

Self-doubt was killing her. As an only child, she normally got what she wanted, when she wanted it. A child hadn't been what she wanted, so she chose a reputable adoption agency to find a family who did, but now, sitting in a house that had been built for her, built for this child, made her question her decision. Other than Kid and Jessie, no one knew she came from the future. That, too, had been her choice. She'd asked Skeeter to just say she was from Hays, and everyone readily accepted the story. Just as they accepted his absence the past few days—no one had questioned his whereabouts. Nor had they voiced their thoughts on the argument they'd all witnessed.

The family along with the ranch hands and diggers were excited to be assisting her and Skeeter as they started their life together. She covered her face with both hands. She'd never felt more miserable. She knew what she was supposed to like, supposed to want, but nothing Professor Rutledge taught had prepared her for what she was experiencing right now. Lately, nothing had turned out like it was supposed to. Maybe it was the pregnancy. She'd read on the internet that women's emotions could be out of whack during this time.

A knock sounded behind her. She ran a hand over her cheeks before turning toward the open doorway and pasting on a smile. "Hello, Hog." The younger brother was a mite shorter than Skeeter, rounder, but the same wide, lopsided grin covered his face. Her heart flopped, and then froze for a split second, aching for her husband.

"Wondering if you're ready for today's cooking lesson." He hovered in the door way. "I cleaned up the breakfast dishes, but saved you some sausage and biscuits."

She rose, patted her stomach. "Some mornings the thought of breakfast just doesn't settle well."

"Oh, well, if you want to wait awhile..." he glanced around the room.

"No, no, I look forward to your lessons." She wasn't lying, she did enjoy cooking, always had. But at the same time, without Skeeter here it all seemed useless.

Hog stepped aside as she shuffled through the door, it took too much effort to pick up her feet. "What are we cooking today?" She tried to sound cheerful. Hog was a wonderful cook and extremely excited to show her how to use all the new appliances her kitchen boasted.

"Whatever you want." He fell in step beside her.

They walked down the stairs from the second story. Her small, compact house had turned into a four-bedroom, double-story lodge. The men had thought her crazy when she asked them to change the design to leave most of the ground floor open. Large log support beams were all that separated the kitchen from the dining and living rooms. The wide staircase made a subtle curve as it lowered into the center of the immense space below. She'd also instructed the hand-hewn wood walls be left exposed and overseen the building of a large breakfast bar, complete with tall stools.

Once everyone else had seen the completed project, they liked it, including Kid. Or maybe he was just being nice to her because she'd quit badgering Jessie. She didn't have time to fret about her sister-in-law; she had her own worries and decisions to make.

"What's it gonna be?"

"I have no idea," she sighed.

Hog glanced her way.

She smiled, at least she hoped it was a smile, and realizing they were talking about two completely different things said, "Whatever you decide. You're Emeril, I'm just the rat."

"Uh?"

She sighed. "Ratatouille, it's a Pixar cartoon."

"A what?"

"Nothing, nothing, I guess my mind was in another place, another time," she admitted as they strolled around the open bar.

"I'm sure he'll be back in a couple of days," Hog said as he pulled a chair away from the table for her.

She nodded but didn't answer because a clank and a bang followed by a groan echoed from the back of the house.

Hog chuckled as he set a plate on the table. "That's Kid. He's trying to install that new wash-out Skeeter ordered."

Lila glanced toward the washroom. The wash-out was quite a sight. The latest invention in indoor plumbing had nearly made her double over with laughter. It was made of sparkling white porcelain and embossed with blue flowers more elaborate than any of the china dishes behind the glass doors of the built in buffet along the side wall of the kitchen. Two wagon loads of furniture as well as the outlandish toilet had arrived yesterday, sent from the mercantile in Nixon.

The heavy, sick feeling of guilt settled deeper in the core of her stomach. Everyone was working so hard on a house that would soon stand empty. She glanced around, wishing things could be different. Wished she'd been born years before—so she could stay in this century forever.

A swift movement made her press a palm to her abdomen. The baby rolled, as if trying to telling her it, too, wanted to stay in the past. The thought was like a double edged sword.

"Lila?" Hog asked. "Lila, are you all right?" His hand pressed against her cheek. "You're awfully pale this morning."

She swallowed, nodded. "I'm fine."

"Don't fret, Skeeter will be back soon."

"I hope so," she sighed.

A noise in the front yard grew loud enough to draw Kid out of the washroom. "Who's here?" he asked.

Hog shrugged, moved toward the window.

Lila pushed away from the table, glanced toward Hog, and then hoping beyond hope it was Skeeter, quickly followed Kid to the front door. He held it open for her to step out first. Moving across the wide veranda she noticed a Conestoga wagon pulling into the yard. "More furniture?" she asked Kid.

"No, it looks like Willamina and Eva." He took her elbow to escort her down the steps.

She'd met Willamina, an old woman who was quite bent over with osteoporosis, and Eva, a young, silent girl, a few weeks ago. The odd couple lived in a sod house near Kid and Jessie. Skeeter had introduced her to them during their trip to Nixon to purchase the surprisingly, comfortable, low-topped boots she wore in place of her flip-flops. She frowned, looked up at Kid. "Why would they be here?"

"Probably just being neighborly," he shrugged as they walked across the dirt.

"Neighborly? They had to travel two days to get here."

Kid chuckled. "Willamina's like family. I'm surprised she waited this long before coming."

A crowd had gathered, and by the time the wagon stopped even Ma Quinter had left her sewing machine to greet the guests. Kid helped Willamina down while Snake assisted Eva. The old woman lifted her head toward the house. A moment later, she pushed the wide brim of her bonnet back, giving her intense stare clear vision. "Well, Lord and all that's holy! That there is one of the finest houses I've ever seen."

Jessie stepped forward, wrapped her arms around the woman and nodded her head. "Lila designed it. Wait until you see the inside, it's breathtaking."

Lila pressed a hand to her warm cheek, unsure why the compliment embarrassed her.

"Well, land sakes! You are as bright as I thought."

This time she gaped.

Willamina stepped forward, took her arm. "Come on girl, show me the rest. I'm itchin' harder than a dog full of fleas to see the inside."

Everyone around chuckled, and for the first time in three days, Lila felt a real smile grow on her face. She waved an arm. "Right this way."

The old woman latched onto her elbow. "The house looks just like you."

"Excuse me?" She glanced down at the woman.

A gnarled, red hand pointed. "The shingles have a touch of red to them. The way the sun is shining on the upper windows reminds me of your green eyes, and the roof over the porch looks like your smile." Willamina's twinkling eyes glanced between her and the house. "Just like you, this house adds a touch of beauty to the prairie fields."

Lila's gaze went from the woman to the house. A silly, warm feeling threatened to make her laugh aloud. She glanced back to Willamina. "Thank you, that's a wonderful compliment."

"A little out of place, but right beautiful," Willamina added.

A frown tugged on her brows.

Before she could comment, Jessie said, "Lila has worked so hard."

Kid cleared his throat, Jessie giggled and left Willamina's other side to hug her husband. Lila felt a hard tinge of jealousy, missing Skeeter even more than before.

"The men have done all the work, I just explained how I wanted things to look in the end," Lila said as they climbed the front steps.

"Well, it looks like they did a right fine job."

Lila became a tour guide, showing all the rooms to Willamina, and proudly presented all of the wonderful furnishings filling the house. Graciously, she pointed out the uniqueness of each room, each touch of care the men and women had used in creating and decorating the showcase. She couldn't have been more proud if she had been the first lady showing off the Whitehouse.

The tour ended near the stone fireplace. Willamina turned to Eva. "Do you have their present?"

The girl nodded, turned toward Kid. He held a large canvas wrapped package.

"Where's Skeeter?" Willamina asked, glancing around as if she'd just noticed he wasn't near.

"He had to go check the bone excavation," Hog said, coming to stand next to Lila. In comfort he patted her shoulder.

"Him and his bones. But I gotta hand it to him, if anyone could become successful finding old bones, it would be Skeeter." Willamina waved to Kid. "Well, bring it on over. He'll just have to see it when he gets home."

Eva walked behind Kid, her footsteps as quiet and shy as her personality. When he set the large load on the wide hearth, the girl carefully removed the canvas covering.

Lila was dumb-struck. "Eva, it-it's gorgeous. I don't know what to say." She stepped forward to touch the edge of the painting. "Thank you."

It was like the one Kid and Jessie had, but of her and Skeeter. His head full of gold-touched curls was slightly tilted back, a wide smile covered his handsome face, and his eyes sparkled with just enough mischief to make her heart skip a beat. The girl had expertly captured his rugged good looks and jubilant personality. His arm, wrapped around her shoulder, held her to his side as she looked up at him.

The breath stilled in her lungs. The woman in the picture was beautiful. Dressed in her lilac covered wedding gown, she had one hand on Skeeter's chest. The expression on her painted face made her heart skip every other beat. The eyes she always thought were dull green looked luminescent as her gaze stared up at his laughing ones. The glint or sparkle Eva painted in them showed exactly how she felt, even though she hadn't yet admitted it even to herself. The young girl's acute talent had found it, and exposed it for the entire world to see. Skeeter Quinter was the love of her life.

She pressed a hand to the tumbles in her stomach, caressing the area as the baby moved. It was several minutes before she tugged her gaze away from the painted couple and looked at the background on the canvas. The moonscape hills of the Badlands and the tall, spiral pillar of Castle Rock rose out of the ground to stretch high into a brilliant blue sky. The faint makings of an eagle floated amongst fluffy white clouds.

Her gaze went to Eva. A soft, timid smile tugged on the girl's lips.

"How?" Lila asked.

Willamina stepped forward. Wrapped an arm around Eva and gave a slight nod, encouraging the girl to talk.

"I-I drew a picture of the two of you the morning you stopped by our house," Eva said in a soft voice.

"But the background, it's-it's perfect."

Willamina nodded. "We camped over that way

for the past couple of days so she could get it exactly as she wanted it. Did a right fine job if you ask me."

"Yes, yes, she did." Lila stepped toward Eva. "I love it, thank you." She wrapped her arms around the girl. "I've never had a gift I've liked more."

Eva hugged her back, her small body trembling as she said, "You're welcome."

"It had just dried enough for us to wrap up when the storm hit yesterday." Willamina said, glancing at the painting as if checking for damage. "That friend of yours liked it real well, too."

"Whose friend?" Lila asked, wondering why Willamina was looking at her.

"Yours."

She shook her head. "I don't have any friends here. Well—I mean besides all of you." Her glance included the family gathered in the living room.

The old woman frowned, wrinkles covered her face. "That feller from Hays. Said his name was Pete somethin' or another."

Lila's world went black.

****

Skeeter dismounted. Cautiously, he glanced over his shoulder and slowly moved forward to examine the flattened grass. Crouched down, he ran a hand over the blades as his gaze went to the horizon. The entire excavation site was visible in the small valley below. A small clump of trees behind him had given cover to whoever had sat here.

He stood, scanned the ground in all directions. The morning dew had already dried from the grass, leaving no noticeable signs of the direction the unknown watcher may have moved. No signs as to who it could have been.

The August sun was a scorcher, heat licked across his shoulders even though it was well before mid-day. He shrugged, rubbed his tired eyes. The long sleepless night left him fatigued. He'd spent several hours sitting with the sentry, waiting for another unusual coyote howl. One hadn't come, and he should have gone to the tent, but for some reason he hadn't—couldn't. An uneasy dread in the air had kept his hackles up.

The rest of the camp hadn't sensed it, and he decided to keep his anxieties to himself. Without a word, he'd ridden out as the sun rose. Behind him the gelding snorted, flicked its tail at pesky flies. Skeeter gazed about. Yellow-brown buffalo grass covered the land, stretched out as far as he could see. Nothing looked out of place. Maybe all that was bothering him was the disarray of his life.

A rustle behind him made him pivot, slap a hand to the holster strapped on his hips. His grasp eased off the walnut-handled pistol as a prairie chicken noisily scampered from her roost. He turned back to the flattened grass near his feet.

Marsh. The man could easily have intercepted Yokel's message to Cope about the new specimen he'd found. If so, the man would have wasted no time in sending spies out to try and steal the bones. Skeeter walked to his horse, mounted. After a final glance around he nudged the gelding forward, searching for other signs the spies may have left behind as he set a course to circle the excavation area.

His mind wandered as he rode—Lila, the baby, the unexplainable man at the tunnel, the Bone War. When had his life become so complicated? Little more than a month ago his only worries had been what type of gifts he should pick up for Buffalo Killer's tribe. A smile tried to tug on his lips. Peaches. Had he known how much the brave liked the canned fruit he wouldn't have wasted his money on colored beads.

As if the mere thought of the Redman could make him appear, a faint figure formed far ahead.

Skeeter squinted against the sunlight. A horseman, with his rifle held high above his head rode toward him. He copied the greeting. Miles apart, it was several minutes before they met.

"My braves saw your man," Buffalo Killer said as his horse stopped. The black and white painted pony glistened with sweat.

Skeeter rubbed against the tickle of hair standing on end at the back of his neck. "My man?"

"From cave."

His head whipped around, scanning the area. "Where?"

Buffalo Killer nodded. "You saw where he slept."

"Where is he now?"

The Indian shrugged, glanced toward the excavation site. "He go when sun rose."

"Were your braves here all night? Talking to each other with coyote yips?"

Buffalo Killer cracked a quick smile, shrugged.

Skeeter didn't comment, already knew the answer the brave hadn't admitted. "Did they get a good look at him?"

"Many hairs on face."

His body tightened so hard the gelding jumped. Pete Hawkins had a full beard and mustache. Skeeter tried to shake the strain gripping his body and patted the horse's neck, calming the mount.

"There are more."

"More? More what?"

"Men."

"Where?"

"Watch diggers."

"Who are they?"

Buffalo Killer shrugged. "Not from future."

He'd been right. Marsh's men were here too. "How many?"

Another shoulder shrug was his only answer.

"Damn it, I wish you'd learn how to talk,"

Skeeter huffed, and pulled his hat off to wipe the sweat dotting his forehead.

A deep scowl pulled Buffalo Killers dark brows together. "I talk." He patted his chest with a fist.

"With one syllable," Skeeter growled. "Why can't you give me a full sentence? Tell me what I need to know without me having to pull it out of you like a hog stuck in the mud."

Buffalo Killer pulled on the mane of his bridle-less horse, twisting it away.

"No, stop." Skeeter reached over, laid a hand on the brave's arm. "I'm sorry."

The arm beneath his hand went lax. "You worry?"

"Yes, I'm worried," Skeeter admitted. "I'm worried about Lila, about the baby, about Pete Hawkins finding her, about Marsh's men attacking Cope's." A deep sigh left his body. "Yes, my friend, I'm very worried."

Buffalo Killer laid his other hand atop Skeeter's still on his forearm. "I help, my friend. I help."

He sighed, glanced toward the excavation site. "Thank you, now if I just had a plan."

Buffalo Killer leaned his head back and an eerie shot ripped up Skeeter's spine as the brave let out several loud, coyote-sounding yips.

Shrugging off the sensation, he glanced around the area as answering yips echoed over the land. One by one mounted braves appeared. Stepping out from behind narrow trees, boulder clumps, and into the horizon's edge circling them.

As the dozen or so tribesmen starting riding closer, Buffalo Killer said, "We help. We help you plan."

Chapter Ten

Confused, fuzzy headed, Lila woke, and needed a few moments before recognizing the rich decorations of her bedroom. A cool cloth lay across her forehead. Heavy lidded, she glanced to the woman sitting on the bed beside her. "What happened?"

"You fainted." Jessie removed the cloth. "Hog said you haven't eaten anything today. Is that true?"

Lila would have searched her mind, checked for memories of eating, if it had mattered, but it didn't, so she simply closed her eyes.

"You know, for someone who claims to know so much about how pregnant women need to take care of themselves, you aren't very good at following your own advice."

She frowned, gazed up at Jessie. Humor tinted the blue eyes looking back at her.

Jessie leaned over, patted her cheek. "I'm teasing. How are you feeling now? Dizzy? Lightheaded?"

"No, no I'm fine." A thump, or thud, or some other odd noise sounded somewhere in the house. The disturbance made memories flood her mind. A hard, tight knot formed in her chest. "Pete! Willamina said she saw Pete." She pressed her hand to the mattress, tried to sit up.

Jessie stopped her movement with gentle

pressure. "Calm down. Just lie there for a moment."

Lila flopped her head against the pillow. "How did he get here?" Despite the heat of the day, a shiver raced over her body. "The tunnel! It must be open again." A burning sob swelled in her throat. "Oh, God! What if he's hurt Skeeter?" She grabbed Jessie's hand. "What are we gonna do? We have to find him."

Jessie wrapped her other hand around their clasped ones. "*We* aren't going to do anything. *You* are going to lay right here until Ma has a chance to examine you, make sure everything's all right."

Jessie pressed a finger to Lila's mouth when she tried to protest.

"Kid is talking with Willamina. He'll find out all she knows and then decide what to do. Don't worry, he won't let anything happen to Skeeter."

Lila twisted her head. "You people can't protect each other like you think you can. We need the police. The FBI. The CIA." Her head swam, and hot, burning tears began to force their way out of her eyes.

Jessie's fair hair pressed against Lila's shoulder, arms wrapped her into a hug. "Shh. Don't cry. Have faith in Skeeter. In Kid. In all the brothers." She sat up, framed Lila's cheeks with her palms. "I don't know who those others are you mentioned. The police, FBI or CIA. But have faith in your family Lila. We won't let you down."

Lila pressed her head deeper into the pillow, closed her eyes. *Faith!* What good was faith? Faith had trapped her in the past right after she'd asked for her ghost back. Who'd turned out to be Skeeter, a wonderful man, but now he was in danger. Deadly danger. If what she'd read on the internet was true, Pete Hawkins had murdered before. He was wanted in connection with a missing girl from Topeka, but since a body had never surfaced, he'd never been arrested. Oh, God, what if Pete had killed Skeeter? What if they never found his body?

A ripping sob tore across her chest. She couldn't live without her husband—didn't want to live without Skeeter. She pushed Jessie away and rolled onto her side as deep cries bubbled out. Pressing her face deep into the pillow, she wept, letting the pain completely absorb her.

Sometime later, cried out and exhausted, she couldn't even muster up a protest as Ma Quinter completed a thorough examination. Afterwards, dressed in a cotton nightgown, her mother-in-law tucked her between the covers.

Turning toward Jessie, Stephanie Quinter said, "She'll be fine. Just needs a day in bed to get her strength back."

The two stepped further away from the bed. Lila closed her eyes. Sleep would be a luxury—one she didn't deserve.

"Damn boy! I'm gonna wallop him good when he gets back. Leaving her here while he goes off to check his bones. That boy never could hold his horses. Can't sit still long enough for grass to grow beneath his feet," Stephanie rambled.

Lila opened her eyes, closed them again. "No, it's all my fault." She rolled her head from side to side, dull thuds of pain pounded at her temples. "Don't blame him." A burning lump scorched her throat. "It's my fault he left."

Stephanie took her hand. "No, it's not your fault, honey."

"Yes it is!" She blurted. "I hadn't told him I'm giving the baby away." A sob burst out. "He was so hurt."

A sputtered cough echoed across the room.

Lila opened her eyes in time to see Jessie grabbed Stephanie's shoulders and guide her to the door. "Ma, please go get Kid, we need to find out what Willamina told him."

Ma Quinter's lips opened and closed, and her face had turned bright red. Lila shut her eyes, rolled onto her side. A second later the door clicked shut.

The side of the bed dipped, and Jessie ran a hand over the side of Lila's face, brushed her hair aside. "I don't think you should talk about that right now."

Pain engulfed her chest. "What if he doesn't come back? What if Pete has hurt him?"

"Shh...don't talk now."

"I love him so much."

"I know you do, and he loves you too." Jessie continued to run a comforting hand over her hair, across her shoulders. "Just rest now."

Exhausted, numb with pain, Lila couldn't do anything except nod.

****

The western sky held the bright sun when she woke several hours later. Shafts of afternoon light shooting through the window, spread a blanket of sparkling diamonds across the top of the chest of drawers where Skeeter's shaving brush sat in a small cup, his razor lying beside it. Her lips twitched. He'd been in her dreams. Smiling, he'd held her in those strong, solid arms, and assured her he was fine.

Lila twisted, glanced to the pillow beside her. It was full, held no indention, yet her dream had been so real, so vivid, and an invisible, yet calm sense of well-being hovered about.

Rubbing swollen eyes, she sat up and glanced around the empty room. Her gaze settled on the closed door and a rock hit the pit of her stomach. Had she told Ma Quinter she was giving away the baby?

"Oh, Skeeter," she mumbled. "I'm so sorry."

She could almost hear his lilting laugh.

"It's not funny. She's sure to pitch a fit." Lila rebuked and hid her face behind her hands, huffed in the cupped air.

Someone must have sensed she was awake because the door latch turned. The click echoed into the room. Lila peeked between her fingers and lowered her hands with relief as Jessie walked in.

"Feeling better?" the woman asked.

She was remarkably better. Lila nodded and flipped the covers aside.

"No, stay there. A day in bed won't hurt you."

"I-I um, I have to go to the bathroom."

Jessie leaned down, pulled a flowered chamber pot out from beneath the bed.

Lila shook her head. "No." She couldn't get used to the idea of peeing in a container that looked like a punch bowl, minus the cups of course.

"Well, all right. Kid got the new one in the washroom installed before he left. I suppose you can use it."

Lila stood, arched the stiffness from her back. "Before he left?"

Jessie nodded, took her elbow to guide her to the door.

"Where did he go?"

"To find Skeeter."

"He did?" Lila paused, not wanting to leave the room just yet.

Jessie smiled. "Yes, he did. Don't fret, he'll find him, and they'll be home before you know it."

"Oh, I hope so. I so hope so."

"They will be. Trust me." Jessie led her out of the room.

From the top of the steps Lila looked down, gazed around the empty area. "Where is every one?"

"Here and there. The hands are finishing up the barn. The chickens and milk cow are settled in, and Joe, our ranch foreman, drove in a small herd of beef cattle today."

Lila nodded, pondering the information as she stepped from the stairs and moved toward the water closet off the kitchen. When she'd agreed to Skeeter's plan of building a house for them, she never imagined it would be so complex. What would happen to all the animals when they went to the future? Chickens, cows, cattle. Hog had made a trip into the small town of Me-lo-te Switch and bought a couple of pigs as well. They now had a complete hobby ranch someone would need to tend to once they left.

It was all so much more multifaceted than she'd imagined it would be. She'd lived on her own for several years, but it was so different in the future. There, all she needed was the local grocery store, didn't have to worry about animals, other than her cat, which in all honesty, wasn't really her cat. Tabby was a neighborhood stray. Everyone fed it, and it didn't call anyplace home, roamed from doorstep to doorstep on its own free will.

Finishing her business, she pulled the chain hanging from the holding tank near her head, surprisingly the highly decorated bowl worked just like the modern ones. She would have chuckled if her life didn't seem so dismal.

Leaving the room, she walked to the kitchen table. "When did Kid leave?"

Jessie stood near the stove, ladling soup into a bowl. "Several hours ago. Would you like to eat here at the table, or back up in your room?"

Her stomach growled, giving her mind no chance to refuse the food. "Here, I think."

"Sit down then. Hog made a pot of chicken soup. It's very good." Jessie set the bowl and a spoon on the table. "Have I told you about his cookbook?"

Lila shook her head as she took a spoonful.

"It has all of his best recipes in it. We were going

to send it to New York to a publisher, but decided they were too good to tell others about. He only shares them with family." Jessie sat down. "I made a copy of it for you. It's in the buffet drawer."

Lila swallowed the last spoonful of soup that Campbell's would die for, before she let her mind wonder to the day's events. Her gaze went to the large fireplace.

"One of the hands framed it and hung it up for you," Jessie said as her gaze landed on the painting.

Her temples started to pound. "Jessie, did I really tell Stephanie I was giving this baby away? Or was that part a dream?"

Jessie sucked in a small gulp of air. "Sorry. It wasn't a dream."

"Oh shit."

"Yeah, that's what I thought too."

****

Skeeter strolled into the excavation site, gesturing to Yokel as he made his way toward the man. They met in the middle of the yard. "We need to talk. But first, where's my brother?" He scanned the men, looking for Bug.

"Bug?" Yokel asked.

"Yes." Skeeter took a closer around the area. "Are one of my other brothers here?"

"No, just Bug, but he rode out not long after you did this morning. He thought you were headed to your house." Yokel pulled the white gloves off his hands. "Why?"

"I'd hoped he was still here." Skeeter sighed. Might as well add Bug to his list of worries. Odd, once a man finds one thing to worry about, others just stack up. He twisted about, pointed to an open-sided tent. "Let's talk over there."

Gathered into bulky wads, the sides of the tent had been pulled back and tied to the four poles holding the flapping roof overhead. The wind tugged on the canvas, tried to lift it into the current and carry it away on the steady breeze. Thankfully it didn't, because the shade it provided from the afternoon heat was much needed. Skeeter wiped his forehead then the back of his neck with his bandana.

Yokel sat, pointed to the other chair beside a lopsided table. "What's wrong? You're making me feel as antsy as a cat on a tin roof."

Skeeter took a breath and sat, steadying the chair on the uneven ground by planting both heels into the dirt. "Where's Johansson?"

Yokel glanced around; an indifferent shrug lifted his shoulders. "Don't know, ain't seen him lately."

"Have you seen him today?"

A deep scowl covered the other man's face. "Now that you mention it, no, I ain't seen him all day." He shook his head. "Not even at breakfast."

Skeeter held the huff of breath growing in his chest. "How long have you known him?"

"Since spring, Cope hired him right before we left Pennsylvania. Said he had good references."

Skeeter nodded. "From who?"

Yokel reached down, picked up a rock to fiddle with. "I don't know. I never asked."

"I think you should have. There's a gang of men. Not many, six or seven, and they've been watching the area. My guess is they're waiting for you to pull out." He paused, made sure he had the other man's full attention. "Then ambush your load."

"Shit!" The rock sailed through the air, landed with a thud in the higher grasses growing beyond the tent. "You've seen these men?"

"Yes, but they didn't see us. Buffalo Killer and his braves are watching them."

"Good, then we can capture them." Yokel shifted, as if ready to rise from his chair. "Send someone for the Sheriff in Collyer."

Skeeter shook his head. "Not yet. I think

Johansson's in cahoots with them." He pointed toward the diggers. "Hard saying how many others could be as well."

Looking startled, Yokel leaned back in his chair. "Surely not the Cavalry men."

"Maybe not, but you must have close to fifty men out here. How many can you guarantee are not in cahoots with Johansson and Marsh?"

Yokel sighed, pinched his chin with his thumb and forefinger. "No more than a handful."

"That's what I thought." Skeeter ran a hand over the table top, drummed his fingers. "I think you should carry on as usual. The braves will let us know if the men plan an attack. In the mean time, ask around a bit, see if you can figure out who else might be in with Marsh."

Yokel nodded. "Was Johansson with the men you saw?"

"No." Skeeter shook his head. Hawkins wasn't with the men either. He wondered if one of Marsh's men had been the man Buffalo Hunter had seen, some of them had facial hair. But the brave insisted none of them were the man he'd seen leaving the tunnel. Feeling a gaze, Skeeter glanced up. Yokel was looking at him questionably. "No, I'm sure he wasn't with them. You haven't seen him, uh?"

"No, and that's odd."

His spine stiffened. "Why do you say that?"

"He's scared shitless of snakes. Hasn't left camp since we arrived."

"Boss! Boss!" A man ran toward the tent. Huffing for air as he stopped near a pole, he exclaimed, "You gotta come quick."

Yokel jumped, his chair toppling behind him. "What? What did you find?"

The man laid a hand on Yokel's shoulder. "A body."

"A body?" Yokel asked doubtfully.

"A man's body."

"Where?" Skeeter stood.

"At yesterday's site. There's a small cave, we went inside to get out of the sun for a few minutes."

"Show us!" Skeeter grabbed the man's arm. They raced across the site, gathering men as they ran. Skidding to a halt beside two men standing guard outside a small opening, he said, "Move aside."

"No, Mr. Quinter, I don't think you should be the one to go in there."

A river of shivers raked his body. "What the hell?" He pushed the man aside, bent over and squeezed through the narrow opening. Once inside he stood again, the area was quite large, but dark. He blinked, tried to focus.

The dank, musty area blazed with light as Yokel stepped in behind him, holding a coal oil lamp. "There," Yokel said, pointing to the far wall.

Unexplained chills raced up his arms and legs as he moved toward the prone body. Recognition hit him like a two-by-four. Fire ripped at his throat. "Oh, God, Bug." He crouched next to his brother's side. The dirt near Bug's pasty face was dark with dried blood. Skeeter ran a hand beneath Bug's head, lifted it. "Bug! Bug!"

Yokel stepped closer, shined the light over the body. Bug's smooth, teenage skin glistened in the glow of the lamp. A jagged, dark gash ran along the side of his head.

A tight knot formed in his chest, stealing the air from his lungs. Skeeter leaned his head down, pressed Bug's face to his neck. Every muscle went tight, his guts churned with bile. "No, not you Bug, not you."

A faint tickle rolled across the sensitive skin below his ear. He pulled his head up, pressed a hand to Bug's neck. A faint flutter rippled beneath his fingertips. His heart leaped into high gear. "Get me a wagon!"

"Mr. Quinter, I'm so sor—"

Skeeter twisted. "He's not dead! Get me a wagon! Now!"

"You men get in here! And send someone for a wagon. This man's not dead!" Yokel shouted. The men instantly scrambled into action.

Skeeter carried Bug himself. Though his brother probably weighed as much as he, the weight seemed slight. The bright sun made his eyes water as he crawled into the back of the wagon and settled his little brother so he could cradle his head during the rough ride. All the while he prayed, prayed like Ma had taught him years ago.

Yokel handed him a medical bag. "I'll send a man with your horse."

Skeeter set the bag beside him, nodded his thanks, and turned to give the driver directions. The words stilled in his throat as two horses skid to halt. Kid and Snake looked at him expectantly.

"It's Bug, Kid. Someone hurt him bad. We gotta get him to the house." He turned to Snake. "On top of that ridge is a small Indian party. Tell Buffalo Killer what happened. Tell him to leave his braves here and meet us at the house."

Snake nodded and spurred his horse as Skeeter yelled to the driver, "Move out!"

****

Lila couldn't stay in the bedroom any longer. Even facing the wrath of Ma Quinter in her holy-roller role would be better than staring at the four walls. After her bowl of soup, Jessie had ushered her back up here. Lila tried to rest, but it was no use, her mind was spinning like a ceiling fan. Everything she knew about herself no longer held true. It was as if she was a stranger—to herself, and didn't know how to relate to this person. Could loving someone change a person this much? Make everything they thought they knew wrong?

She moved to the window and pulled aside the heavy curtain. The retreating sun barely peeked over the horizon, calmly slipping away after having done a full day's work of heating the western plains. The cool night air washed over her, lingering long enough to make her skin prickle, and a heavenly scent filled her nostrils. Whether it was the clean, freshness of the country side or the appetizing smell of whatever Hog was cooking, she didn't take time to decipher, but pivoted on one foot and walked to the wardrobe.

She slipped the nightgown over her head, stepped into a flowing grey skirt and pulled on a loose-fitting, ruffled, white blouse. Ignoring the boots sitting near the bed, she padded across the room barefoot. As she grasped the door knob, she took a deep fortifying breath, hoped it would help in the encounter with Stephanie, and stepped out the door.

Low murmurs came from the kitchen. She eased down the staircase, stalled near the base. Jessie, standing near the breakfast bar, smiled and gestured toward the table. A small amount of tension slipped from Lila's shoulders, allowing her to lift her head as she moved forward.

Stephanie twisted in her chair, following Jessie's gaze with her own. "Oh, honey, are you feeling better?" She rose, stepped forward and grasped Lila's elbow.

Lila found an ounce of courage for the confrontation, and willed her knees to stay strong. "Yes, thank you."

Holding out a chair, Stephanie aided her onto it. "Good, sit down and have some supper. Hog cooked a wonderful venison stew."

Her knees didn't fail her, but nonetheless, she sank gratefully into the chair, and was even able to smile at Hog as he set a plate in front of her. Patting her shoulder, he settled onto the chair beside her. Willamina and Eva sat across from them with Jessie and Stephanie seated at the ends of the table. No one spoke, and Lila followed suit, chose instead to eat her meal. Before coming to the past she'd never had venison, or rabbit, or prairie chicken, but now she found they were quite tasty. Then again, Hog could probably make anything become quite tasty. He was a master chef. She lifted her gaze, glanced toward her brother-in-law. A rambling thought took hold. Hog should come back to the future with her and Skeeter, and Jessie and Kid. There he could open a restaurant, and folks were sure to travel for miles to eat his specialties.

Hog met her gaze with a kind smile. She returned it, and resumed eating. It wouldn't be fair to take so many family members away from Stephanie, she'd be quite lonely. Then again, maybe Stephanie, Snake and Bug would want to come, too. Oh, but that would leave Willamina and Eva here alone. She could imagine the younger generation accepting the future, but Stephanie and Willamina would have a hard time with it all.

When her plate was empty, she rose to carry it to the sink, pondering if she could convince the whole Quinter family to travel through the tunnel.

"You sit down and rest. I'll help Hog clean up," Stephanie instructed.

Lila quivered, returning to the present with a snap. The woman was being much too nice. She'd expected the opposite. How on earth was she going to explain an adoption agency to Ma Quinter? Shaking her head, needing a few minutes to straighten her wandering mind, she said, "No, I'm getting stiff from lying around. I need the exercise."

Before Stephanie had a chance to answer, a loud commotion sounded from the front yard. Everyone leaped to their feet. Ma Quinter was the first to get to the doorway, her large double-barrel shotgun in hand as she threw the door open.

Lila peered over the woman's shoulder, and her heart somersaulted. Skeeter jumped from the back of the wagon before it even stopped rolling. She stepped forward, ready to run out the doorway when Kid flew off his horse to help Skeeter lift something out of the wagon.

"What's up?" Stephanie shouted. "Who's hurt?"

"It's Bug, Ma. He's hurt bad," Skeeter said.

Stephanie threw the gun, it skid across the floor as she raced out the door. "My baby? Who hurt him? How bad is it? Dang-gum it, boys, hurry up, get him in here!"

Lila pressed both hands to the rapid thuds in her chest. Jessie wrapped a hand around her shoulders, but her gaze was on Skeeter. His eyes met hers. They were dull, sad, not a hint of joy could be seen. A sob choked her as she looked at the lifeless body he and Kid carried up the stairs.

Jessie tugged, pulled her out of the way as the men crossed the threshold. Leaving Lila to stand alone, away from the crowd, Jessie bustled forward. "Bring him upstairs, I'll get the bed ready."

From the kitchen area Willamina said, "I'll get some water, Eva get some rags and bandages."

Lila retreated further out of the way, feeling useless, like a fifth wheel. She had no idea what to do. In her time, they'd call nine-one-one, or drive to an emergency room and wait, huddled together in a sterile waiting room, for a doctor's diagnosis. Heavens, no one here probably even knew CPR. She did, she'd learned it in ninth grade health class, but had never used it—did she even remember the basics?

The scuttle around her continued—Jessie bolted up the stairs. Skeeter and Kid, gently maneuvering their load, followed with Ma right on their heels. Willamina rushed from the kitchen, a basin of steaming water in her hand. Eva went up the steps next, carrying a handful of white cloths.

Lila brushed her hair away from her face, irritated by the stray curls. She was the only one who'd gone to college, probably the only one who'd graduated high school, yet here she stood—without a clue as to do what to do—feeling as dumb as a box of rocks.

A man, one of the diggers, walked in the doorway. He glanced around then handed her a squat leather bag. "Here's the medical bag from the site. Maybe there's something in there they'll need."

She wrapped her fingers around the handle. Still unsure. Hog appeared at her side, a tapestry satchel in his hand. He touched her shoulder. "Come on," he coaxed her to trek up the stairs ahead of him.

Her steps were slow, shaky. Hog's arm settled on her shoulders, gently steadying. She glanced his way, her eyes settled on the bag in his other hand.

"It's Ma's medical bag," he said.

She nodded, recognizing it from when Stephanie had examined her earlier. It was full of small bottles and pouches of herbs, balm, and other things she quivered even imagining what they might be. Did they still bleed people with leeches in this era? Did Ma Quinter have a bottle full of bloodsuckers in the tattered bag? A shiver tickled her flesh. Why hadn't she studied medicine instead of Information Technology? At least then she'd be some help.

Hog patted her shoulder. "Ma's knows what she's doing. Before Doc Fields arrived a couple years ago, Ma doctored all the folks around Nixon."

She swallowed against the thickness forming in her throat and topped the stairs. Eva hovered in the doorway of the room down the hall. Tears trickled down the girl's face. With fingers trembling as hard as Lila's, Eva wiped her cheeks, and stepped aside to let Lila and Hog pass.

Stephanie and Willamina stood near the head of the bed, blocking her view of Bug. His long legs stretched to the foot of the bed, stocking toes flopped sideways. Jessie, wrapped in Kids arms stood on the other side, one of her hands gently rubbing Bug's knees.

Skeeter stood on that side of the bed, near the headboard, his hand on Bug's shoulder. She wanted to go stand beside him, wrap her arms around his solid waist, but there wasn't enough room to squeeze past Kid and Jessie. She stared, willed him to look her way. But he didn't. His eyes watched whatever Stephanie and Willamina were doing.

Hog left her side, moved to set Stephanie's bag on the table beside the bed. Lila clutched the handle in her hand, her teeth trembling, pinched her bottom lip. Hog returned, took the bag from her hand and then carried it to the table too.

Running footsteps echoed off the stairs and seconds later Snake bound into the room. Breathless he asked, "How is he?"

Kid glanced his way, gave a slight shake of his head. Jessie buried her face deeper into his chest, and Lila, gasping for air glanced to Skeeter. He still didn't look her way.

"Ya'll get out of here," Stephanie said, her voice extremely calm. "Willamina and I got work to do."

No one protested, but each of the boys touched Bug before they turned to meander toward the door. Hog put his hand on her back, pushed her toward the door. She appreciated his kindness, but it wasn't his touch she wanted. Fighting the urge to shrug off his hand, she walked through the door.

As each person stepped out of the room, they stopped outside the door, forcing her to move further down the hall. She soon found herself near the door to her room. When Skeeter stepped out they were separated by everyone else. She stepped forward, ready to nudge past Hog to get to him when Snake said, "Buffalo Killer is outside. He won't come in a white man's house."

Skeeter took his hat off, flattened his hand over his forehead, squeezing his temples with his forefinger and thumb. Lila squelched an urge to thrust through the crowd, silently begging him to look her way.

He didn't. With a solemn nod he moved toward the stairs. "I'll go talk to him."

Hog and Snake followed him. Kid, Jessie still clutched to his side, went toward the room they'd been staying in, and Eva shot down the hall to the room she and Willamina had been settle in.

Lila stood there until loneliness and sadness quaked her body so hard she became fearful of collapsing. With a sob she turned and stumbled into her bedroom. She was sad Bug was hurt, certainly didn't want him to die. But what about her? Why wasn't Skeeter comforting her like Kid was Jessie?

A gut wrenching, sick and sour, taste filled her mouth. She hadn't changed. She was a selfish, horrible person who thought of no one but herself.

Trembling from head to toe, she buckled onto the edge of the bed. The last bit of sunshine provided just enough light to cast the room with a fog-like haze. The room swirled, and she covered the wrenching sob bubbling out her mouth with her hand.

In the future it hadn't seemed so awful. For years she'd been taught that's how people her age behaved, accepted it factually, with no need to question or change it, but here, where everyone cared so much for one another, helped each other without the slightest thought of what was in it for them, her behavior was appalling.

A warm, soft tumble happened in her stomach, and she laid her palm against it. She wasn't completely selfish. After all, she was giving her baby away so it could have a good home. Knew that's what was best for the baby. Or was that what she'd told herself? Maybe the real reason she was giving the baby away is because it would be too much work to keep. Isn't that what everyone in the future had told her? The flutter happened again. She'd believed them. Without completely examining the decision, she'd taken what her friends, the doctor, and social worker had said as gospel. Having a baby as a single, college student was not a wise decision—giving the baby away was.

She rose and walked to the window. The moon had risen to replace the sun's light with a shimmering glow. It bounced off the hills of prairie grass, casting dark shadows across the land. No one had said traveling to the past was a good idea, but here she was. Twisting, her gaze settled on the large group of men gathered near the barn, Hog and Snake, surrounded by ranch hands and a few diggers. Their heads hung as they conversed amongst themselves, clearly worried about Bug.

Bright red, new paint on the barn glistened in the pale light. She frowned. These men had all left their duties behind to come build the house and barn for Skeeter and her. They weren't construction workers who were paid for their time and skill. Sure, some were employees of Kid's, and he probably still paid their wage, but even the diggers had left the excavation site just to come and help. This era certainly put more effort into helping each other than helping themselves.

Near the wagon parked in the middle of the yard stood two other men, her heart thudded as her gaze settled on her husband. His hands gestured as he spoke with Buffalo Killer.

She crossed her arms, hugging herself. Maybe it was time she learned to think for herself; to consider how her actions affect others—time for her to rethink her decision.

****

Skeeter trudged up the front steps, his feet heavier than two good size anvils. He paused at the door, almost fearful of entering. Images of Bug's pale face tore at his mind and heart. Buffalo Killer would gather more braves; send them out to search the area for both Johansson and Hawkins. He was certain it was one of them who'd injured his little brother, and they'd pay. Of that he had no doubt.

The door swung open easily, and he entered the deathly quiet house. Coal oil lamps flickering here and there along with the streaks of a full moon provided a welcoming glow. He sighed, lifted his head to gaze about.

Windows circled the entire span of the lower floor. At first he wondered about not having walls to separate the rooms, but once completed, he really liked the feeling the space gave of living on the prairie with as few barriers as possible. He loved the wide open plains and the design fit perfectly. The way the stone fireplace fit between two of the windows reminded him of Castle Rock.

His heart flipped, hitting the inside of his ribcage with the tremendous jolt. A huge painting, well over three feet square hung above the mantle. He stepped closer, gapping as he took in the artwork. The heat of passion swirled with the softness of love from head to toe as he stared at Lila's image.

Her beautiful face gazed up at his. Radiant eyes sparkled and butterfly lips were crested into a happy arch. An avalanche of emotions tumbled over him. The minute he'd seen her tonight he'd wanted to crush her to him. Feel her soft curves fused with his.

Smell her hair, taste her lips. But he'd had to see to Bug. Had to get his brother settled so Ma could assess his injuries, and then, in the bedroom, when the gut wrenching reality of Bug's seriousness hit, he couldn't go to her. If he had, the red hot tears burning his eyes would have flowed. In her arms, he would have cried like a little boy with wet britches. Stone cold determination of not embarrassing her like that is what held him at bay.

He'd seen the fear in her eyes, the feelings of helplessness as she watched everyone scramble about. She was so vulnerable in this harsh world. Her time must be gentler, not as violent. Thoughts of the useless tunnel tugged at the back of his mind. Turning to the staircase he moved, grasped the banister. If he had to dig more tunnels than a prairie dog town had, he'd find a portal to get her home. Return her to the world where she could be happy and carefree.

The door to Bug's room was still closed. He paused, but no sounds filtered through the thick wood. He stopped at the threshold to his room, their room. The one he would share with Lila, at least until he found a way to get her back to the future. Through the open door way, he let his gaze linger at how magnificent the room looked furnished. It was somewhat ironic. He, Skeeter Quinter, who'd never thought of having a glamorous home, a beautiful wife, a barn full of livestock, now had it all.

His eyes stopped, took in her image as the emotions swirling in his blood stream made his veins throb almost painfully. Her head was tilted down, focused on using the flint stick to light the lamp on the table beside their bed. He moved cautiously, a thick rug absorbed the sound of his heels as he stepped up behind her. She replaced the glass chimney of the lamp, and his hands reached out, wrapped around her waist.

Instantly she twisted, wrapped her arms around him and molded her frame to his. Each curve found a matching one, making him feel as if he'd just been cocooned with a warm, fragrant blanket. He let the air leave his lungs and basked in her embrace. They stood like that for several seconds, and then her lips began to run kisses along his skin exposed between the undone top buttons of his shirt. Her lips crept upwards along his neck.

His hands rose from her back to her face, his fingers raked through the silky hair over her ears, and with an out of control longing, he took her mouth. The hot, moist fusion sent a river of shivers through his body. With a deep groan, he plunged deeper, needing her more than a dying man needed grace.

Chapter Eleven

His lungs, burning for air, forced him to end the kiss sometime later. He filled his chest with a fresh breath and trailed her face with smaller kisses. It was amazing how one kiss from her could refuel his body. He no longer felt drained, but renewed with energy so strong he knew this craze he had for her would never wane as long as he lived.

A frown of confusion tugged on his brows when their gazes met. Tears trickled from the edges of her eyes, slowly dripped down her cheeks.

"I'm sorry. I'm so sorry." She crushed her face into his chest. "I've been so selfish."

The anguish in her voice hung in the air. His fingers moved through her hair, tugging gently on the back of her head so he could see her face. "Selfish?"

She nodded, eyes deep with sorrow. "All I've done is think about myself. It seems that's all I ever think about." Her hands slipped from his waist, and she took a step back. "I can understand why you'd hate me. I've behaved horribly, and I'm so ashamed."

"Honey—" he started.

"Just please give me a second chance. Please forgive me." She pushed against his chest and took another step back. "I don't think it's all my fault, it's how I've been taught to behave. I know that's just an excuse, but since I was born, people have said only children are selfish, and Professor Rutledge said millennials are the most selfish generation." Her head twisted, forcing his hands to let loose their hold. "After living here, I've realized how wrong that is. Everyone here cares about each other so much."

Skeeter's tired mind tried to follow, but when she started talking about millennials he always felt a little confused.

She brushed the tears from her cheeks and paused near the foot of the bed. "I promise I can change. I'll do anything if you'll just forgive me." Her chest heaved as if she was holding in deep sobs.

One step is all it took to pull her back into his embrace. He kissed her sweet smelling curls, ran his hands over the smooth contours of her back. "Lila, I'd forgive you if you stole the sun out of the sky. But, honey, there's nothing, absolutely nothing you need to ask forgiveness for."

Her body shuddered with a gulp. "Yes there is. All I've done since I arrived is thought about what I needed, what I wanted." She glanced up at him. "Professor Rut—"

He pressed a finger against her lips. "Doesn't know everything. Just because someone tells you how you are suppose to think or behave doesn't make it true. And it certainly doesn't make you the person you are." He gathered her in his arms, settled them both onto the edge of the bed. "It doesn't matter when a person was born, not the month, not the year, and not the generation."

Her mouth opened.

He shook his head, pressed a hand to her chest. "It's what's in here that makes a person who they are." An encouraging smile formed on his lips, and he touched her temple. "And what's in here. You are a smart, beautiful, wonderful lady. One who has a heart of gold. No matter what some old professor told you, you're not selfish. No one around here believes that, and most certainly not me." Framing her face he said, "I love you, Lila. I love you just the way you are. I don't want you to change one little thing about you."

She shook her head. "I'm not smart either. Everyone else knew what to do to help Bug. I didn't. I just stood there like a lump on a log. And I'm the one who went to college."

He chuckled. "Honey, a university isn't the only place to gain knowledge. Everyone knew what to do because they've done it before. Learned what to do by experience."

Her gaze searched his face, as if she studied to see if he told the truth.

He ran a thumb over her cheek, wiping away a single tear. "I've missed you so much these past few days."

She closed her eyes, took a deep breath before re-opening them. "I've missed you too, and I love you. I love you more than I ever thought imaginable."

A quiver of joy encompassed his body from the inside out. The kiss he initiated was long and loving and ended only because a faint knock sounded on their open doorway. Skeeter twisted, looked toward the opening. The oppressive silence of the house reminded him of other worries raking his mind.

Willamina, one hand braced on the doorframe, leaned into the room. "Come downstairs so I only have to repeat Bug's condition once."

He nodded, assisted Lila to her feet, and together they moved toward the door. She wrapped an arm around his waist, and he tightened his hold around her shoulder as they stepped into the hallway. The door to Bug's room was still closed. Willamina, her aged, hunched frame seeming more slouched, was further down the hall, knocking on other closed doors, but Ma was no where in sight. A sour taste filled his mouth, his stomach churning at the thought of his little brother dying.

Dull throbs began to beat against his temples, and his back teeth clenched together. This gut wrenching pain and the anger sizzling his body was as new to him as the soft, exciting sensations loving Lila gave him. When they stepped off the last stair, he took her tightly in his arms one more time, tasted the sweetness of her lips. How could a man love and hate the world at the same time?

Lila opened her lips, deepening the fierce kiss Skeeter initiated at the bottom of the stairs. She could feel his pain and his love, and wrapped her arms around his neck, held his head in place. Fate was cruel, the way it played give and take with a person's life. She had so much thinking to do, so much to figure out, but the one thing she didn't question was him. He was her anchor, and if the tether holding them together ever broke, she'd die on the spot.

The opening and closing of doors, or some such scuttle noise made her ease her hold and let him break the contact. His eyes glistened, not with mischief or joy, but with tell-all sadness. She shut her eyes at the sight. The soft brush of his lips touched her forehead before he turned them toward the kitchen area.

In no time, the entire family had gathered in the room. Willamina sat at the head of the table, Eva, Snake, and Hog sat in three of the chairs and Kid, with Jessie cradled on his lap sat in another. One open chair waited for her and Skeeter. He sat, pulled her onto his lap as Joe, and several other ranch hands as well as a couple of diggers lined up along the wall.

Lila settled upon Skeeter's solid thighs, leaned against his chest. Jessie, her blue eyes rimmed red, reached over to clasp her hand. She returned the hold, wrapping her fingers around Jessie's, as all eyes went to Willamina.

"Well, it ain't good," the woman started, patting the solid table top. "Someone dang near split his head open, and he's lost a lot of blood." She tugged on one floppy earlobe and continued, "Stephanie got the gash sewed up, and we set an herb poultice on the worst of it."

"Did he wake up?" Kid asked.

She met his gaze with a serious frown. "Nope, and we can't say if'n he will."

Lila blinked at the tears stinging the backs of her eyes. Bug was so young, and though she hadn't gotten to know him as well as Snake and Hog, he'd been extremely kind to her. He looked a lot like Kid with dark brown hair and eyes. The other boys resembled Skeeter with lighter hair and hazel-green eyes. But like Skeeter, Bug was always smiling and jumping to do something or another for someone.

"What can we do?" Skeeter asked. His hold on her hip tightened.

Willamina shrugged her stooped shoulders. "Wait. Hope. Pray."

Eva gasped and smothered a sob with her hand. Snake reached over and ran a hand over the girl's shoulder. He looked at Skeeter. "Who did this?" His eyes became little more than slits.

"I can't say for sure, but..." he paused, looked around the room. "There's a man from the dig site I want to question. Buffalo Killer and his braves are searching for him."

"Johansson?" One of the diggers asked.

Skeeter nodded.

An eerie feeling tickled her neck, she twisted against it, and her gaze landed on the painting above the fireplace on the far end of the great room. Instantly, she recalled what Willamina had said. Pete was out there. Could he have done this to Bug?

He was certainly capable of something this dreadful.

"There's always been something fishy about that feller," the digger said.

"Like what?" Skeeter asked.

The man shrugged. "Can't really say for sure. It's just a feeling."

Lila turned, ready to tell Skeeter about Pete when Hog stood up, his chair scraping the floor as he slapped the table. "Well, then let's go find the bastard!"

The room erupted with commotion as the ranch hands and diggers started talking amongst themselves, nodding and gesturing.

"I'm in," one of the ranch hands said, stepping toward the table.

"Me too," added a digger.

"Hold up," Kid said with authority. "We don't even know where to start looking. We're better off waiting to hear from Buffalo Killer." He glanced toward Skeeter. "Don't you think?"

"Yeah, he's sending out a scouting party tonight. He'll give us a report in the morning." Skeeter rubbed at his temple with his free hand and glanced toward Willamina. "Maybe by then Bug will wake up, give us more to go on."

"I hope so." Her narrow eyes remained solemn as she added, "But can't promise nothing."

Lila bit her lips. She couldn't tell him about Pete. He had enough on his mind already. And she really didn't want all of the brothers, ranch hands, and diggers to know it was her fault Bug was upstairs—dying.

She lowered her head. Here she was only thinking about herself again. Could she change? Skeeter's hand touched her cheek, tucked her head beneath his chin. She twisted, hid her face in the cotton of his shirt. It didn't matter really. Bug's condition wouldn't change whether Skeeter knew

Pete was here or not. Her self-rationalization kicked back. But it might be easier if he knew Buffalo Killer's men should be looking for Pete and not some digger.

"Ah, hell," Hog's voice echoed the quiet room. "If I can't go chasing the bastard, I might as well cook something. You fellas must be hungry."

"No, not really." Skeeter's voice made his chest rumble beneath her ear.

"Well, you'll eat anyway," Hog answered, sounding remarkably like Ma Quinter.

Skeeter leaned back in the chair, she lifted her face. His eyes were closed. She moved to slip off his lap. His hold tightened and his lids lifted. "Where are you going?"

"I'll help Hog."

"You don't need to."

She rested her hands on his shoulders, leaned forward to kiss his cheek. "Yes, I do." It would give her hands something to do while she thought—came up with a way to tell him Pete had somehow made it through the tunnel and was responsible for Bug's condition.

He twisted, caught her lips for a quick peck before she stood. His half-cocked smile was meant just for her, and tugged at her heart. The tired, stained looking lines around his eyes pulled harder. What she wouldn't give to see him as happy as he had been that first day in the cave, when he talked about Buffalo Killer and his peyote buttons. A smile tried to twist her lips into a comforting reply, and she hoped it showed how much she cared for him. She gave his cheek a quick caress before moving to the counter where Hog had started piling an assortment of cooking utensils.

"The rest of you grab some chairs off the porch and make yourselves comfortable. I'll make enough for the lot of you," Hog said.

Ranch hands and diggers alike took no time in following his orders. Jessie and Eva were soon delivering cups of coffee while she rolled up her sleeves to make a pan of sticky buns. Hog had plunked the recipe in front of her and nodded his head as if he didn't need to say anything else. He didn't, she'd made a batch the day before, and they'd turned out quite well. Coarse, brown sugar and thick, fresh butter made the bits of bread dough tastier than any she'd ever eaten from the Cinnabon kiosk at the mall.

The thought of doing something constructive, showing Skeeter she wasn't helpless, filled her with determination and confidence. Measuring ingredients into a bowl, she puckered her lips and concentrated on her task.

It was several hours before the men cleared out of the kitchen, and Skeeter settled a hand on her hip to tug her toward the staircase. He'd excused himself earlier to use the big outside tub Snake had built, and his freshly shaven cheek rubbed hers. The contact sent a warm rush of pleasure all the way to her toes.

She hung the dishtowel over the edge of the sink and wrapped both arms around his waist as they walked across the polished wood floor. They paused here and there for him to snub out the lanterns. A faint scent of coal oil spiraled into the air along with fine wisps of black smoke. The scent wasn't unpleasant, but then again, her nose was busy reveling in the smell of the spicy soap her husband had recently used. Her body, tingling from head to toe, couldn't wait to enter their bedroom on the second floor. Walking around the stairs for him to extinguish the lamps in what she called the living room, her gaze went to the painting above the fireplace.

With his free hand, he rubbed the arm she had

wrapped around his midsection. "Eva painted that," he said.

It was a statement, not a question. She nodded. "Isn't it gorgeous?"

He kissed her temple. "Yes. Yes, it is."

"I asked her to make another one, but smaller. Eight by ten or so." She flinched at the memory. Again, she'd been thinking of herself, hadn't considered the amount of work it would be for Eva. But, knowing the big one wouldn't fit through the tunnel, she'd asked for a smaller one she could take to the future.

Skeeter twisted. His hands flowed over her upper arms, gently caressing. She tried not to meet his gaze, but he made it impossible by lifting her chin. A quizzical expression covered his face. "What's wrong?"

"Nothing, I—uh..." She couldn't think of an excuse.

One of his hands roamed down, his fingers threaded with hers. "Come on, my little wife. It's time for you to get some sleep."

She started to protest sleepiness, but knowing her words would be selfish, held them and followed as he blew out the last two lamps. "You must be exhausted," she said instead, focusing her thoughts on him.

He tugged her closer as they walked up the steps. "Yes, I'm tired. But I can't wait to crawl into that big bed of ours and hold you next to me. I just can't seem to sleep without you by my side."

"Really?"

A low chuckle left his chest as they topped the staircase. "Yes, really."

She almost said, 'me too,' but that too, would have been self-centered. Her mind mulled, wondering if something that made them both feel good was selfish on her part or not. A conclusion hadn't formed by the time they entered their room.

He shut the door behind them and before she had a chance to take another step, he tugged on her hand, twisting her back toward him. His hands pulled her close, and his mouth covered hers with slow, easy delight.

Her mind went blank for a split second before it became engrossed in his taste, smell, and touch. Time stopped and flew at the same time. The next thing she knew they were on the downy-soft feather tick, their clothes left a trail from the door to the edge of the bed, and her body sang with the joy and pleasure of his sensual, thorough lovemaking.

****

The bright, red hues of the new day peeked through the window, filled the room with an innocence of hope he could relate to. Skeeter eased his arms from Lila's sleeping form. He was renewed, ready to face the day fate was descending upon them. As long as he had her, he had the world, and could survive anything thrown his way. He leaned down, placed a soft kiss on the top of her head. Together they *would* survive anything, everything. Silently, he flipped her discarded clothes over the foot of the bed. Then retrieved his, stepped into the britches, and carried the rest to the door.

Glancing back to her sleeping form basking in the early morning glow, his mind kicked in. He'd have to tell her about Hawkins. Didn't want to, but would have to. His gaze darted around the room, bounced off the big headboard, across the tall chest of drawers, and large ladies closet he'd ordered, and finally landed on the curtains and quilted covering his mother had made. It was a spectacular room. Almost seemed impossible it was his. Damn, he was going to miss it all when they left for the future. Going to miss his family, the wide open land, the discovery of bones, he'd even miss Buffalo Killer and his tribe.

She twisted, buried her face deeper into his pillow. A smile grew on his face. The simple pleasure of holding her close was worth leaving it all behind. He'd gladly follow her to the end of the earth without a single regret.

He spun around, pulled open the door. There were just a few things he needed to take care of. After he'd settled the score for Bug's attack, he'd start digging on the tunnel. Closing the door behind him, he caught Kid's gaze as his older brother walked toward the door to Bug's room. Kid paused, waited for him to slip into his shirt, tug on his socks and boots, before opening the door.

They stepped in, looked expectantly toward the bed, and then glanced to their mother sitting in the chair no more than a foot from the edge of the bed. She shook her head. "No change. He's still out like a stump. But he's breathing and got a good pulse."

Skeeter walked to her side, wrapped an arm around her slender shoulders. The woman acted as if she was as solid as rock and as tough as nails, but deep down she was as gentle as a kitten. His new wife had taught him that too. Loving Lila allowed him to realize how much he cared for the other people in his life. He kissed Ma's gray hair. "Did you get any sleep?"

She ran the heel of her hand over both eyes. "Yeah, I dozed."

The door cracked open. Willamina poked her head in before pushing the wood wider to step in. "Hog has coffee going, why don't ya'll go down? I'll sit with him for awhile."

Ma started to protest, but Skeeter took her hand. "Come on. He'll be fine for a few minutes. Come have something to eat."

She turned to Willamina. "You'll holler?"

The old woman nodded, smiled. "Like a jackal."

Ma, straightening her dress as she went, walked out of the room ahead of him. She paused in the doorway, turned around. Her gaze settled on the bed, on Bug's pale, still shape. "I love all of you boys. Everyone one of you is a right fine man." Tired, red-rimmed eyes glanced between him and Kid. "But-but Bug's my baby." Tears started to flow down her aged-soft cheeks. "He's my baby."

"Aw, Ma." The words burned his throat as he wrapped his arms around her.

Her small body shivered as she wept against his chest.

It was a first. He couldn't ever remember his mother crying. It tore at his heart, but hardened every muscle at the same time. "Bug's going to be all right. Just give him a day or two to heal." His gaze met Kid's.

Water was welled in the bottom of his brother's dark eyes, and his nostrils flared with each breath. Kid bit his lips together and gave a slight nod. The pensive, stiff movements said his older brother felt exactly as he did.

"And we'll find who did this, Ma. We promise, we'll find them," Skeeter vowed.

Ma twisted her head, wiped her nose on the sleeve of her dress then nodded. "I know you will." She straightened her back, and as stiff as a door she walked toward the stairs. "That son-of-a-bitch chose the wrong family to mess with."

He couldn't control the slight smile tugging at the corners of his mouth and was relieved when the same grin covered Kid's face. His brother slapped his back as they followed their mother's stomping feet down the curved staircase.

Snake, tall and willowy, and looking as determined as Skeeter felt, met them at the bottom of the stairs. "Buffalo Killer's here."

"Already?" Skeeter glanced toward the front

door.

"Yup, he won't come in."

"I'll go talk to him."

"Good luck with that." Snake's gaze went to the door.

"Why do you say that?"

"There's no carrying on a conversation with the guy. I tried yesterday. He doesn't say more than two words at a time."

He slapped Snake's shoulder. "Indians are men of few words."

"I figured that out." Snake nodded. "Hey, did you know they call you Bone Hunter?"

"Yeah, they have for some time now."

"I should become friends with them. Any name would be better than Snake."

A rough laugh came from the kitchen. "Oh yeah? Try Hog for a while." The white apron tied around Hog's broad chest added to the humor glinting in his eyes.

"You boys quit frettin' 'bout your names. Your Papa gave you those names, and you should wear them proudly." Their mother insisted as she took a chair at the table, wrapping both hands around a cup of coffee wafting steam.

Skeeter chuckled and moved toward the front door. His brothers wouldn't get anywhere trying to insist being called by their given names of Scott and Howard. Their dad had given them all nicknames shortly after birth, and since his death going on ten years ago, their mother refused to let them go by their given names. As his hand settled on the doorknob, the squabbles continued from the kitchen, and his gaze went to the second floor, where Brett, nicknamed Bug, still struggled to survive. A tinge of guilt stung his chest. It would hurt them all when he and Lila left for the future.

He shook off the thought, placed it in the back of

his mind, and pulled open the door. Buffalo Killer had braided several long, white feathers amongst his long strands of black hair. The wind whipped them about as the brave stood proudly in the middle of the yard.

Skeeter raised a hand in greeting. Buffalo Killer lifted the rifle braced across his chest and thrust it high in the air. There were few Indians left on the plains, and most of the ranch hands and diggers who'd spent the night had gathered near the barn door to gaze at the brave. Skeeter nodded a greeting to them as he walked to the center of the yard.

"You want scalp?" Buffalo Killer asked in an overly loud voice.

Skeeter all but stumbled to a halt. "What?"

"You want scalp?"

Chapter Twelve

A slight twinkle sparkled in the brave's black eyes. Skeeter glanced at the painted pony. Nothing out of the ordinary hung from its mane. He forced a grin to stay at bay. "Who are you trying to scare? You didn't scalp anyone." He kept his voice low.

Buffalo Killer shrugged, but his eyes glanced left, toward the barn.

"No you keep it," Skeeter said in a loud voice, keenly understanding how important it was for Buffalo Killer to appear frightful. The brave wasn't arrogant or conceited, but proud to be who he was, and Skeeter didn't mind helping the man keep the over exaggerated tales of the Sioux alive.

The men eased back into the barn, but their gazes stayed on the yard. Buffalo Killer smiled, nodded.

Skeeter shook his head in disbelief. The brave never ceased to amaze him. "Now that they are all scared shitless, you want to tell me what you found?"

Buffalo Killer chuckled, clearly amused with himself. Then his face became serious, a steely gaze filled his eyes. "The man."

"Where? Where is he?"

"Staked. Guarded."

He clenched his fist, holding in the want to tell the man to spit it out. "Where?"

"Near bone site."

"Who is he?"

"Not from future."

Shit! He'd hoped they'd found Hawkins. "One of the diggers?"

Buffalo Killer gave a single head nod.

"Any sign of the other man? The one from the future."

The brave shrugged.

"Are your men still looking?"

Another single head nod was his only answer.

"All right. We'll have some breakfast and then ride out to your camp. See who this man is."

Buffalo Killer stared at the house.

Skeeter knew his interest was piqued. "Will you come in? Eat with us?"

A scowl formed over the brave's dark eyes.

He twisted, glanced toward the house. Lila, in a shimmering gold dress walked onto the porch. Her red hair was twisted back into a bun, but several short, fine tendrils fluttered around her elegant neck and in front of her ears. His heart jolted. The image of her on the steps of his house filled his chest with pride. Skeeter laid an arm on Buffalo Killer's. "I've entered your teepee, shared a meal with your family. Please come share one with mine."

"Wife?"

"Yes, we're married."

"I wanted."

"But I said you can't have her." Skeeter grinned, knowing the man was teasing. "Besides you already have a wife."

Buffalo Killer shrugged.

A serious, raw strain pulled at his throat. Skeeter lowered his voice, though Lila still stood on the porch, he didn't want the wind to carry his words. "The man from the future wants to kill Lila."

Buffalo Killer's head snapped about quickly. He squinted then gave a nod of determination. "I eat."

His black eyes grew darker with anger. "Then we find future man. Scalp him."

Skeeter couldn't ignore the shudder that raced across his shoulders. This time he knew the brave wasn't kidding.

Lila smiled as Skeeter and Buffalo Killer walked up the porch steps. She held out one hand. "Hello, Buffalo Killer. It's good to see you again." The Indian no longer frightened her, and she was happy to see him again. She felt so recharged with happiness this morning she could rival the Energizer bunny.

The Indian looked at her hand for a moment before he patted his chest with one of his thick palms. "Buffalo Killer." A finger pointed to her. "Badland Woman." Then he took her hand in both of his. "Friends."

She glanced toward Skeeter, lifted a brow in question. "Badland Woman?"

He nodded. "It's what he's decided to call you."

"Sheesh!" Snake who stood in the doorway behind her said. "Even she gets a good name."

She frowned in confusion, glanced toward the younger brother. Snake stomped back into the house, and as she turned to Skeeter he gave a slight chuckle. "What's that all about?" she asked.

"Nothing," he said. "Buffalo Killer is joining us for breakfast."

"Oh, wonderful." She waved an arm toward the door. "Come on in."

Buffalo Killer glanced toward Skeeter. "Big Teepee."

Skeeter laughed and wrapped an arm around her. If possible, her body swelled, feeling the huge, exciting, overwhelming sensation of his love. She snuggled her shoulder beneath his arm, fitting flawlessly against his side as they walked into the house.

The meal became a festive time. Buffalo Killer

enchanted the entire family, and by the time breakfast ended he'd renamed every one of them. Hog gleamed with pride as Buffalo Killer thanked 'Cooks with Pride', and Snake even cracked a smile when he was referred to as 'Earth Man.'

When the dishes were cleared, and the men began strapping the holsters to their hips, Lila grasped Skeeter's arm, a cold sweat tickling her skin. "What are you doing? Where are you going?"

The room grew quiet. He glanced about, before guiding her into the living room. "Buffalo Killer's men found the man who might be responsible for hurting Bug. We're going to his camp."

Her knees began to tremble. She grabbed his waist for support. Could it be Pete? Her breath grew shaky. "Don't go. You don't have to go. Let the others go. You stay here."

He took her shoulders, held her steady. "Honey, I can't do that. I have to go." One finger hooked beneath her chin, lifted her face to look at him. "Don't worry, Joe and some of the cowhands will still be here. You're safe."

"It's not me I'm worried about. It's you. What if something happens—"

"Don't worry. Nothing is going to happen to me."

Tears burnt her eyes. "Promise me. Promise me, you'll come back."

"Of course I promise. I'll come back safe and sound."

She glanced to the doorway. The brothers, Kid, Snake, and Hog as well as Buffalo Killer stood, waiting for Skeeter. They were a formidable bunch. Reminded her of a group of men she'd seen starring in a western movie. Wyatt Earp or some such show. They looked rough and mean, but didn't scare her in the least. She raised a finger, pointed at them. "You all better make damn sure nothing happens to him."

Shocked gazes covered their faces.

"Nothing better happen to any of you." She lifted her chin, met their stares straight on. "You got that?"

"Yes, ma'am," Hog and Snake answered.

"We'll take care of him, Lila," Kid responded.

"See that you do."

"Badland Woman fierce," Buffalo Killer stated.

Jessie and Stephanie Quinter came to stand beside her. Skeeter kissed her lips, a short quick peck, before he kissed his mother's cheek and patted Jessie's. Then he turned and nodded at Buffalo Killer. "All of the Quinter women are."

Lila would have followed him out the door, but Ma Quinter touched her arm, a soft but controlling touch. She glanced to Jessie. The woman gave a slow shake of her head. Understanding rang clear. The men had to leave, and the woman had to stay behind, strong and solid. She folded her arms across her chest. "They better take care of him. If he comes back with one scratch on his head there's going to be hell to pay."

The echoing beat of departing horses rumbled into the house as the other two women glanced at each other and then back at her.

"What?" she demanded. Now that she had decided to remain in the past, she wasn't about to let something happen to her husband.

"Nothing," Jessie said. With a wide smile, she moved toward the kitchen, but before she got more than two steps a door slammed from above.

"Stephanie! Come quick! He's waking up!" Willamina shouted.

One behind the other, dresses hoisted above their knees, they raced up the steps, and into the room.

Bug moaned a low, pain-filled groan. The dark crescents of his eyelashes fluttered as the lids strained to open. With another groan, he lifted his head a touch, but then it lobbed back on the pillow.

"Bug, Bug, honey, it's Mommy. Can you hear me?" Stephanie rubbed his cheek.

Lila almost chuckled. For some reason, she just couldn't imagine any of the Quinter boys calling the woman mommy. The baby in her womb tumbled, and a smile covered her face. In a few more months this little one would be calling her mommy and Skeeter daddy.

A frown tugged on her brows. When had she decided to remain here? It must have been sometime during the night, for when she woke up this morning she knew with certainty she was staying, here—in the home built for them. Where she was no longer expected to behave as others said she should, but where she could, for once, be herself.

Bug gave a feeble sounding cough and weakly croaked, "M-ma?"

"Yes, baby, I'm here. You're going to be fine, honey. Just fine."

"M-my hea…"

"I know your head hurts. Don't try and talk. I'm going to give you something to ease the pain. And then you go back to sleep. When you wake up again you'll feel lots better." Stephanie shook a small amount of white powder into a glass of water and encouraged Bug to drink. "There, that's good, a little more. Good job, Buggy-Boy."

"M-ma?"

"Yes, honey?"

"Ske—"

"Skeeter is just fine. Don't you worry now. You just need to get some more sleep."

Bug seemed to relax and with a low moan fell back to sleep. Ma Quinter looked up, tears glistened her eyes. "He's gonna make it, girls!" A wide grin covered her face. "Your baby brother is gonna be just fine." She stood and held open her arms.

Tears tumbled down Lila's face, she wasn't quite sure what the tears were for, Bug, or her decision, or just because, but nevertheless, she stepped forward. Ma Quinter embraced her and Jessie at the same time. The three of them, held onto one another as they cried with what Lila assumed was joy and relief.

Lila glanced toward the bed, noticed Willamina standing by her side. She reached out and pulled the woman into the hug. It was empowering, this sharing of emotion, and she tightened her hold on the women.

After her tears were cried out, she took a moment to wipe her cheeks. The others copied her movements, laughing with amusement while doing so. And Lila realized she belonged to the most wonderful family on earth. They may be a touch unconventional, but they were hers.

Stephanie grabbed each one of them separately and planted a big kiss on everyone's cheek before she said, "Come on, let's get out of here and let him get some sleep."

Jessie with her arm around Willamina walked out of the room.

Stephanie wrapped an arm around Lila, patted her side as they took one final glance back at the bed. "No matter how old they get, sweetie. They'll always be your babies. Even as big and strapping as my boys are, they're little more than infants in my eyes." She twisted them toward the door. "A momma's love is the strongest thing on earth."

When the door closed and they stood in the hallway, Stephanie continued, "You know what I mean, don't you?"

Lila glanced to the door, her hand absently running over her abdomen. "Yes, I think I do, Stephanie."

"Stephanie?" She let out a deep guffaw. "It's ma

to you. Don't you know I love you girls just as much as I love those boys?"

A warm bubble floated up her chest, and Lila smiled. "Thank you, Ma."

Ma laughed. "Come on, lets go have a cup of tea, and then I got to get back to sewing. I have a couple wool skirts to finish up for you for this winter. As well as some warm buntings for the baby."

Lila stumbled, brought her feet to a sudden stop. It had been wrong of her to think of taking them all to the future, selfish. They fit into this world perfectly, where Ma could sew from the time the sun came up until it went down. The past is where she belonged too, but there was still the fact she was carrying a baby that didn't belong to her husband. She glanced around, settled her gaze on the small settee at the end of the hall, in front of the wide window there. "St-Ma, could we talk for a moment?"

"Sure, sweetie."

They walked to the window, sat down. Lila swallowed the lump in her throat. "Ma, you know this baby isn't Skeeter's."

Stephanie nodded, waited for her to continue.

"Well, I've been thinking I want to keep the baby, but that's not really fair to him. I mean, considering how the baby came to be and everything, it's not right that I expect Skeeter to raise it as his own."

"It sure as hell is."

If anything, her mother-in-law was blunt, and Lila didn't know what to say.

Stephanie took her hands, squeezed them between hers. "Lila, it's not important how this baby came to be. What's important is the love this little one gets once it's born." One hand lifted to cup her cheek. "And I know my son. He loves you and this baby with all his heart. Just like the rest of us do."

Lila scrunched her eyes closed, holding in tears.

Vulnerability burned her throat. "I'm scared, Ma."

Short, solid arms wrapped about her shoulders. "I know you are honey, but we're all here to help you. We'll never let you down."

Lila believed the words, but doubt and fear of childbirth in the eighteen hundreds was hard to overcome.

****

Skeeter dismounted, let the reins of his horse fall to the ground as he walked toward the man tied to a thin, spindly, sandstone pillar. Johansson's ruddy face had turned beet red from the sun's fire-hot rays.

The pillar stood in the middle of a small clearing where more than a dozen of Buffalo Killer's braves mingled about. Their scantly clothed bodies looked ominous covered with the bold, red, yellow, and black stripes and markings of war paint.

The camp had been made in a small gully, well hidden by little more than tall grass and few scraggly bushes. Invisible to the naked eye, he hadn't noticed it until they'd ridden in.

"Quniter! Am I glad to see you. Tell these heathens to untie me immediately." Johansson screeched.

Skeeter shook his head. "No." He glanced about. Clearly visible in the bright blue sky Castle Rock stood a mile or so to the west. The badlands stretched out behind the structure. He watched the heat of the day bubbling off the tips of the rocks for a few minutes. "No, not yet."

The man struggled against the leather straps wrapped around his torso. "Why the hell not?"

Skeeter kicked at a clump of dirt. It dissolved into a cloud of dust for the wind to carry away. "What were you doing outside the dig site?"

"Scouting." The man tried to sound dignified.

He raised a brow. "For what?

195

"For new excavation sites. What else would I be scouting for?"

Skeeter took off his hat, wiped away the sweat on his forehead with his sleeve. "Sites for Cope? Or for Marsh?"

The man's face faded to a light pink. "M-marsh?" He cleared his throat. "Why would I scout for Marsh? He's the enemy."

"You want scalp?" Buffalo Killer walked passed him toward Johansson.

Johansson's eyes bugged, sweat poured down his face. "Okay, okay, I'll tell you what you want to know. I-ah, I-ah, M-marsh p-paid," he stuttered, clearly unsure where to start.

"So you're getting paid by both Cope and Marsh." Skeeter glanced at Buffalo Killer. "Not yet."

The brave let the sun glisten off the blade of his knife. The rays bounced onto Johansson's face.

"Yes, yes, I am. And I can tell you why." Johansson wet lips the sun had baked dry, and turned his neck, trying to get away from the gleam of Buffalo Killer's knife.

Skeeter stepped closer, holding the man's gaze with an unyielding one. "I'm sure you can. But first I want to know why you hit my little brother in the head."

"Your brother?" The man frowned with confusion. "I didn't hit your brother. I haven't hit anyone in the head."

Skeeter let out a deep breath. Not really surprised. His gut told him it had been Hawkins who hurt Bug, not Johansson. His cheek twitched. Where the hell was that man? Johansson was a waste of time. He had to get this over with and start searching for Hawkins.

"You want scalp now?" Buffalo Killer asked.

Skeeter glared at him, no longer interested in the game. The Indian shrugged and stepped aside.

"I swear, Quinter, I didn't hit your brother. He was still sleeping when I left camp. Everyone was." Johansson squirmed against his tethers again.

"When you left camp to meet the ambushers?"

Johansson hung his head.

Skeeter slapped his hat back on his head. "Damn it, man! Old bones aren't worth killing people."

"Marsh and Cope—" the man started.

"Are a couple of stupid, rich men. Money's not a reason to kill either."

"What was I suppose to do? They both want—"

"I know what they both want. To be world renowned in paleontology, and will stop at nothing until it happens. Well, it's not going to happen on my watch. I'm not going to let this Bone War of theirs kill anyone else. Not here anyway."

"How are you going to stop them? They're obsessed with it."

Skeeter glanced at Castle Rock, thought for a moment before answering, "I'll tell you what *we* are going to do. Several of Buffalo Killer's braves are going to ride you over to the ambushers. There *you* are going to call the ambush off, turn those men around, and ride like the wind to Dodge. My brother," he paused to search his mind for a savage name to further frighten the quivering man, "*Kills like a Snake* is going to follow to make sure you board an east bound train. Trust me, you make even the slightest detour, and I *will* have your scalp."

Johansson's Adam's apple bobbed like a cork in a pond as he nodded.

"Once you get to New York you tell both Marsh and Cope neither of them is welcome here— anywhere around here. There'll be no more digging in Kansas. Their damn Bone War isn't going to exist here."

"What about the site. What we've already

found?"

"Yokel plans on leaving soon. Another group of Buffalo Killer's tribe will follow them as far as Dodge, and see they get on the train. My partner in New York will settle up with Cope." He knelt down, stared Johansson in the eyes. "You better make damn sure both Cope and Marsh know their men are not allowed in this country. If they show up here, Buffalo Killer will have enough scalps decorating his lance it'll look like a horse's tail. And I'll personally track you down so yours can be at the top."

"I'll tell them. Th-they're finding a lot of stuff up in the Dakotas." Johansson nodded. "I'll convince them to go there."

Skeeter shook his head, wondered how some people could be so dense. "There's a lot of Sioux in the Dakotas. I'd suggest you find a new line of business if you want to keep the little bit of hair you have."

Sweat run down Johansson's temples. "Oh, uh, yeah, yeah. You got a point there."

Skeeter stood, looked at Buffalo Killer, and nodded. The Indian turned to his men, began conversing and gesturing with his hands.

Pressing a hand to the throbbing in his temple, Skeeter turned to Snake. "You mind riding with them?"

"Kills like a Snake go," Snake, eyes dancing, said in a deep voice.

He almost laughed aloud, glad Snake didn't mind the impromptu name, but the seriousness of the situation overlaid the humor. "Snake, don't get separated from the party. Hawkins is out here somewhere. We still gotta find him. I know he's the one who hurt Bug."

Snake grew somber, nodded. "I know what he looks like. I'll keep an eye out."

Confusion pulled his brows into a frown. "You

know what he looks like?"

"Yeah, Willamina gave us a description."

"Willamina?" He glanced to Kid then Hog.

"Yeah, she and Eva ran into him over by Castle Rock before they came to your place," Hog supplied.

His body became so tense he felt like he was tied to the pillar instead of Johansson. He glared at Kid. "When the hell was someone going to tell me?"

Kid shrugged. "That's what we were doing, but then Bug was hurt, and you were already taking him home. Once we got to the house, I figured Lila told you."

"No, she didn't tell me." Fear, hotter and moving faster than a range fire shot up his spine. "Ah, hell! He knows where to find her!"

His feet barely touched the ground as he flew to his gelding and sent it into a gallop. From the saddle, he leaned along the neck of the swiftly racing horse to gather the reins whipping in the wind.

Chapter Thirteen

Lila raised her hands over her head, stretching the kink in her back. Kneading bread dough was more of a workout than any gym equipment they had at the health club. She flexed her arms, feeling the burn of strained muscles.

"Looks perfect," Jessie said.

"Thanks." She smiled and laid a cloth over the top of the half dozen loaves. They'd rise in no time in the noon heat, and then she'd punch them down one more time before they'd be ready for a final rising and baking. The whole process was quite intriguing. She had a bread machine in her apartment, a couple of times she'd dumped the ingredients in and left for school, when she came home a fresh, small loaf of bread had waited for her arrival. But once the newness had worn off it all seemed like too much hassle for a loaf of bread she could buy at the convenience store.

Here it didn't feel like a hassle or work, more like something that just needed to be done, like brushing her teeth. That was another thing she was impressed with. She'd never wondered when the toothbrush had been invented, but they had them here. They had three rows of stiff bristles that Skeeter said came from the back of a hog. She still wondered if he'd been teasing her. Nonetheless, the brush along with the brushing powder that came in a small, tin can worked as well as her Oral-B back home.

A clatter from above made her turn toward Jessie. They glanced at one another before rushing to the steps. Ma had been taking a nap in her room and beat them both to the door of Bug's room. He sat on the edge of the bed, holding his head with both hands.

"What are you doing?" Ma scrambled to his side.

"I gotta go to the privy," Bug said.

"I got a chamber pot right here." Ma pulled a flowered, porcelain bowl out from beneath the bed.

"I ain't using that." His pale cheeks grew pink. "I'll go outside."

Ma wrapped her arm under his arm pit. "Kid installed that new fancy one downstairs. I'll help you to it."

"Where are my boots?" he asked.

"I don't know. You didn't have any when they hauled you in," Ma said.

"That bastard stole them didn't he?"

"Who?"

"The man who hit me. Bet he stole my horse too."

"I don't know, the boys didn't say anything about your horse either," Ma answered. "Come on, I'll help you to the wash room."

"I ain't using that one either." Bug stood, took a moment to gain his balance. "I don't care what Kid says, I ain't," he glanced toward her and Jessie, "doing my business in the same house I eat in."

"Bug, that's silly," Jessie insisted.

Lila hid a smile and stepped forward. That was the same thing Skeeter had said when Kid suggested he order the new toilet. "Come on, Bug, I'll get you a pair of Skeeter's boots and help you to the outhouse."

"Thanks, Lila." Bug offered a slight smile.

With Ma on the other side, they got him down

the stairs, and after he slipped on a pair of boots, helped him out the back door and into the little house with a half moon shape cut on the front door built on the far side of the back yard. She had insisted on the cut out, and again everyone thought her crazy. She assumed since the beginning of time the little shape had been cut into the wood on outhouses. Now it seemed she was starting a trend because Snake claimed he was going to cut one in the door back home.

"Oh, that gall-darn wind. It's got my sheets twisted around the line again," Ma said, pointing across the yard.

"Go ahead, I'll wait for Bug," Lila said, sitting down on a stump a few feet from the outhouse.

Ma started walking toward the sheet, saying over her shoulder, "I'll be right back. Don't try to walk him back to the house by yourself."

"All right, I won't."

Lila watched until Ma disappeared amongst the huge white sheets flapping this way and that. The wind tossed the grasses about, rustled through the small grove of trees behind the outhouse. An odd sound caught her attention, and she turned. The men hadn't rolled the grass down all the way to the trees, in places it stood over three feet and swayed like waves. The branches of the trees and even the trunks bobbed and weaved in the strong gusts. She brushed the hair from her face and turned back. "You okay in there, Bug?"

"I'm fine," he grumbled through the wood.

She chuckled, realizing she shouldn't have asked.

All of sudden, her head snapped back and a hard hand covered her mouth. A vile stench filled her nose. She tried to scream, but a fat palm wouldn't let any sound emit. Fear raked her body. Kicking and flaying her arms, she tried to break the hold. A deep, nasty, whispered chuckle hit her ears—made her body freeze.

She twisted her neck. Her heart stopped as she stared into the most menacing eyes she'd ever seen.

"Yes, it's me, Lila." Pete Hawkins' mouth was so close to her face, his lips touched her cheeks when he spoke.

Bucking like a wild horse, she flopped about fighting against his brutal hold. She tried to bite at his palm, but couldn't open her mouth wide enough. The stump beneath her wobbled and then fell, knocking them both to the ground. The air swooshed from her lungs. By the time she sucked a full breath back in, his hand had landed on her mouth again. The tiniest bit of a scream emitted.

"Lila? Lila, you all right out there?"

Pete jerked her to her feet. She clawed at his hands, kicked like a mule at his knees, all the while screaming into his stinking palm. The rotten stench of his skin made her stomach churn. The hand tighten, pulled her head back, tucking it beneath his chin, and one of his fat legs wrapped around hers, stifling her kicks.

Something shiny flashed sunlight into her eyes. Her body tensed, grew stiff as a tree when the long blade of his knife lowered to her neck. A sharp pinprick of pain stung the skin below her chin, and the cold steel of the blade settled heavily against her neck.

The door of the outhouse flew open, and Bug wobbled as he grabbed the doorframe. His mouth opened but before a sound emitted, Pete instructed. "Don't say a word, or I'll slice her throat."

Bug's eyes turned as cold as ice, but he clamped his mouth shut.

Pete tugged her backwards. Tears of fear poured down her cheeks. The wind, whipping about as usual, splattered them back into her eyes, making them sting harder.

"Not quite as talkative this time, are you Quinter?" Pete said. "That little head butt I gave you got you scared or something?"

Bug stepped away from the outhouse. Eyes dancing left and right, he braced his legs like a man ready to fight. He shook his head slowly. "There's only one person I'm afraid of."

"Oh?" Pete sneered.

Bug raised an eyebrow and nodded once. "Yup, I call her Ma, and she's standing not ten feet behind you."

Pete twirled her around so fast Lila became dizzy. The world seemed to spin out of control. Vomit rose up her esophagus. She gagged trying to swallow as the double barrels of Ma's giant shotgun appeared before her eyes.

"Put it down old lady or she's dead!" Pete bellowed.

Her ears rang from his shout, and her stomach revolted again. She couldn't hold it in. Half-digested breakfast spewed between her teeth out her lips. It hit his palm, splattering back onto her face.

"Shit!" Pete exclaimed. His hand left her mouth, and she doubled over, emptying the rest of her stomach on the ground.

A loud crack filled the air, followed by a thud. Glancing up as the last bout of foulness left her mouth, Lila saw Pete sprawled out on the ground.

Ma stepped closer, lifted her pink, paisley skirt to kick his boot. "Sorry bastard picked the wrong family to mess with." Then she lifted her gray head and shouted, "Good shot, Jessie! You got him right between the eyes."

Lila pivoted. Her sister-in-law, followed closely by her dog, ran across the yard. A rifle was tucked beneath one arm as she held the roundness of her stomach with the other. Weakness rippled Lila's body, and her vision blurred before she slumped to the ground to easily accept the blackness closing in on her.

****

The ranch was in sight when the unnerving pop of rifle fire hit his ears like a cannon. Skeeter whipped the gelding with the ends of the reins, kicked at the horse's belly with the heels of his boots. Men ran from the barn toward the backyard, and he almost trampled a couple of them as he steered the gelding around the house.

His heart stopped dead in his chest when he saw her. Lila laid flat on the ground, his mother, Jessie, and Bug knelt beside her. He all but fell from the flying horse, stuck his boots in the hard ground to keep upright. His heart kicked back in, thudding with pain, it threatened to beat right out of his chest. He ran and stumbled at the same time.

"She's all right," someone said. It could have been Ma, Jessie, or Bug, the ringing in his ears couldn't decipher the voice—just the words.

He knelt down, gathered her in his arms. "What happened?"

"She fainted. Hawkins had a knife to her neck..."

As they talked, he cradled her limp body and assessed each inch with his eyes. Someone told him the story of Hawkins, the knife, Jessie shooting him. They were still talking when he stood, began to walk to the house.

Buffalo Killer stepped aside, and Skeeter met his dark eyes. "Scalp him."

The Indian's head snapped up, his eyes wide.

"Dispose of the body. I don't want it anywhere on my land."

Buffalo Killer waved a hand, motioning his braves to step forward, and Skeeter carried Lila to the house.

Someone held the door open. He stepped in, and Ma rushed past him. "Here, lay her on the couch," she said.

He shook his head, walking toward the stairs. The fear and anger that had consumed his body slowly seeped out, but he couldn't talk yet. If he did he'd either break down crying like a baby or lash out screaming like a madman.

All he wanted was to be alone with her. She was alive. Soft gusts of air slipped from her parted lips and fluttered against the sensitive skin of his throat. He needed to lay her down, run his hands over her body, make certain nothing was broken or injured.

She was still out when he settled her on the bed. Her body was limp as he positioned a pillow under her colorful curls. He ran his hands up and down, over every limb, making certain the flesh was warm and unmarred.

Ma scurried in the room as he straightened. "I have some fresh water and a cloth for her head."

He held out his hands, took the items. "Close the door on your way out." The words burned his throat.

Ma handed him the items. "I'll go see how Bug's doing."

He moved to the wash station, poured water from the bucket into the wash bowl and the rest into the pitcher, then dipped the rag in the bowl, wrung it out, and moved to wipe her face. He rinsed it out, folded it and laid it over her forehead.

Still somewhat shaky, he leaned down, brushed a kiss over her lips. As long as he lived, he'd never forget that split second he thought her dead. He'd wanted to die himself. Right then and there he'd felt as if his life was over. Straightening, he glanced toward the window, thanking the good Lord she'd survived.

Movement tugged his gaze to the bed. One of her hands was reaching for the cloth covering her eyes.

He sat down beside her, lifted the rag. "Lila, honey?"

Her eyes snapped open. "Skeeter?"

"Hi, sweetheart."

She pushed herself upright, and threw her arms around his neck. "Skeeter!"

His lips brushed her forehead, fluttered over her eyes. When they lowered, she twisted away, hiding her face in his shoulder. "Honey. Honey, are you all right?"

She nodded.

His hands combed into her hair, lifted her face to look at him.

"Don't kiss me," she whispered.

His heart slammed into his ribcage. "W-why not?"

"Because I have to brush my teeth." Her cheeks turned bright red. "I threw up."

He chuckled. Kissed the tip of her nose.

She took a deep breath. "Pete—"

"You'll never have to worry about him again."

"I know," she said. "Jessie killed him."

Skeeter nodded. "She had to."

"I know. It all happened so fast. He grabbed me. He had a knife. Ma had her shotgun, and, and Jessie had her rifle." She glanced at his face. "Bug? Is Bug all right?"

He nodded. "Yes, Bug is fine."

She twisted, tried to climb off the bed. "I better go see, make sure his wound didn't open back up."

"Ma's seeing to him."

"Oh." She slipped her feet onto the floor. "Well, then, I better go check on Jessie."

"Kid's doing that." He stood, walked to the water basin and pitcher stand near the window and began to gather items.

"Oh. Well, I probably should go check on my bread."

He shook his head. "Hog's probably putting it in the oven as we speak."

"The laundry on the line needs to be carried in."

Carrying a glass, her toothbrush, and the tin of brushing powder he said, "Willamina and Eva will see to it."

She scratched her head, as if she was trying to come up with another excuse to leave the room. Glancing between the items in his hand and his face, she said, "So there's nothing I need to do?"

He dipped the brush into the tin, handed it to her. "Nothing except brush your teeth so I can kiss the daylights out of you."

She giggled, took the brush. "Oh, well, that's sounds more fun than anything I suggested."

"It certainly does. Now hurry up, you have exactly fifteen seconds. I'm counting."

She shook her head, talked around the brush in her mouth as she rose. "A dentist once told me you have to brush for a full three minutes."

"Three minutes?" He didn't think he could wait that long.

Lila giggled, took a mouthful of water and swished the cinnamon tasting powder from her teeth, then spat the water back into the glass. Setting it and the little bristle brush on the water basin stand, she twirled around and leaped into his arms. "I'll brush a full five minutes tonight to make up the difference."

"Thank you," he murmured as their lips met.

She knew she should go downstairs to check on the others, maybe even act a bit more distraught over what just happened, but at this moment in time, she wasn't going to do any of that. Right now she was going to be very selfish, and keep her husband all to herself—maybe for an hour or more.

****

Four days later, standing on the front porch,

Skeeter hugged Lila close, her tears dampening the front of his shirt as his family, including Willamina and Eva, and the ranch hands, pulled out of the yard. The wagons they drove were empty, except for personal possessions, including Ma's sewing machine which weighed more than a full grown steer. "Shh, don't cry," he encouraged. "We'll see them again before we go."

She stiffened in his arms. "Before we go?"

He nodded.

"Where are we going?"

He hadn't yet told her about the tunnel, that he hadn't found the portal. Buffalo Killer had said he'd have some braves work on it, dig a few more off shoots of the main channel. He let his gaze settle over her head, searching for the right words to break the news.

A flash caught his attention, he tilted his head. The sun reflected again before he realized it was a rifle held over a rider's head. "Looks like we have more company riding in," he said, thankful for the distraction.

She twisted, glanced up to follow his gaze. "Who is it?"

"Buffalo Killer," he said, now able to make out a painted pony.

The bareback rider bee-lined toward the wagons, they stalled for a few minutes in conversation. The group looked like painted silhouettes on the prairie. Still, he knew the Indian was bidding farewell to the new friends he'd made.

Lila stood quiet, watching, and his mind raced, wondering if Buffalo Killer had found the portal. He couldn't deny the time would come. Heaviness pressed on his shoulders. Soon the day would arrive when he'd have to say good-bye to his family, his friends, forever. He swallowed, tried to make the lump in his throat disappear. It would be fine. He'd rather have the pain than know she did. Though she hadn't spoken of them recently, he knew she missed her parents, her life in the future.

It scared the hell out of him, this future she talked about, but he'd survived. As long as Lila was at his side, he could endure anything.

Buffalo Killer rode into the yard, raised his rifle over his head. Skeeter raised a hand. The Indian slipped to the ground, walked toward the house. "Family go home."

It wasn't a question, yet he answered anyway. "Yes, they're all going back to their houses."

The Indian patted his chest. "Buffalo Killer," he pointed to the house, "go big teepee."

"Yes, yes, come in," Lila said. "I'll make you some coffee. And just this morning I made sticky buns."

Buffalo Killer frowned.

Skeeter chuckled. "You'll like them. Trust me they're as good as canned peaches."

Buffalo Killer's eyes grew wide, his feet picked up pace as he strutted across the yard and up the steps.

After the Indian had eaten the entire batch of buns, and licked his fingers until Skeeter wondered if the skin would come off, the brave asked, "Need help?"

Skeeter frowned. "You need help?"

"No, Bone Hunter need help?"

He shook his head. "No, Yokel and his troop are leaving in a few days. There'll be no more bone hunting."

Buffalo Killer shook his head. He glanced around. "Help. Big teepee."

Lila, sitting in the chair beside him, covered his hand with hers. "I think he's asking if we need help here, with the ranch, the farm," a happy giggle left her lips, "whatever we call this place." A smile covered her face. "Our home."

The Indian nodded. "Old braves like cow. Taste buffalo."

After the ordeal with Johansson, Skeeter had given Buffalo Killer a couple of steers in payment for the braves who rode with Snake to take the ambushers to Dodge. Those braves were still on the trail, should have arrived in Dodge yesterday, but evidently the rest of the tribe had liked the beef. It tasted like the buffalo they loved so much.

His mind hummed with thoughts. He could use some help. He'd bought a sizeable herd from Kid, and if he trained a few braves as to how to raise them, the tribe would have meat for years to come. When the time came for he and Lila to leave, he'd give the land, as well as the dwellings to Buffalo Killer, and leave Kid enough money to assure the herd kept growing to feed future generations.

He ran a hand over his chin. In the meantime, before they left and when he did have to travel, either to the dig site, the tunnel, or even to town, it would be a comfort to know someone else was here with Lila, especially now that she was growing rounder every day.

"Bone Hunter need help?" Buffalo Killer asked again, his voice sounded almost like a plea.

"Yes, yes, my friend, I need help."

"Two, three, braves?"

"No." Skeeter held up his hand. "Four braves and one woman to help with the housework.

Buffalo Killer closed one eye as if he was counting in his mind. He held up one hand. "Five cow?"

Skeeter shook his head. Five cows wouldn't feed the tribe through the winter. "Three cows a month."

"Month?"

"Moon. Three cows a moon."

Buffalo Killer looked at his hands. His fingers

fluttered, and his eyes popped open. "Three cows one moon?"

"Yes, every moon your tribe will get three cows."

"Big cows?"

"Yes, full grown cows every moon."

Buffalo Killer leaned back in his chair, folded his arms across his chest. "Done."

Skeeter almost chuckled. The brave acted as if he'd just fought a hard bargain. But it was the love in Lila's eyes as she gazed up at him that brought a smile to his face. He couldn't stop the grin any more than he could stop the sun from shining. Full of happiness, he leaned over and kissed her lips.

Buffalo Killer shuddered at the action, and Skeeter laughed aloud. "You should try it my friend, it's wonderful.

Dark brows lifted as the Indian looked at Lila.

"With your own wife," Skeeter added.

Buffalo Killer shuddered again.

****

The days flew past, weeks turned into months, and before she knew it, fall was upon them. Lila waited daily for word of the arrival of Kid and Jessie's baby. Her own belly was becoming quite large, and her lap had all but disappeared. The days were busy, too busy for her to focus on how to tell Skeeter she planned on staying in the past. And at night, when she did bring up the subject, he'd stiffen and change the course of the conversation, or make her forget totally by skillfully leading her body into a frenzy only he could satisfy.

She stepped onto the front porch and wrapped a thin shawl around her shoulders. Buffalo Killer's braves were working out remarkable well. They'd ended up with six instead of five. Two of the men were married and brought along their wives. The other two were young, still teenagers, but hard workers and more than willing to learn all they could. She'd even become their teacher, each day she spent an hour or more showing all six how to read and write.

At first it had been just the women, Silver Fox and Yellow Dove, who wanted to learn so they could do more than browse through the magazines and books Jessie sent through the parcel post at Me-lo-te Switch on a regular basis. But once they began to learn, as well as speak more English, the men began stopping in the house, asking for a sticky bun and loitering long after they'd eaten the batch.

It was very exciting, being a part of the process that would assist their tribe in the years to come, and Lila filled with pride each time one of her students accomplished a new task.

Silver Fox and her husband, Runs with Horses, had a four-year-old little boy, Red Elk. His laughter filled the house with such a sweet sound Lila grew more anxious every day for the arrival of her baby. Yet, the fact she couldn't share her excitement with Skeeter made it all seem like a huge black cloud hung over her head.

The sky was growing dark, and she glanced toward the teepees erected several yards behind the house. Skeeter had cut down more trees, and a long bunkhouse had been built perpendicular to the barn. Yellow Dove used the space to cook for the workers, said the building was nice because it stopped the wind from blowing out her fire, but they all refused to sleep in it, even when it rained.

"Don't fret, it looks like the storm played itself out before arriving. Shouldn't be much more than a light rain." From behind, Skeeter's hands wrapped around her, splayed across her stomach and rubbed wide circles.

"I know, but I wish they'd move into the bunkhouse."

His lips pressed against the top of her head for

several minutes before he said, "It's not their way. We can't force them to use it."

"I know, but it doesn't stop me from wishing."

"Nor worrying. You have to be the biggest worry-wart on earth."

She patted his hands still caressing her stomach. "No, just the biggest woman."

"No," he said. "I think you are..." His hands went to her shoulders, twisted her around. "The prettiest." He kissed her eyebrows. "The sweetest." His lips lowered to brush her lips. "And the most wonderful woman on earth." He kissed her again, harder, tasting her lips with his tongue.

She melted against him, opened her lips while circling his neck with her hands. After several minutes, she needed air and pulled her face from his. Smiling, she leaned her head back, looked at his handsome face. "Hmm...how about the luckiest?"

He smiled. Her heart and the baby somersaulted at the same time.

The small mound of her belly was pressed against him, and Skeeter felt the baby move. His eyes lowered and one palm slipped between them. He ran his hand back and forth, over the wool of her skirt wanting to feel it again. "Does it hurt?" he asked.

"No, it's wonderful."

He nodded, smiled, but his mind went into a thunderstorm of turmoil. Buffalo Killer's braves had dug more than a dozen off shoots from the original tunnel, and still he found no portal to the future. Not once had she asked about it, nor voiced her fear about giving birth in this time, but he knew it was there.

The other thing that was also there was her want of giving away the baby. They hadn't talked about it again since that morning in the wagon. More than once she'd brought up the subject, but he'd sidestepped, quickly changing her thoughts in anyway possible. He'd not only fallen in love with her, but was in love with the baby as well. The thought of someone else raising the child ripped his heart into pieces.

"Skeeter," she said.

He knew she'd read his mind. A lump the size of Castle Rock formed in his throat.

"Promise me you won't change the subject," she said.

"Lila, I gotta—"

She interrupted before he came up with a suitable excuse. "We, Skeeter." A no-nonsense gaze met his. "We have to talk."

He bowed his head, nodded and followed her into the house.

Chapter Fourteen

She went to the living room, sat down on the long, horse-hair divan. He went to the fireplace, loitered by casting a couple small logs into the bed of coals. Using the poker, he stirred the red embers until blue tipped flames licked at the sticks of wood.

"Come sit down," she said.

He squared his shoulders, shrugging off the goose bumps rising beneath his shirt. "Lila—"

"Please, Skeeter, just come sit down, let me say what I have to say."

He blew out a breath of air. Why didn't she ask him to cut off his right hand? It would be easier, less painful than giving up the baby. Hell, he'd cut off the whole arm; even had a leg or two he could do without.

She stretched out an arm to him, fluttered her fingers.

He took her hand, surprised by how warm it was, or maybe it was because his felt ice cold. The couch felt hard, uncomfortable as he sat down. Other nights while she read or sewed, he'd stretched out on the long lounger, relaxed into its softness. But tonight, the hair seemed to poke through the material of his britches, stinging his skin like sandburs in July.

"I-uh, I..." she started.

"Can I say something first." He rubbed her hand

with both of his.

"You'll change the subject."

"No, I won't. This is about the baby."

Her deep heavy sigh flowed between them. The sound hung in the air.

He had to say something before he burst. "Lila, I know how this baby came to be. And, honey, I'm sorry. I'm so very sorry for what Hawkins did to you." He swallowed against the hatred the sound of the man's name made grow in his gut.

Her face scrunched as she squeezed her eyes closed and sniffled.

"Yet, I can't blame this baby for the man's cruelness. I know it has to be hard for you to love a baby that came from," he flinched, hated saying the word, but continued, "rape."

Tears began rolling down her face. They tugged at his heart like a solid lasso. "Honey, I'll do everything. I'll feed it. I'll change its dirty diapers. I'll stay up all night when it's crying and can't sleep."

She glanced up. An odd look covered her face.

He grasped her cheeks. "Please, Lila, please don't give this baby to some strangers. Please let me raise it."

"You raise it? What about me?"

"I'll try to keep the baby away from you. And maybe as it grows up, you'll learn to forgive it, and possibly like having it around."

Lila couldn't believe what she was hearing, and began to tremble from head to toe. She pushed his hands away from her face. "Forgive it? Like having it around?" Cold, raw anger swept across her mind and body. "This is *my* baby you're talking about." Jumping to her feet, she stomped across the room. "Is that what you think? That I hate my baby because of what Pete did?"

Skeeter didn't move, other than his mouth fell open.

"I didn't know you thought so little of me." She twisted about, ran for the steps leading to the second story. "I thought you'd understand."

"Lila!"

"Leave me alone!" Tears fell from her eyes, making everything blurry as she raced up the stairs and into their bedroom. The door slammed hard enough to rattle the windows as she threw herself onto the bed.

She'd tried so hard. For months she'd tried to show him how she could put others first, and yet he thought she was an awful person. Her own husband thought she hated an innocent little baby.

"Lila?" he said.

"Get out!"

"Honey—"

She sat up, pointed a shaky finger at him. "I said get out. Get out of this room. Get out of this house. Just get out and leave me alone!"

He hovered in the doorway for a few seconds before he hung his head and turned, pulled the door shut behind him.

Lila flopped back down, pressed her face into the pillow and cried.

It could have been minutes, or hours, she had no way of knowing when the tears finally slowed, then ceased to fall. Sniffling she sat up, looked around her room. Blinking she forced her burning eyes to focus through the murky darkness filling the room. She twisted, climbed off the bed, and let her fingers search the nightstand for the flint box and matches. When the lamp filled the room with flickering light, she moved to the window.

One window in the bunkhouse glowed in the dark night. It had to be Skeeter. He must have left the house as she'd asked, gone to the bunk house to sleep. She folded her arms across her chest. Well, that was fine with her. Goosebumps tickled her forearms, and she rubbed at them, silently admitting, no, it wasn't fine with her.

She took a deep breath. What was her problem? One hand covered her mouth. *She really was a drama queen!* He'd said he wanted to raise the baby. A smile pulled at her cheeks at the thought of him changing dirty diapers. Her mind went back to the living room, to the other things he'd said.

A half-groan, half-mewing sound tumbled in her throat, and her hands left her face to press against the pitter patter of her heart. Skeeter wanted this baby as much as she did. She bowed her head. Yet, she'd turned it all around—hadn't listened. Her mind had been so consumed with what she thought he'd say she hadn't really heard what he had said. Matter of fact, she hadn't really heard what people had been saying for some time. She'd been too caught up trying to figure out who she was, why she behaved the way she did. If she hadn't crawled through that tunnel she'd probably never have realized it. Here, with Skeeter, she'd matured, not in age, but in a way that had developed her into a valid person—someone she could relate to, and understand. And perhaps, most importantly of all, see what she'd somehow lost. The knowledge that everyone has the ability to live their own life.

How had it all happened? When had she forgotten everything her parents had taught her about being her own person, following her dreams, *making* the life she wanted? They'd always said she could do anything if she put her mind to it. They were the ones who'd taught her to be independent, showed her how to love, and be loved. Mom and Dad were wonderful parents, so why had her life become so out of sorts, skewed with misconceptions and disbeliefs?

Memories flooded. The one where she'd told her parents about her change in majors stuck out front and center. Her father had said it was her choice, but he'd also said, he'd hoped it was what she wanted in her heart. At the time she'd scuffed it off, but now she understood what he'd meant. Information Technology hadn't been her dream, early childhood really hadn't either. But children had been. More than once her mother had assured her what had happened with baby Charles had simply been an act of God, not the norm. But that incident, the memory of that mattress full of blood strung her along, when it was truly nothing more than a onetime scary incident. In fact, around the world women gave birth every day, had been for generations, and would continue to do so for as long as the world existed.

She closed her eyes. Yes, it had been a scary experience for her and her parents, but people overcame things much worse all the time. When had she let it take control? Truth be told, she hadn't thought about that night in years and hadn't realized the event had such a hold on her until she'd considered changing majors and...

A chill filtered her spine. "Damn you, Professor Rutledge! All your talk of generations did nothing but turn me into a person I never was," she shouted, twisting about in the empty room. "I don't care what you said. It doesn't matter what year a person was born, that doesn't make them who they are." Her gaze settled on the miniature painting sitting on the tall chest of drawers. It was identical to the one hanging above the mantle downstairs. And Skeeter was right. Sometimes a person gained more knowledge outside of college than in it.

"You, Professor Rutledge, are a spiteful old man who never married, and found delight in twisting facts to torment every young person you encountered. No wonder Mom and Dad wanted me to switch schools. But I wouldn't listen, already too full of your misguided beliefs." A wave of deep sorrow filled her. "I thought you were just a lonely old man who needed a friend, like Tabby the cat."

She walked over, picked up the miniature painting and moved back to the window. Skeeter was the best thing that had ever happened to her. He'd saved her life—in so many ways. Would he be able to forgive her? She'd treated him so badly, and he'd never been anything but the most wonderful man. One who loved her—truly loved her for herself. Something not even she had been able to do. The air in her chest stalled, and a quiver raced over her skin.

She glanced back down at the picture. It wasn't Professor Rutledge's fault either. It was her. All her life she'd felt alone, like she didn't fit in. She blamed it on being an only child, homeschooling, and even her generation, when truth was, it was her. Deep inside her there had always been an empty spot that nothing could fill. Nothing, until she crawled through that tunnel. Since then she'd felt whole, like she'd finally come home to the one place in the world she belonged.

Her gaze went from the bunkhouse to the horizon. The night sky obscured her view, but she knew exactly where Castle Rock stood. Behind it were the badlands, the cave, and the tunnel to the future. Willpower, stronger than she'd known before, filtered into her system, and she filled her lungs with air.

Clutching the framed painting to her chest, she closed her eyes. "Dear Lord, it's me again, Lila. I know I promised to never ask for anything again that day in the tunnel, when you gave me my ghost back. But that day, I'd also promised to find this baby the perfect family, and now I realize I need a little help in making it all work out. If you'd be so kind as to help me, I think it's time to completely fulfill that promise."

****

Skeeter woke stiff and sore. The straw mattress on the short bed in the bunkhouse crinkled loudly as he flopped his feet over the edge. He rubbed his tired eyes and cringed at the pain. They felt like a bucket of sand had been poured in them. Pressing the butts of his hands to sore temples, he hung his head. What the hell had happened last night?

Jumping to his feet he shook his head. No use going down that road again. He'd gone over every word he'd said to her a million times while the light rain fell on the roof all night. It was no use. She hated Pete so much so couldn't forgive the tiny life growing inside her womb.

He walked over, splashed water on his face. There was no solution. He'd have to let her give the baby away. It was what she had to do, so therefore it was what he'd have to do. He'd just have to accept it.

After drying his face, he slipped on his boots and left the building. The morning air was crisp, sent a shiver up his spine as he sprinted toward the house. Shutting the backdoor, he glanced about and let his gaze linger at the top of the staircase.

Hoping the sounds might stir her, he moved about, building a fire and then noisily started a pot of coffee. When the strong, rich aroma filled the air, he pulled the pot from the burner and filled a cup. The warm brew and the heat from the stove helped, he soon felt more like himself.

His gaze had gone to the stairs several times, and his ears had been tuned in for the slightest sound, but the ongoing silence continued to be deep, deafening. He set the cup on the table and moved across the room to climb the stairs.

Cautiously, he pushed open the door to their room. His fingers slipped off the knob as the emptiness of the room filled his gaze. The bed was neatly made. He backed out of the room, looked up and down the hall. By the time he got to the third bedroom, fear was tickling his spine. Slamming open the fourth door did little more than display one more empty room.

He twisted, ran down the stairs, and searched about before he went to the washroom. It too was empty.

Wrenching open the back door he shouted, "Lila!" Her name echoed over the plains like a mocking bird. He choked on a breath of air. Burning coughs tore at his lungs as he leaped down the steps.

Black Hawk walked out of the barn. Skeeter shouted to him, "Have you seen my wife?"

The brave shook his head.

He ran to the outhouse, ripped the door open, and letting it bounce in the wind, swirled about. She had to be in the house. He must have missed her. Maybe he didn't notice her tucked beneath the covers. His feet barely touched the ground as he sprinted over the grass.

Once inside, he searched again. Pulled the covers off the beds, let them tumble to the floor. As he bolted out of the last room and down the hall, something about their room tugged at him. He stalled in the doorway, searching for the unknown. A rock landed in the pit of his stomach as his gaze settled on the chest of drawers. The miniature painting of them was gone.

He crossed the room, pulled the chest away from wall, hoping it had fallen behind the piece of furniture.

It hadn't.

A deep, pain-filled moan rumbled out of his chest, echoed throughout the empty house.

She'd left him.

Chapter Fifteen

Lila crawled out of the tunnel. The dirt on her hands turned to mud as she wiped at the tears falling down her cheeks. Her body shook uncontrollably, and she gulped for air. Exhausted, both mentally and physically, she scooted away from the opening and hugging her knees, bowed her head.

It had been harder than she'd imagined. But she'd done it, and prayed her parents would understand. She missed them terribly, always would, but her life was here now—in the eighteen hundreds badlands with her husband and their soon to be born child.

The first sunrays of morning snuck into the cave. The light made her shiver harder. Shortly after she'd left the house last night the storm that had been brewing all evening had arrived. The walk to the cave had been long and cold. Her heavy, wool skirt was still wet. A frown tugged on her brows. That had been stupid! Why hadn't she started her car? The heater would have dried out her skirt while she planted the note to her parents in her backpack.

She glanced about, a supply of firewood sat along one wall beside several boxes and crates. Rubbing some warmth into her icy hands, she stood and began searching for a flint box. A small fire would warm her enough to make the long trek back to the house. Hopefully, Skeeter was still sleeping, wouldn't notice she'd been gone all night.

The hinged lid of the first crate creaked as she opened it. Crinkled straw filled the box. She grabbed a handful to throw into the rock lined fire pit. Her nails brushed against something below the straw. With both hands she dug into the box and lifted out a long, round cylinder. Her eyes grew wide. She read the writing on the side of the box, one word, painted in bold red letters. Dynamite.

Her mind swirled. She glanced back to the tunnel. If she blew it up there would be no chance of going back. No chance of anyone ever accidentally finding the portal again. That certainly would convince Skeeter she meant business. She loved him beyond all else and was here to stay, she and the baby. People in the eighteen hundreds didn't give children up for adoption. At least she hoped they didn't.

By the time she was ready to light the long fuse, streams of sweat rolled down her back. The box of dynamite had weighed a ton. It had taken every muscle she'd ever imagined she owned to pushed the box deep into the tunnel. After that she'd climbed back down the cavern again to lay out the long rope fuse she'd found in another box.

She didn't know much about explosives, but had seen enough old westerns to know the fuse burned quickly. Wanting to be as far away as possible when the flame hit the box, she used two rolls of the rope, strung it all the way up the tunnel and across the floor of the cave to the wide, natural doorway.

Bent down, she struck a match to the flint box and carefully held it to the end of the fuse. The rope sparked then hissed as the fire raced over the thick braided threads like a Fourth of July sparkler. Turning about, she hitched her skirt to run, but her feet dug into the hard sand as her eyes locked onto a broad, bare chest.

Lifting her face higher, her gaze settled on Buffalo Killer's dark features. A look of surprise covered his face as she screamed, "Ruunnnn!"

She bolted down the sloped hillside, stumbling as her feet slipped now and again on the still damp grass. A large hand grabbed her upper arm and her feet left the ground. Her butt landed on the bare back of the painted pony and Buffalo Killer's thick arms held her in place as they raced down the hill.

When they started to slow, she lifted her feet dangling over one side, held them out of the way of the horse's stout legs, and shouted, "Don't stop! It's gonna blow!"

Buffalo Killer frowned, glanced back to the hill. "Blow?"

"Ka-boom!" she screamed.

"Ka-boom?"

The wind whipped her hair into her eyes. She shook her head, trying to see through the strands. "Like dig site. Ka-boom!"

Buffalo Killer's arms tightened around her like steal bands, and he kicked at the pony beneath them.

They were just rounding Castle Rock when the explosion happened. A deafening racket filled the air, cracking and echoing louder than a bolt of thunder could ever hope to sound. The horse, Lila, and Buffalo Killer all squealed at the same time.

She had no idea how it happened, but the next thing she knew, she and Buffalo Killer were on the ground. Still wrapped in his stronghold, what should have been a hard fall had been little more than a soft thump. They both stared as the painted pony flew across the prairie faster than a Kentucky racehorse.

The earth beneath them rumbled with after shocks and a dust-filled cloud floated above them. Little pebbles of sand and rock tumbled from the sky, pelting like fine drops of rain.

Buffalo Killer slightly eased his hold. His lips moved.

She shook her head, trying to regain her hearing. "What?"

"Are you all right?" he shouted.

"Yes, yes, I'm fine. How about you?" She answered equally as loud.

"I'm fine. What the hell did you do?"

"I—" She frowned, twisted her head slightly to see his face more clearly. "When did you learn to speak English so well?"

"I—" He clamped his lips shut.

She shook her head, waved her finger before his nose. "Your secret's out buddy."

He bowed his head, curled one lip up.

"You've been acting this whole time?"

A silly smile touched his face as he shrugged.

"Who taught you?"

He shrugged again and said, "Your husband."

"Really? When?"

"Well, he didn't teach me as much as I just picked it up from him. We've spent the better part of the last two years together." He scrunched his face. "He doesn't know. It's kind of funny how frustrated he gets at me."

She giggled. "I'll tell you what, you don't tell Skeeter I blew up his cave, and I won't tell him you speak very good English."

He glanced back to the cave. Rocks still fell from the sky, bounced like hail across the ground. "That cannot be kept a secret. They probably heard it in Denver."

She wrinkled her nose. "You might be right."

Their ringing ears didn't hear a horse approaching until heavy snorts blew across their necks. She and Buffalo Killer turned at the same time, glanced past the horse's nose to see Skeeter's look of shock.

His gaze went from the dust still rising in the air to the two of them. His face hardened. Her cheeks burned as she realized she still sat on Buffalo Killer's lap.

She lifted one hand, fluttered her fingers. "Hi."

His face must have turned to stone, not the slightest crack of his adorable grin emerged as he dismounted. He grabbed her arm. The tug wasn't hard, but it wasn't gentle either, as he pulled her off Buffalo Killer's lap. She started to make a comment, but the coldness of his eyes made her bite her tongue instead.

Star Gazer and Black Hawk rode in, Buffalo Killer's paint trailing closely behind them. She didn't have a chance to even smile a greeting, Skeeter's hands wrapped around her waist and unceremoniously, he planted her into his saddle. Not daring to move more than necessary, she eased one knee around the saddle horn.

He pointed to the paint and without a word Buffalo Killer walked toward the horse. Skeeter mounted the gelding, tucked his thigh beneath her hip. His gaze went to the site of the blast.

Her chin dropped. Who would ever have thought six sticks of dynamite could do so much damage? One would have been plenty. The whole side of the cliff was gone, and what was left of it had canyons the size of swimming pools. Sand and dirt still trickled down the steep slope and dust continued to rise from the ground.

He flipped the horse around, and she latched onto his arm as they galloped back toward the house. She'd just wanted to block off the cave, not destroy the hill. Skeeter certainly seemed upset by the damage she'd done. Maybe he'd had dinosaur bones in there. The dynamite must have come from the excavation site; maybe they'd stored some other things in there too. She bowed her head, having never thought of that. It would take diggers years to uncover them now. That is if they'd survived the blast.

Skeeter's mind and body fought. His flesh was already responding to the warm, supple body in front of him, but images of her wrapped in Buffalo Killer's arms, sitting on the brave's lap as pretty as you please, ate at his brain.

He slapped the reins across the gelding's rump, forcing the animal's speed to increase. Her fingers dug into his forearm, and he gave the reins a slight tug, eased the pace into a smooth lope. It wasn't safe for her to travel too fast.

Out of the corner of his eye, he noticed Buffalo Killer's gaze kept bouncing toward him. He ignored it. A damn fool, that's what he was. Once again, he'd thought he could trust the brave.

When they arrived at the house, he dismounted, looked at Buffalo Killer and pointed to the house before he reached up to lift Lila down. Her hands settled on his shoulders, and the touch made his knees grow weak. Their eyes met. Hers were somber, cloudy. The rock in his stomach grew to the size of a boulder.

He removed his hands from her sides, clenched them into fists as she slipped hers off his shoulders and turned to walk toward the house. At the stairs he took her elbow, making sure she didn't slip on the boards the sun had yet to dry.

Buffalo Killer held the door open. He shot the brave the evil eye as they walked passed, toward the table. Lila sat on the first chair, flattened the material of her dress over her knees. He gestured to Buffalo Killer to sit down next to her.

The anger ripping his guts apart couldn't be quelled any longer. "Damn fine friend you turned out to be."

The brave, half-squatting, still lowering himself onto the chair, snapped his head up. With a humph he stood, patted his chest. "Buffalo Killer friend."

"Like hell you're my friend!"

The Indian folded his arms across his chest, stared angrily across the room.

Skeeter stomped forward, stopped nose to nose. "A friend doesn't steal another friend's wife."

The stern look on Buffalo Killer's dark face went lax before his eyes squinted, snapped with anger. "I didn't steal her! I saved her from blowing herself back into the future."

Skeeter felt his chin drop, turned to Lila.

"Back to the future?"

Her lips opened and closed a couple times before she pointed at Buffalo Killer and said, "He can talk in full sentences."

Chapter Sixteen

Skeeter frowned, looked back at the brave. Buffalo Killer had spoken in a full sentence. But the information made no difference. He snapped his head back to Lila. "You were going back to the future without me?"

"No!" Her face twisted. "No, not going, went. I went back to the future—I had to. And when I came back I decided to plug the portal and—"

"You went to the future?" His ears rang. He moved, stepped closer to her so he could assure he'd heard right.

She nodded. A sad glint glistened in her green eyes. "I had to leave a note for my parents. I had to let them know I'm okay."

He squeezed his eyes shut, pinched the bridge of his nose. "How?"

"I left it in my backpack. It was in the backseat of my car." She stood, took a hold of his arms. "It would be too hard for you to go to the future. You don't have a birth certificate. You'd never be able to get a social security card without a birth certificate. And you'd never get a job without a social security card. And, and then you'd need a driver's license, which you wouldn't be able to get without a social security card either. Oh, and then the government would wonder why you never filed income taxes before so we'd surely be audited."

He held up a hand. Her explanation was doing little more than make his head swim.

Buffalo Killer took advantage of the moment of silence. "I go now."

Skeeter pointed at the brave, but then let his hand fall to his side, having no idea what he wanted to say. Still, wanting the man to know he wasn't happy, he said, "I'll talk to you later."

The Indian huffed a breath of air. "I not steal wife."

Skeeter glared at him, let him know his secret was out.

"Fine!" Buffalo Killer threw his hands in the air. "I didn't steal your wife. I have my own wife. What the hell would I do with two of them?" His broad back stiffened as he walked to the door. "I'll stop by and see you tomorrow."

The door slapped shut, and Skeeter's mind instantly returned to Lila. "You went back to the future?"

"Yes, I had to leave a note for my parents." She shrugged. "I had to."

"How did you get there?"

"Through the tunnel. How else?"

"The tunnel didn't work. I tried it."

"It worked just fine for me."

"Which one?"

"Which one? There's only one."

"No there's not. Between Buffalo Killer's braves and myself there had to be over a dozen tunnels, and not one led to the future."

She stepped forward, wrapped her arms around his waist. He couldn't resist her touch, her closeness, and enveloped her body. Tingling with want, his hands ran over her shoulders, down her back. Her temple pressed against his chin. "I only found one, and it took me right back to the future. Everything was just as you said. My car was in the same spot."

"But how'd you get through the house. I know it collapsed."

"The stairwell was still standing. I had to be careful not to trip since most of the rest of it was a pile of rubbish." She straightened, dug in a pocket of her dress. "I had this on the way back." A small, red cylinder sat in her palm. She folded her fingers around it, pushed her thumb on a small silver button and the end lit up like a miniature sun.

Intrigued, he took it to examine closer. With the slightest touch on the button the light would disappear then come back again.

She giggled. "It's a flashlight. I thought you'd like it."

He set it on the table, pulled her back into his arms. "I would have gone with you."

"I know." She pressed a kiss to the front of his shirt. "But I had to go by myself. I knew I could get back, but I worried if you would be able to."

He shook his head. "No, I mean I would have moved there. Stayed in the future with you."

She laid a cheek to his chest. "I couldn't do that to you. Couldn't make you live in the future. You belong here."

"I belong wherever you are. Always will." He grasped her upper arms, tugged her tighter to his chest. The aftershock of fear still racked his body. "I was so scared when I realized you'd left. Please don't ever do that to me again."

"I'm sorry. I hoped to be back before you woke." She lifted her face, kissed his chin. "And I won't ever leave you again. But I hope you understand that I had to leave the note for my parents. I don't want them to worry about me."

He sighed, thinking of how badly her disappearance must hurt her parents. "Honey, I don't think a note will ease their worry."

She nodded. "Yes, it will. I also gave them the

miniature picture Eva made of the two of us. I told them how happy I am here. How I had to choose between the past and the future." Her hands cupped his cheeks. "I chose the past. I'll forever choose you over everything else life has to offer. They'll understand that."

If a heart could physically grow in size—his did, swelled to fill his chest until it hurt. But it was a sweet, everlasting pain. He lowered his face, tasted the lips he'd forever hunger for, and never tire of sampling. Her mouth opened, encouraging him to delve deeper and sip her heady nectar.

The way her hands combed through his hair, the curves of her body molded against his, filled his veins with fire. Skeeter broke the kiss, ready to lift her into his arms and march up the stairs to their bedroom.

She stopped his hands before they hoisted her. "I also told them about the baby."

His hands went limp. "What did you tell them?"

Her teeth clamped down on her bottom lip until it went white. She swallowed, and looked up at him with pleading eyes. "I told them not to worry. That I have the most wonderful husband on earth, and that we already love our baby more than they could imagine."

He blinked against the pressure on his eyeballs. "I do you know."

"Yes, I know. I do too."

"You do?" He grasped her cheeks. "So we're keeping the baby?"

A smile curved her lips. "Is that okay?"

He whooped like a brave on the warpath. Grabbed her waist and twirled them both around before he realized the motion may not be safe for the baby. Setting her back on her feet, he bent and locked her lips with his.

A shock wave took away his breath, and he

grabbed her cheeks, held her face still so he could gaze into those green eyes. That's when he saw it— she was whole. He closed his eyes for a moment with utter thankfulness, knowing without a doubt his little bird had healed. Whatever had been broken, whatever had been gripping her insides with pain and doubt was gone. A new wave of gratitude filled his heart, for even though she had flown away, she'd come back—to live with him, forever.

****

Lila looked out the window. Time had flown by. It was hard to believe it was Christmas Eve. The sun shining down on the barren ground heated the air well above freezing and meadowlarks took advantage of the spring-like temperature to peck for hidden seeds in the back yard. She ran a hand over her huge stomach. Her load had lowered, made even the simplest movements difficult. She knew she must look like a duck as she turned to waddle to the tree Skeeter had hauled in and helped her decorate.

Gaily wrapped gifts for the brothers, Ma, Jessie, and her and Kid's baby boy, Joel, sat beneath the bottom boughs of pine needles. A couple weeks ago, she'd been sluggish and hadn't had the energy to get the presents ready for the post, and now that a burst of vigor fueled her, it was too late. They'd have to be sent after the holiday.

Joel was three months old now. She wanted to see her nephew, but her loving, doting, husband wouldn't permit her to travel that far. He was right of course. Their baby was due any day now. She still had apprehension about giving birth in the eighteen hundreds, but Jessie had survived just fine, and she had Skeeter. He wouldn't let her down, of that she was certain.

The smell of gingerbread drew her toward the kitchen. Stocking footed, since her huge belly made putting on her shoes very difficult, she padded to the stove and pulled open the oven door to check the cookies. A large bowl of frosting sat on the table, ready to decorate the different shapes as soon as they were done, and cool.

Her heart tightened, wishing her parents could join them for the holiday. It was impossible, and she found satisfaction in knowing her parents knew she was happy. Besides, they were most likely vacationing someplace sunny. Even though her family had settled in Hays for her to attend school, the traveling bug had never left her parents, and Christmas time was always vacation time. Skiing in Colorado or snorkeling in Hawaii was how they usually spent the holiday. The trips had been fun, but she'd always secretly longed for the Christmas's her friends groaned about. Houses full of family and wonderful events. This year she'd become determined to make traditions her children could carry on.

Skeeter thought her crazy as she decorated the tree singing Rudolph the Red Nosed Reindeer and Jingle Bell Rock. She couldn't carry a tune in a bucket, never could, but he didn't mind. A smile tugged at her lips. Once she'd taught him the words, she'd heard his deep baritone singing under his breath as he helped her decorate. Huge red bows lined the wide staircase and knitted stockings Ma had made hung from the mantle. Her parents would be proud of the home she had, the roots she was putting down.

The heaviness left her chest as she gathered a hot pad and retrieved the cookies from the oven. A smile filled her face. She'd made her choice and didn't regret a minute of her life in the past.

Slipping the hot treats onto a cloth to cool, she lifted her head as the back door opened. A frown tugged at her brows as Skeeter backed in through the open area, struggling to bring something through the doorway.

She set down the pan and waddled over to hold the door. As he backed in further a beautifully carved rocking chair came into view. "Oh, my! Where on earth did you get that?" she exclaimed.

He turned about, set the chair down. "Try it out," he said. His grin went from ear to ear.

Running a hand over the richly grained wood, she twisted and ungracefully lowered her huge frame into the seat. The rockers instantly began to move, and she leaned her head back, closed her eyes. "It's wonderful." She grasped the hand rails, rocked back and forth. "I love it. Could sit here all day."

"I'm glad you like it," a familiar voice said.

She snapped her eyes open. "Snake?"

Her brother-in-law, smiled, leaned down, and kissed her cheek. "Merry Christmas."

Mouth agape, as he stepped aside, she watched the trail of people stepping into the house. Snake, Hog, Bug, Ma, Willamina, Eva, Jessie, and Kid, carrying a baby in his arms soon had formed a circle around her.

She glanced to her husband. He tried to hide the smile on his face as he shrugged.

"We didn't tell him we were coming," Ma said. "He looked as shocked as you do when we pulled in the yard." Stephanie patted one hand still clutching the arm of the chair. "You're time is near, and no little girl of mine is going through labor without her Ma here."

"Or her Aunt Willamina." Willamina's gnarled hand pointed at her chest.

"We thought you might like to meet your new nephew," Jessie said, stepping forward to give a quick hug.

Lila had to blink to keep the tears at bay. "Thank you. Thank you all so much. This is perfect." She glanced about, smiling. "This is the Christmas I always wanted."

"Well, then you just sit there and enjoy your new chair," Ma said as she slipped off her knitted shawl. "You boys go get everything out of the wagon. Jessie you sit down there with Lila, Joel must be about ready to eat again. Hog, you and Eva start decorating those cookies on the counter..."

Ma kept giving instructions that others quickly followed as Skeeter stepped in front of the rocking chair and knelt down. "I didn't know they were coming."

She leaned forward, cupped his handsome cheeks. "It's just what I was wishing for, a house full of family for the holidays." She looked around before her gaze met his again. "My family—our family. It's perfect."

His lips met hers, but with Ma still barking orders, they couldn't linger. "I love you," he whispered then stood to slip out the back door seconds before his mother would have hit him in the backside with the straw end of the broom.

Lila giggled, it didn't matter how old the Quinter brothers were they would forever be little boys in their mother's eyes. She relaxed against the back of the chair, took in the organized chaos as Jessie pulled up a chair. A dark-haired, little head emerged as her sister-in-law unbundled the blanket-wrapped baby in her lap.

"Oh, please, may I hold him?" Lila asked.

"Of course, he's been waiting to meet you."

"Not as much as I've been wanting to meet him, I assure you." She took the baby, snuggled him beneath her chin, and kissed the downy softness of his head. "He's beautiful."

"Yes, he is. Looks just like his daddy," Jessie said, running a finger across the baby's cheek.

"Yes, he does." She kissed the baby again. "He's perfect." Glancing around the room, she added, "And this is awful, but I think I'm going to be really selfish and sit right here in my new chair, holding my nephew for the rest of the day."

And she did. Well, almost all day, she had to give Joel to Jessie when an hour or so later he started to fuss, ready to eat. By then Hog had a meal fit for royalty covering the table.

Gratefully, she accepted Skeeter's aid to rise and walk to the table. A dull ache had formed low in her back. The short jaunt across the kitchen did little to lessen the pain and she arched, rubbing at the area.

"You feeling all right?" he asked.

She smiled, nodded. "Just stiff from sitting too long."

He eased her onto a chair, kissed her cheek before sitting down next to her. "You can take a nap after we eat."

"I will not, not with all this company." She glanced at the family taking seats around the table, her heart thudding with excitement. "Isn't this wonderful?"

Halfway through the meal, the ache in her back increased and began to send small, sharp fingers of pain around her hips. She cringed a bit more with each one, wiggled to find a more comfortable position. Skeeter grasped her hand. "What's wrong?"

"I think I need to get up, walk around a bit. My back really hurts."

He stood, pushed his chair out of the way and helped her rise. She'd only taken two steps when she stalled, gasping. Warm fluid rushed down her legs, soaking her socks as it pooled into a puddle below her skirt. Suddenly, a gripping pain shot across her stomach, made her double over.

Lila didn't have time to straighten before the room became a whirlwind. Skeeter hoisted her into his strong arms as Ma shouted, "It's time! It's time!"

"I'll set some water to boil," Willamina yelled.

Bug's voice said, "I'll get your medical bag, Ma."

Jessie rushed past, "I'll get extra linens for the bed."

Lila's heart picked up speed. She looked at Skeeter. "It's time?"

"You'll be fine, love. Just fine," Skeeter said as he carried his wife up the stairs. The smile he planted on his face was meant for her reassurance, and did little to suppress the way his stomach had started to roll. The time had come, the moment anxiously awaited for, and feared at the same time. He forced his arms not to tremble as he shouldered his way into their room, and waited for Jessie to pad the bed before lying her down.

Turning to the door, he shouted, "Hurry up, Ma!"

"Hold your horses, Skeeter. It's gonna be awhile afore this little one makes their debut. First ones always take the longest." His mother walked to the bed, tugged on his arm. "You go on downstairs, there's nothing more you can do here."

Lila's hand stretched toward him. "Please don't leave me."

He wrapped his fingers around hers, leaned down to look into her pleading green eyes. "I'm not going anywhere, ever."

"You're just as bad as your brother," Ma said. "He wouldn't leave Jessie's side either. I'll tell ya just what I told him. Stay out of my way while I work."

He kept out of the way, but stayed close to Lila, even helped as she was undressed and re-clothed in a nightgown trimmed with purple lace. Every so often she'd grip his hand and huff through the pain he knew was bearing down on her womb.

In some ways time sped, in other ways it trickled.

He fluffed her pillows and waited.

Ran a cool cloth over her head and waited some more.

When the sun had long since set and the moon no longer glowed through the window, she was weak and tired. He rubbed her back, gave her sips of water to moisten her lips drying out from laborious breathing.

The pains became closer together. She barely had time to relax before the next one tensed her body again. Ma sprinkled some powder onto a spoon, held it up to Lila's lips. "Here, sweetie. This will take the edge off the pain."

Lila nodded, opened her mouth like a little bird. After she swallowed, she said, "You wouldn't happen to have an epidural in that bag of yours, would you?"

"A what?" Ma asked.

She shook her head, sucked in a deep breath as another pain set in. "Never mind," she groaned between gritted teeth. When the pain ended, she flopped back onto the pillow. "I don't think you gave me enough powder."

"I gave you a full dose," Ma said.

"Yeah, but I think my pain is worse than most women. I need some more."

Ma patted her arm. "It takes a few minutes to work, you—"

"Make her give me some more," Lila interrupted, her eyes pleaded at him.

Skeeter felt as helpless as a scarecrow. "Give her some more," he said, grasping Lila's hands with trembling fingers, his palms covered with sweat.

"Like I said, it takes—"

"Now, Ma. Now!" He could tell by the vigor his wife squeezed his hands another contraction was already upon her. If only he'd taken her back to the future, she could be having their baby with the comfort of modern medicine. He didn't know how they could make childbirth comfortable, for he'd certainly never seen someone in so much pain. With all his heart he wished there was some way he could absorb it from her.

Ma shook her head, but gave Lila another spoonful, and she'd barely swallowed it when her eyes grew wide. "I either gotta push or go to the bathroom!" An ear wrenching screech escaped her clenched lips, filling the room and running along every nerve in his body like a bolt of lightning.

Ma threw aside the sheet, bent Lila's legs at the knees. "Yup, it's a comin', honey, I can see the head. Push, sweetie, push hard."

Lila grunted, "I am pushing!"

"Push harder," Ma said.

Sucking in a deep breath of air, Lila screeched, "I am!"

Skeeter, having no idea how to help her, twisted to sit behind her on the bed, and wrapped his arms around her shoulders. "You're doing great, honey. Just push a little harder. You can do it."

She huffed, and closed her eyes, pushing with all her might. A loud scream filled the room, and he tighten his hold, used his shoulder to support her back as the baby slipped from her womb into his mother's waiting hands.

"Oh my God," Lila moaned as her body slumped against his.

"It's a girl," Ma said, holding up a tiny body. Red and wrinkled little arms and legs flayed about.

Skeeter was glad he was sitting down, for he'd never been so light-headed. The room swirled before his eyes, and he felt almost as if was a ghost again, floating about. Lila lifted her chin. The lovely smile covering her face made his daze fade and pulled him back to earth. He kissed her lips, while wrapping her into a solid hug.

"Here's your daughter," Jessie said a second later.

Lila lifted her arms, and he repositioned, making enough room for her to cradle the baby. Tiny orange curls were plastered to the little head, and as the miniature, scrunched, red face settled into the crook of his wife's arm, he bent down to kiss his daughter's forehead.

"Oh, my, it's a mini-me," Lila giggled.

"She's beautiful, just like her mommy," he whispered.

After a few minutes, Ma said, "Let Jessie bundle her up now, then Skeeter you can take her down to show your brothers while we get Lila cleaned up and settled."

He glanced to his wife. She gave a slight nod. He could see exhaustion overcoming her body. Carefully, he took the precious baby from her hands. The tiny head barely filled his palm. He twisted and gently laid her onto the pink blanket Jessie had spread out on the side of the bed.

An expert from recent practice, Jessie had the baby diapered and bundled with a few swift movements. She snuggled the baby to her chin for a few seconds before handing her back to him. "You can come back in a few minutes. It won't take long. Lila will be fine, I promise."

He hadn't realized his fear showed on his face. With a slight nod, he turned, kissed the top of Lila's head before he folded his arms around the baby and vigilantly left the room. He forced his feet to walk slow and steady, knowing he'd never carried anything so valuable in his life.

By the time he stepped off the stairs, he felt stronger, more sure of himself. Pride squared his shoulders, filled his chest as he walked into the living room. "Take a look at this, fellas!"

The Quinter brothers, and to his surprise, Buffalo Killer gathered around, oohing and ahhing his prized cargo. He instantly knew, from this moment on his daughter had every Quinter man and the fearsome brave wrapped around her little finger, and always would.

A short time later Eva appeared at his side, shyly whispered, "You can go back up now."

He nodded and strolled up the stairs, the whole way telling his daughter about the pony he'd buy for her, the kittens she could play with in the barn, the flowery fields she could toddle through, and that her daddy would always be there for her.

Entering their bedroom the words stilled in his throat. Lila, more beautiful than she'd ever been, sat against an array of pillows. She smiled, patted the open space on the bed. He sat near her knees, handed the baby to her.

Ma stood on the other side of the bed, ran her hand over the tiny head. "Boys are wonderful, but there's something about a little girl that just makes your heart sing, isn't there?"

He gaped, wondered how she'd nailed his feelings. "Yes, there is. Thank you, Ma. Thank you for being here tonight."

"I wouldn't have missed it for the world." She nodded then said to Lila, "Go ahead and put her to nurse, she's got to learn how to do it right away."

Lila pushed the wide neckline of her gown down, exposed a breast to her precious daughter. The tiny face rutted for a moment before the petal lips opened and clamped on. Lila sucked a breath at the shock of force the little mouth had then raised her gaze to look at her husband.

That adorable grin, the one she loved with all her heart, covered his face. Grey-green eyes glistened with solid, strong devotion. His brows furrowed as he asked, "How do you feel?"

"Wonderful," she said truthfully. "Come sit by us."

He bent down, took off his boots, and then

scooted up to sit beside them. One arm wrapped around her shoulders as his other hand went to gently caress the baby's back.

"I'd like to name her Kendra Stephanie Quinter. After my mother and yours," she said. Her glance followed his, to where his mother stood near the door.

Ma pressed one hand to her chest, wiped at her eyes with the other.

"That sounds like the best name in the world to me," he said.

Stephanie smiled. A pink blush covered her cheeks. She wiped her eyes again, turned to Jessie and said, "Come on, let's leave these three alone for a bit."

Jessie wrapped her arm around their mother-in-law, and winked back toward the bed as she pulled the door closed with her other hand.

Skeeter's warm lips brushed her temple before he said, "You sure you feel all right?"

"Yes, I feel perfect. My life is perfect."

"I love you," he said. "I love you both."

She snuggled closer, rested her head on his shoulder. "I know," she said. "I love you too, and I also know you'll never let us down. Never."

Epilogue

Christmas Day 2008

Charles Scott eased the car to a stop, cut the engine with the flick of his wrist before he glanced toward his wife. Even though the last six months had been wearing, she still looked as beautiful as she had the first day he'd met her, almost forty years ago.

He reached over, took her hand. "You doing okay?"

Her gaze settled on the small cemetery in front of the car. She nodded, let out a slow breath of air. "Yes."

Giving her hand a final squeeze, he released it, and twisted to open his door. She followed suit, and they met at the front of the car. Hand in hand, they walked along the faint trail to the aged-old grave markers. The Kansas wind swirled past, carrying a warm temperature that almost mocked the calendar saying it was December.

Stepping through the wrought-iron gate, his breath stilled in his chest when he noticed a person bent over, lying flowers near the base of a large headstone. His wife's grip tightened, letting him know she too had noticed the girl. The slender frame and long red curls reminded him so much of their daughter his body began to tremble.

As if she knew they stared at her, the girl stood, turned their way.

"Lila?" Kendra whispered.

The girl cocked her head, looked at them quizzically. Her features were close to Lila's but not identical. Her eyes were a grey-green instead of the bold, spring green their daughter's had been.

He tugged on Kendra's hand, forcing her to step forward as he did. "Excuse us, we didn't mean to disturb you," he offered.

The girl smiled. It was a smile he'd seen before. "You aren't disturbing me. I brought flowers to my great-grandmother's grave." Her gaze went to the large headstone.

He walked closer, until he could read the names engraved in the granite. Lila and Steven "Skeeter" Quinter, July 4, 1950 was etched below the names.

He took a deep breath to get past the chill rippling over his body. She hadn't died until nineteen-fifty. If they had moved to Kansas as youngsters they may have met her—known their daughter as an old woman. His mind twirled. The whole escapade was so intriguing. He believed in parallel universes, knew they existed, but to know his daughter lived in one was mind boggling.

Kendra let go of her husband's hand. Stepped closer to the girl who could almost have been her daughter's twin. "Lila Quinter was your great-grandmother?"

The girl nodded. "I'm named after her."

"Lila. Your name is Lila?" she asked, questioning if she'd heard right.

The red curls bobbed as the girl nodded, then she frowned as her gaze settle on the picture Kendra clutched in her hands. "Hey, we have that exact same picture. My mother recently had it restored." She shrugged. "It had been in the attic for years, but now it hangs over the fireplace. The exact spot it did when Lila and Skeeter built the house."

Kendra flipped the picture around to gaze at the smiling face of her daughter, the happy, handsome face of the son-in-law they never met. She swallowed the lump forming in her throat. "The house they built?"

"Yes, it's only a few miles from here. Been in the family since they built it." The girl glanced between Charles and her. "Are you two extended family? The Quinter's are a large bunch, come across a new one every now and again."

"Your mother was Lila's child?" Kendra's heart lifted with a warm flow of joy.

The girl shook her head. "My grandpa was their oldest son. They had six children, Kendra was the oldest, next was Charles, my grandpa, then Steven, Alex, John, and Grace."

Kendra grabbed her husband's elbow. Their daughter had named her children after them.

"Where do you guys live?" the young Lila asked.

"Hays," Charles sounded like he had a frog in his throat.

"Oh, I'll be attending college there next fall." She bent down, rearranged the small bouquet of flowers the wind had already twisted about. When she stood she said, "Are you two going to stop out at the ranch?"

Kendra wished she could say yes, but said, "Oh, we wouldn't want to impose."

"Impose? You wouldn't be imposing. The house is so full two more won't be a problem. Lila set the tradition, every year family from all over gathers here." She glanced to the headstone. "The town was named after them you know."

"It was?" Charles asked.

"Yes, they made friends with the band of Indians who'd been keeping folks from settling the little town that was then called Me-lo-te Switch.

Once folks were no longer afraid of the natives, people began settling in, and after Skeeter found oil on his land the town became quite well-known."

"Really?" Charles bent down to pick something up from the ground. He twirled a little black thing between his fingers.

"Oh, you found a Mosasaurs tooth," Lila said.

"Yeah, I guess I did."

"I find them every now and again. That's why Skeeter bought the land in the first place," she said, pointing around. "For the fossils. But the Bone War became too dangerous, and he put a stop to the excavations."

"You seem to know a lot about your great-grandparents," Kendra said.

"Yes, I've read Lila's diaries so many times, I have them almost memorized."

Kendra's heart was racing. The note her daughter had left for them to find in her backpack had been hard to believe at first, but during the last six months, she and Charles had come to believe every word. Believe Lila had found a portal to the past and fell in love with the man of her dreams. The authorities, unable to find any clues to her or a man by the name of Pete Hawkins, had closed the missing person case, said the two must have ran off together.

Only she and Charles knew the truth. That Pete had been stalking her, had followed her into the past where he lost his life. She glanced to the headstone. The past was also where Lila had found her life, and lived it with all her heart. A warm, happy wind brushed over her, made her skin tingle. She knew the breeze was her daughter, letting her know everything was going to be fine—in both the future and the past.

Charles wrapped his arm around her shoulder. His smile said he felt the breeze as well.

"There's one really odd thing though," Lila said.

"Oh, what's that?" Kendra asked.

She pointed to the headstone. "They died together. Just went to sleep in their bed one night and never woke up, we know that from family history. But there are no birthdates on the stone because Lila didn't have one. Nowhere does anything ever say when or where she was born. We know she was from Hays and met Skeeter at the Badlands, because he called her his Badland Bride, but we've never found any information about her before then." Lila shrugged her shoulders then pointed to the picture. "My mother would love to see that. She's as obsessed with family history as I am." She glanced at their faces for a moment. "Tell you what. I'll go wait by my car, let you two look around a bit, and when you're ready you can follow me to the ranch."

Kendra followed the direction Lila pointed. On the other side of the fence, a bright red Mustang, exactly like the one in their garage in Hays, was parked in the shade of a weeping willow tree. Her gaze floated to her husband.

Tears glistened in his eyes, and he gave a slight nod.

"You're sure we wouldn't be intruding?" she asked, fighting the water in her eyes as well.

"Of course not! Once a Quinter always a Quinter."

Kendra smiled. The first real smile she'd felt in months. "Thank you, Lila. We'd love to meet the rest of your family."

"Your family." Lila stepped forward, laid a hand on her arm. "You'll be meeting the rest of your family."

Kendra knew the words to be true. Somehow Lila had orchestrated this moment, had devised a plan for her parents to meet her great-grandchildren, their great-great-grandchildren.

Only Lila, their considerate little girl, could have orchestrated this so perfectly.

She had always put others before herself, and evidently, still was.

A word about the author...

As a young girl I remember spending warm summer days and long winter nights with Nancy Drew and Laura Ingalls Wilder. As the years slipped by the books evolved into romance novels by Kathleen Woodiwiss, LaVyrle Spencer and a host of others.

In 2000 when my husband said I should write one, I took the challenge and have loved every moment of the journey. To create characters from once upon a time and lead them through a life that ends in happily ever after is such fun. Of course, you have to torture them a little bit along the way, and just like real-life children you often have to clean up after them. But, just like real children, they are worth it.

My husband of more than twenty-five years and I live in Minnesota, have three grown sons and the most precious gift ever—a granddaughter, Isabelle. I work as the resource development manager for our local United Way program, am a lifelong Elvis fan (yes, I've been to Graceland) and love spending Sunday afternoons watching NASCAR with family and friends.

Contact Lauri at Lauri@izoom.net

Other Cactus Rose titles to enjoy:

OUTLAW IN PETTICOATS
by Paty Jager
Maeve Loman has had her heart crushed before; she isn't about to have it happen again. Zeke Halsey has wanted Maeve Loman since he first set eyes on the prickly schoolteacher. Offering to help her find her father, he hopes to prove he's not going anywhere. Neither one knows the extent to which they will stoop to get the answers they crave.

SECRETS IN THE SHADOWS
by Sheridon Smythe
The lovely widow Lacy had taken in two young children—and the rambunctious little angels wasted no time getting her into trouble with Shadow City's new sheriff...

STANDOFF AT THE WATERIN' HORSE
SALOON (Rosette) by Stacy Dawn
Bridget Schneider has a few things to say to the cowboy who stole her heart over a year ago and never came back—but she's not about to let her anger be hog-tied by sudden...distractions. Jonas might've stolen her heart, but she's sure as shootin' gonna get her pride back.

A LAW OF HER OWN
(Miniature Rose) by Linda LaRoque
When Charity Dawson resigns her father's corporate law firm to pursue a career as a trial lawyer, she gets more of a change than she wanted. She finds herself transported to 1888 Texas in the middle of a murder trial.